DISTRACTING ACE

Caroline Bell Foster

Scan for free reads

ISBN-13: 978-0993067334

Publisher: Sunshine Publications
Cover design by: Coral Elliott Endsor
Editor: Alec Hawkes

To my dad, who continues to be my biggest fan.

CONTENTS

CHAPTER ONE

'*Kill me now!*' Nina pressed her head against the cool glass of the windowpane and watched, with what should have been *scenic excitement*, as the panoramic skyline of New York City whizzed by to her right.

The Statue of Liberty was just a thin, blurry, one-inch line in the distance.

A few hours, and what should have been the best solution for getting to New York from Baltimore, had turned out to be the journey from hell.

If hell could be described as sitting in an ancient model American car with loads of metal at the front and back, no air conditioning, the windows unable to go down and cracked leather seats that scratched the back of your legs-then this was it.

If hell was occupied by fraternal twins Shereece and Nicola sitting up front, continuously bitching because they had to have dinner with their grandmother, then Nina was definitely in hell. Add her once favourite Gwen Stefani song, *Hollaback Girl,* being on loop for the last hour, and she was ready to open the door and fling herself into the flames.

Nina shared the back seat with the twins' friend Devonia; an elfin like Chinese girl who could be the 'poster child' for travel sickness! Devonia was doped up and sleeping with her head thrown back against the head-rest; her long hair in braids and bunched up at her neck, acting like a satin pillow as she slept. Devonia had tagged along at the last minute and, because of her, they'd had to pull over countless times while she brought up her stomach lining. The car still reeked of vomit. Yes, her trip to hell had begun at six o'clock this morning. She would have been better off taking the bus, Nina thought once again, but had craved another *All-American* experience, a road trip, in a Cadillac no less, before she left for Europe in a few days.

"Nina?"

Nina tried not to grimace as Shereece turned in her seat to address her.

"We're just going to pull into a convenience store, or gas station, to get some flowers for the old lady, drop them off, then New York is ours!" She ended on a flourish, raising her hand to her sister Nicola, who had taken her hand off the steering wheel to slap Shereece's palm in a hi-five.

Nina made a tooting horn gesture and stretched her lips into what she hoped was a smile.

Her phone vibrated in her hand and a genuine smile lit her face as she rapidly began texting her best friend, Andy. Her flight had arrived, and she was currently taking a taxi to their hotel.

Nina couldn't wait to see her; it had been three months. They'd never before gone more than a month without seeing each other. Now her time as an overseas student at the University of Maryland was over; she had two nights and three days in the city with her best friend to look forward to, then back home to England. Nina couldn't wait. She liked America, had enjoyed her stay on campus, but nothing beat the nightlife of Essex. Both she and Andy were born and raised Essex girls, and proud of it.

Screams, and a screeching of tires, jolted Nina out of her daydreams and she watched in horror as the heavy car fishtailed, in what seemed like slow motion, stopping a hairsbreadth away from a silver SUV with darkly tinted windows that had been about to park in the same spot.

They were too close to the other car for Nina to open her door so, taking off her seatbelt, she scrambled across Devonia, who was looking around in a daze, and rushed around to the front of the sky-blue vehicle.

Shereece was already in the face of a tall, athletic-looking guy. If the scene weren't so tense, Nina would have taken a moment to appreciate the man's thick shoulders, displayed in a black 'muscle shirt' and his long muscular legs in khaki shorts, but Nicola was now out of the car, and the three of them were screaming at each other. The twins were like yapping, blonde, cheer-leading Chihuahuas; the man like a fierce German Shepherd.

"This is disabled parking!" The man blazed down at the girls for the tenth time, stabbing a finger in the air.

Nina looked around, spying the blue disabled parking sign you couldn't miss, as there was one smack bang in front of each parking bay.

"Oh yeah," Nicola stood up on tiptoe, getting in his face. "You don't look like a cripple to me!"

Alarmed, Nina watched as the man practically turned purple, and she quickly squeezed between them all, pushing Nicola out of the way.

"Stop it!" She yelled above the din of accusations, placing her back to his chest and shooting daggers at the girls before turning to look up at the man. "I'm really sorry," she soothed, taking a chance and touching his forearm.

He looked down at her, his sharp frown not detracting from his handsome face. *God, he is a looker*, she thought, taking in his dark blond hair, straight eyebrows and blue eyes. She wanted to starfish her fingers and trail them over his chest. "I'm sorry," she apologised again. "Nicola, move the car," Nina ordered over her shoulder.

"Not before we get those flowers," Shereece huffed adamantly, before flouncing away, Nicola close behind as they went into the shop without a care or thought of an apology.

"Friends of yours?" The man drawled, capturing her hand and turning slightly, so they both could follow the drama of the twins as they squabbled over the dismal selection of bouquets.

"Certainly not," Nina clarified, stepping away. "Look, I'm ever so sorry. If the car weren't so big, I'd move it myself." She stated.

He was looking down at her with a sparkle of interest, his mouth tipping up at one side as he stepped into her personal space. She thought she heard him mumble something about being surrounded by fucking Brits, but she couldn't be sure.

Nina stepped back; she was tired, hungry, and had reached her wit's end. Cute guy or not, she wanted to get to the hotel right now.

"Where are you from?" He asked, tipping his head to the side.

Shit, she really wasn't in the mood for this conversation and smiled briefly, before spying Devonia who, now that it was safe, had gotten out of the car.

"England," she said rapidly, in a tone that didn't invite further conversation as she edged towards the car. "I should say they," she nodded towards the sisters in the shop. "Don't normally act like that, but I'd be lying."

He grinned at her, then looked at his own vehicle as though remembering something.

"Don't worry about it." He walked to his SUV, got into the drivers' seat and, as the engine had still been running, swiftly reversed and manoeuvred the vehicle into the next bay, then with another smile sent her way and a tip of the head, made his way into the shop.

With her mind made up, Nina turned to Devonia, who was leaning against the bumper, looking pale.

"I'm going now."

"Now?" Devonia turned to her.

Nina opened the door on her side of the car and checked the pockets to make sure she hadn't left anything behind in the door and seat pockets before pulling out her bag. She didn't want to have any reason to seek the twins out ever again in this lifetime or the next.

Opening the boot, or trunk as she was told to call it, she heaved out her rucksack, placed it on the ground and slammed the door shut before glancing down at her clothes. She'd dressed for comfort this morning, grey leggings and trainers, but her white crop top wasn't really appropriate for public transport so, rummaging in her rucksack, pulled out her favourite T-shirt with the university logo on the front, and without thought, quickly stripped off her top and pulled on the T-shirt over her bra.

She thought she felt eyes on her, but Devonia was dramatically panting into a paper bag and *Cuteness*, as she now called him, was chatting and laughing with the twins. Men, Nina thought, shaking her head, were so bloody predictable.

"You're going?" Devonia asked between huffs.

"There's a subway station over there," Nina pointed. She'd spotted it earlier. "I'm sure I can find my way into the city from here."

"Maybe I should come with..." Devonia started.

Nina knew it wasn't for her benefit. Devonia was a follower. She never made a decision that was her own. How she managed in this world Nina didn't know, but what she knew, with absolute certainty, was that this escape she was making by herself.

"Nah, I'll be fine," Nina deliberately misinterpreted her meaning and hoisted her rucksack onto her back before giving Devonia a quick hug. "Tell them thank you for the lift, but I'll make my way from here." She instructed, hoping to make her escape before the girls came out of the store. She turned away after watching Devonia go into the shop.

"Oh, thank God." She breathed in relief as she checked her phone. Andy had arrived at the hotel and was ordering a bottle of champagne for them. Nina grinned.

"You forgot your bag," someone said behind her, as she was about to set off and cross the street.

Startled, Nina span around, looking for the person behind the deep voice.

"On the bonnet."

Nina turned to see the top half of a man's face looking at her. Everything below his lips was hidden behind the tinted window. She hadn't even realised there was someone else in the SUV. She couldn't see much of him as a navy baseball cap, as they said in America, was pulled down low on his face, shadowing his eyes. The hair peeking out at his neck was dark, and a single thick curl played in his ear. He was very masculine; all hard angles and she could see the start of a neatly trimmed shadow of hair framing his face. A tiny gold earring caught the sun, winking at her.

He must have seen her get dressed, she thought. Creepy.

"Pardon?"

"On the bonnet," he nodded towards her car. "Your bag."

Knowing he was watching, Nina moved to pick up her bag, bounced her knees to reposition the heavy rucksack, before placing her other heavy bag on her shoulder. "Thanks," she turned to him and watched as he dipped his head in acknowledgement.

Reluctant to move, she stepped close enough to see that his hair was chocolate brown and his facial hair a mixture of colours. Mario's *Let Me Love You* was playing softly in his car.

"Erm, do you know how long it will take to get over there?" She pointed to the famous skyline.

She thought he wasn't going to answer and turned to go when he said. "On the train? About an hour or so."

He was British, West London if she wasn't mistaken, but as she hated when this kind of thing was pointed out to her, decided not to mention it.

"Thank you."

His head dipped in acknowledgement again before adding with a smirk. "It was a good thing you changed."

Nina gasped. He had seen her and was letting her know that he had. Oh my, his smile changed his face, Nina thought, feeling a warm blush creep up her neck and she crossed her arms over her breasts as her body reacted to him. She took another tentative step closer.

"Erm, I'm sorry about the parking thing—" she began, but he turned to the front, giving her a quick view of his profile before the window slid up and Nina only saw her reflection looking back at her.

His rudeness took her breath away and, with lips puckered with annoyance, turned and walked to the subway.

On the other side of the street, she turned and, because she knew he was watching, waved before descending the subway steps.

CHAPTER TWO

"Oh my God, it's so good to see you!" Nina exclaimed once again to Andy, who was laying on the opposite table as they both had a massage.

Andy hadn't been joking about the champagne or the 'Before You Head Out' package she had treated them both to. They'd been waxed, plucked, rubbed and polished to within an inch of their lives, and they still had something called the 'Rain Forest' shower experience to have, then nails, hair and make-up.

"I know," Andy exclaimed with a grin. "I don't know why your parents thought it would be a good idea for you to go to America."

"We'd been going out too much,"

"I told you that weekend in Marbella was a bad idea," Andy stated.

Nina laughed, remembering the infamous weekend when they'd taken off to the Spanish coastal city at the last minute, with two other friends, and spent three nights partying hard. Hard. So hard, she didn't remember one night at all.

"You wouldn't have met Gareth if we hadn't gone though, would you?" Nina reflected.

Andy sighed with a stupid grin on her face. "I think I'm in love."

"I know," Nina answered. Andy fell in love quickly and often.

"Who'd have thought it?"

"I knew you'd think that, too."

"You aren't offering much to this conversation, are you?"

Nina giggled, "I only met him that one time after Marbella and that was just before I came here, so I never got the chance to vet him, but he seems okay."

Andy turned onto her back and waved the masseuse away. "Thank you, but that's it," she dismissed with a smile, sitting up.

"He's a bit clingy." She revealed.

"Clingy, how?" Nina asked, following suit and wrapping the huge, white, hotel towel around her lightly oiled body, as she helped herself to another glass of champagne and handed one to Andy, too.

Andy shrugged, but Nina knew her friend too well and asked again.

"He thinks you're a bad influence," Andy admitted ruefully, with a twinkle in her eyes. "And that you'll introduce me to a gorgeous American footballer type with massive shoulders this week."

"Is that on your wish list, Andrea Duke?" Nina asked, with her hands on her hips. "How could he think I'm a bad influence?"

"I told him it's the other way around, but he remembers that night in Marbella when you danced on the bar and dragged me up there with you."

That was the night Andy had met him.

"Didn't you tell him it was your idea?"

"Sort of." Andy evaded.

Nina laughed, not the least bit perturbed by her friend's evasiveness. Nina did get blamed for all of their escapades, mainly because she was the one to follow through on Andy's dares, with Andy herself somehow never getting caught. It was the blue innocence of her eyes, added to her dark straight hair, pale skin and sunny disposition–you couldn't fault her friend for anything, and Nina wouldn't have had it any other way. Andy was the little sister she had never had. Although, technically speaking, Andy was older by twelve days.

"It's a good job I love you." Nina hugged her tight as they moved into the living area of the suite and flopped onto the huge suede sofa that faced the flat-screen TV. The whole suite was white, with brown and gold soft furnishings throughout—all very five star.

Nina's parents had treated them to two nights in the hotel, flying Andy over to be with her before Nina returned to England.

"I know." Andy tucked her legs under herself, picked up her

phone and started playing Snakes.

"Can I ask you something?" She asked, after a moment, putting her phone into the pocket of her complementary white hotel robe.

"Since when have you ever had to ask permission?" Nina went on but sat up straight when she noticed how serious Andy had become. "What is it?" She asked, her forehead creasing in concern.

"Is everything okay with your mum and dad?"

"Yes, why?"

Andy bit the inside of her cheek; she'd been deliberating whether to ask or not. Ever since Nina had been in America, her parents had been acting strange.

"There's a rumour going around that your parents have filed for bankruptcy."

Nina laughed. "That's ridiculous,"

"I'm serious, Nina. Your dad has put the house you have in Cornwall on the market."

Nina frowned. She'd been speaking to her parents every Sunday, like always, and they hadn't even hinted that they had money worries. *How could they have money worries, anyway*? She thought. They'd opened a new Caribbean restaurant just last year, bringing their outlets to twenty-four around the country.

"We hardly go to that house anyway, so maybe he's just getting rid of it." She reasoned.

"Your mother loves that house. Why would he sell it?

"I don't know, do I?!" she replied sharply, then reached for Andy's hand. "I'm sorry. I didn't mean to shout."

"It's okay. Maybe it's nothing. Forget I even mentioned it." Andy grabbed the complimentary basket off the glass coffee table and placed it between them. "What do you want?" She asked, rummaging through the indulgent calorific goodies.

"No more snacks!" Nina shouted, slapping her friend's wrist playfully. "What are we having for dinner?" Nina asked, feeling a little light-headed. The champagne had landed on top of the chocolate bar she'd bought in the subway station that morning;

she needed proper sustenance.

Andy was the organiser; she always had been, and Nina referred to her when it came to organising her life. It had always been like that. They worked so well on every level, and they both knew they couldn't cope without the other.

"We're eating dinner in the hotel," Andy paused dramatically. "And then we're going to that Irish pub I told you about."

"Irish? You don't want to go to a sports bar? Check out the jocks?"

"Yes, Irish. Do they even call men jocks anymore? It sounds so ancient,"

Nina shrugged. This was how they were, conversations all over the place.

"I don't know. It's a great word."

Andy rolled her eyes. "I take it you're still into this whole linguistic thing?"

"It is what I've been studying all these months, you forget?"

"Nah, but that gap year to travel around the world kind of made me forget." Andy went on as she picked up a brownie from the complimentary gift basket, unwrapping the delicate tissue paper it came in, and took a bite. "Mm." She rolled her eyes to the back of her head and sighed. "Lush."

"As if you weren't there with me," Nina went on. "Remember the time you started chatting up that cute customs officer in Indonesia? We ended up having a full-body drug search!"

"How was I supposed to know that's what drug mules did? He was so cute! Dimples and everything!"

"And—"

There was a knock at the door.

"Saved by the knock," Andy chimed, going to the door. "Time for that Rain Forest thing."

***

While waiting for dessert, and Andy, who had gone to the loo, Nina took a moment to remember her earlier conversation with her dad. She'd rung him as she was getting ready for dinner.

He'd been happy to hear from her; listing everything that had happened that day with meticulous detail, as he always did. When she'd asked him about the sale of their holiday home, he said yes, they'd decided to get rid of it as they were buying a newly built six-bedroomed, four-bath roomed, detached up the road. He said it made better economic sense and that their coffers were still overflowing.

He always used the term coffers instead of money, and she'd laughed, reassured that all was well. She'd reminded him of their flight times and rang off with a chorus of I love you's down the phone.

Andy came back to the table just as their dessert arrived, 'spotted dick' for Nina and 'key lime pie' for Andy. As soon as she sat down, Andy began talking about Gareth again.

"What do you mean, he's hiring a personal trainer?" Nina said, interrupting Andy's animated flow of words.

"Yeah, he says he loves my body, but wants me to get fit."

Alarmed, Nina put down her spoon and focused on her friend. "What do you mean, he wants you fit?"

"Yeah, that's what he said." Andy shrugged her shoulders and looked down at her pie. "Maybe I shouldn't eat this, huh?"

"Back up, missus," Nina said. "You don't think something is wrong when a man tells you *he wants you fit*?"

"It's not like he called me fat, Nina," Andy answered, pushing her plate away, leaving three-quarters of her pie. "Not everyone can be five seven and a size eight." She defended cattily.

Nina frowned over at her friend. Something was going on, and it all pointed to Gareth.

"I'm sorry." Nina soothed, pushing her plate away. She was not going to fight with her best friend over a man, especially tonight. Their time in New York was about the two of them. When they got back to England, it was back to their busy lives, Andy working for her parents' party planning business and Nina, hopefully preparing for the next chapter of her life.

"I'm sorry too." Andy apologised, her phone buzzed, and she

picked up the pink metallic Motorola and flicked it open. "It's Gareth," she said unnecessarily.

Nina watched as Andy bit the inside of her cheek, something she always did when she was anxious. When she glanced at her, she snapped her phone shut and, with what Nina knew was forced brightness, asked.

"How was it, anyway? Did you meet anyone? Have rampant sex with an American jock?" Andy made bunny quotations over the word 'jock.'

"It wasn't how I thought it would be," Nina admitted, ready to change the subject.

"No sex?"

Nina shook her head.

"Feeling up of your perky bits?"

Nina chuckled. "Nope."

"Oh dear, three months without getting any?"

"It was okay, really. Everyone was nice—"

"The word *nice* is insignificant. It doesn't have much of a meaning you told me so yourself. You said nice was up there with—"

"Moist, yes, I know," Nina rolled her eyes at her friend. "I just wasn't attracted to anyone, plus—"

"What?"

"There's a different kind of atmosphere here." she looked around the room, seeing all the affluent people of different nationalities, and leaned in close. "I felt my blackness."

Andy, who had also leaned in close, reached for her friend's hand.

She had been Nina's friend since forever, well from the age of seven. Nina had been one of three black kids in the entire school. It got better when they went to boarding school in France, but not by much. She'd had to wipe her friend's tears when she had been referred to because of her skin colour by stupid, insensitive white people. But things were so much better in Europe nowadays, especially in England.

"I'm sorry," Andy squeezed her hand.

"It's okay," Nina shrugged, moving back into her chair and sipping her wine. "I buckled down." she took a deep breath. "And applied." She revealed softly.

Andy gasped, knowing instantly what she was referring to. "Oh, my God! You did?!"

Nina grinned and nodded, catching her friend's excitement. Andy was the first person she'd told.

"I'm so flipping proud of you. Oxford; I can see you now." Andy picked up her napkin and dabbed at the corners of her eyes.

"Are you crying?" Nina asked, spying the tears.

"No, it's an eyelash," Andy sniffed. "When will you know?"

"I'm expecting an email any day now."

"Oh my God," Andy said again. "We need to celebrate." She signalled the waiter.

"How about we head out?" Nina suggested. Although the hotel was beautiful, it was too exclusive. She was ready to let her 'Essex' out.

"To the pub it is!" Andy grabbed her hand and pulled her from the table, took a few steps, then looked at what they were both wearing. "But we have to change. Essex has come to New York!" She laughed, knowing exactly what she was going to dress them in, and rushed them over to the elevators.

CHAPTER THREE

"This place is amazing," Nina said again, slamming down another shot glass. She'd lost count of how many she'd had, maybe five or maybe seven. But she knew she hadn't yet reached her limit. The fiasco in Marbella was her measuring stick from now on. There was no way she would ever drink to the point of passing out ever again. Get to the buzz, drink water, maintain the buzz. That was her new motto. She should get a T-shirt printed, she thought.

"Glad you like it!" Andy shouted over the music.

They were in *Heathers,* an Irish pub in Manhattan. Andy had been here once before and knew the atmosphere was just what they needed to celebrate Nina applying to Oxford University. Oxford! It was huge! What an achievement.

Nina had always been super-intelligent, forever on the 'Talented and Gifted' programmes throughout school and was one of those irritating people who never really applied herself, but always managed to pass exams with flying colours. While Andy's parents had to employ every tutor for every subject, to ensure she got a passing grade. Nina going to Oxford to study linguistics was massive. She was so happy for her.

"You know what this place reminds me of?" Andy said.

"No, what?"

"That bar in Coyote Ugly," she explained, looking around, spying a bunch of bras hanging from the ceiling alongside glittery, home-made four-leaf clovers. "You know the one with the girls dancing on the bar, pouring drinks and singing—" she flapped her hands with excitement as they both burst into song. "Can't Fight the Moonlight!"

***

Ace watched from the far corner. He'd seen them when they'd walked in, and he'd been unable to pull his gaze away from her ever since.

She was as beautiful as he remembered her to be. He'd felt a pull then when she'd apologised for her friend's rudeness that morning, and he felt an even bigger pull now; dressed as she was in a deep red pair of shorts that cupped her ass and showed off her toned legs, and a black, sparkly vest type thing that clung to her breasts; no man could resist that package! She was fucking supreme, he thought.

Her skin was brown; a perfect, deep, sun-kissed brown that looked both smooth and healthy. He'd been admiring her body while she talked to his cousin that morning. A year ago, he would have been out of the car like a shot, and she would have been under him right now. Those long legs of hers wrapped around his hips as he fucked her. Last year, that was.

Ace snarled, raised his beer bottle to his mouth and watched as she bumped hips with her friend, threw back her head to laugh —showing him the long kissable column of her throat—touched her glass to her friends and drained the glass before slamming it on the bar in triumph.

The group of men milling around them cheered, egging them on. One guy even put his hand on her ass, and Ace felt possessive anger stake him. He was relieved when she removed the dick's hand and wagged her finger in the guy's face. *Good*, Ace thought, pulling on his beer as he continued to torture himself by cataloguing everything she did.

What the hell was he doing here, anyway? He looked around; it was his fucking pity party to help him make up his mind. Time was running out. His cousins had dragged him out because, as they put it, he was wallowing in self-pity and needed to get his dick out. Their words. How the hell could he be any fun when he was like this? He slapped his thigh. Didn't they know what he was going through? And if he wanted to—*Jesus fucking Christ*! He interrupted his gloomy thoughts; someone had turned up the music, and the girls had climbed onto the bar to dance.

***

Nina graciously took the hand that was offering to help her off the bar. She and Andy had danced, taken some shots and danced some more. Knowing her limit was near and the height of the bar making her dizzy, she climbed down. It was time to pull back and have a glass of water, she thought.

"Thank you," she told the guy, only looking at him when he didn't let go of her hand. "Hey, it's you!" She grinned up at him.

"Yeah, it's me."

"*Cuteness*."

He raised his eyebrows and smiled. "If you say so. You took off before I could get your number," he said in her ear, wrapping an arm around her waist, but looking over his shoulder as he pulled her flush against him.

"You're so full of it," she told him playfully, pulling out of his embrace. "You already have the twins' phone numbers. Why do you want mine?"

"Ah," he touched his heart dramatically. "You broke my heart today and didn't give me a chance to get to know you." He wiggled his eyebrows, feigning innocence. "Can I get yours?"

She shook her head.

"Who's your friend?" Andy said, sliding awkwardly off the bar to stand beside them.

"I met him earlier," Nina explained. "When we almost crashed into his car."

"You didn't tell me about any crash," Andy gasped. "What happened?"

Nina watched as *Cuteness* slung his arm over Andy's shoulders, leaning heavily into her to tell her about their earlier mishap.

Nina took that moment to go and freshen up in the bathroom.

After using the facilities, she patted her face with a tissue and looked at herself. She looked good. She wasn't vain or anything like that, but she knew she was pretty and had a fabulous body. Gymnastics and ballet all her life made for a toned body. She could drop into the splits with a gust of wind if she wanted to.

The hair and make-up team had done an excellent job on her. Her make-up wasn't as obvious as she liked to wear it in England, but it was nice; her eyes smoked up and lined with black liquid liner, layers of mascara and fake lashes. Her hair had been washed, and her extensions replaced. She looked good.

Turning on the tap, she ran water over her wrists for a moment and thought about the other blonde guy in the SUV today. *Cuteness*–she really needed to ask him his real name–was here. Maybe his friend was too. Hmm, perhaps she would get a chance to tell him off for his rudeness.

Turning off the taps, she dried her hands, and with renewed determination, walked out. She was on a mission. Nina didn't like bad manners.

Andy was by herself when she came out. "Where is he?"

"Who?"

"Cute-the guy I left you with?"

"He was too busy talking to my girls." Andy looked down at her boobs.

"Since when has that been a problem?"

"I didn't like him, okay?" she replied sharply. "Want a shot?"

Nina frowned at her friend; something was off. "Did he make a pass or something?"

"It was the 'or something'."

Nina could see the tears threatening in Andy's eyes and pulled her friend close. Andy was a big girl. In England, a shapely size eighteen and all lush curves. In body-conscious America, she would have to shop at a specialist shop for clothes.

"Do you want to go?" Nina asked with concern, forgetting her mission.

"No, he's an arse." Andy wiped her eyes and grinned. "Let's dance!"

They danced with each other, they danced in groups, and they danced with different men. They only stopped dancing when the music changed to slow songs and, sitting at the bar and fielding offers of drinks and more dancing, Nina looked around.

That's when she saw him.

***

Ace watched her all night; his jaw was aching from all the clenching he'd been doing, and he'd wanted to smash his cousin's face in when he'd gone over and talked to her when he'd specifically told him not to.

Now, his brother and cousins had gone on to another bar, reluctantly leaving Ace behind when he told them he *'didn't need a fucking babysitter'*.

All night he'd remembered the man he used to be. He held the record for getting laid the fastest out of all his cousins, he reflected without humour, remembering the night he'd talked up a woman and was deep inside her up against a wall, in eighteen minutes flat. His cousins had timed him, he remembered. Now he was sitting here, limp as a squid, stalking a woman who didn't know he was here.

Ace didn't even know why he was torturing himself like this. It wasn't as though he was going to walk over and talk to her or take her to bed. He rubbed his leg as he continued to watch her dance. God, she had moves, he appreciated. He decided he'd get pissed, then go home.

She turned suddenly and looked straight at him.

Shit! Don't do it, don't do it. Don't. Fucking. Do it, Ace thought in a panic. She did it anyway. She walked over to him and he, dumb shit that he was, had nowhere to go.

She sat down without asking if the seat was taken, even though the table was full of empty beer bottles and shot glasses that he couldn't have drunk by himself.

God, she was beautiful. She needed to leave. Fucking Christ, he was all over the place and needed to get a grip, he thought, trying to calm his heart rate down.

"Help yourself to a seat," he drawled, in what he hoped was a casual sounding voice. She tied him in knots, and she hadn't even said a word yet.

"I was hoping you'd learned some manners between this morning and now," she answered, leaning back in the chair and drinking him in. He was wearing a darkly coloured shirt, open at the neck. His shoulders were broad, and his shirt sleeves rolled up, showing his hard forearms. *When had forearms ever been sexy*? She thought, fighting the urge to touch him.

"And why would you think that?" Ace weaved his fingers together and placed them at the back of his head in studied casualness.

She crossed her arms over her chest, dragging her eyes off the column of his throat and shrugged. "Oh, I don't know, slamming the door in someone's face is the epitome of rudeness, maybe?" She challenged.

He frowned and leaned forward, placing his right forearm on the table, pushing the bottles forward. "We must have been at two different places, lady," he drawled coldly. "Because I didn't slam no doors."

Nina tipped her head to the side, not only listening to what he was saying but also how he was saying it. He was British, but he'd lived in America a long time. His words and sentence structure were Americanised, she noted curiously.

"Winding up a car window is akin to slamming doors!" She retorted. This was a weird conversation. "Aren't you going to offer to buy me a drink?" She asked playfully, edging for normality.

If she had reacted to him by seeing just half of his face this morning, seeing him full-on like this, without the baseball cap, was making her all hot and light-headed. She clenched her legs together.

He was beautiful, the low lighting cast shadows over his face, but what she could see she liked. The angle of his chin, his lips, oh my, they weren't smiling at her, but there was some sort of teasing movement going on, as though he was holding it in. His eyebrows were thick, with a small landing strip leftover from an injury scarring the right brow. His nose was long and his hair thick and shiny. He must have had it tied back in his baseball cap, she thought, as it was now touching his broad shoulders in dark waves.

"You've had enough to drink." He answered.

She gasped, jolted out of her appreciation of him. "You've been watching me?"

"No."

"Yes, you have," she teased, placing her elbows on the table and cupping her cheeks. She'd been feeling eyes, other than those close by, on her all night. Now she knew why.

"It was hard not to,"

He made it sound as though she'd been eating fire and prancing around naked.

"Do you want to dance?" She suggested, hearing Mario's *Let Me Love You* for the second time that day.

"No."

"Shame. What's your name?" She'd never had to work so hard to get a man's attention in her life, but she couldn't, wouldn't, leave it alone. Mario playing was a sign.

"Ace."

She laughed and rolled her eyes. "And I'm the Queen of Hearts."

He frowned at her. "Seriously, my name is Ace."

"Nina," she held out her hand and waited. Just when she thought he was going to leave her hanging, he moved forward and grasped her hand. That's when she realised why he didn't want to dance and why he hadn't got out of the car that morning.

He was in a wheelchair.

CHAPTER FOUR

He had to give it to her she didn't flinch or falter as his large hand engulfed hers.

"Nina Mae," she repeated, with a smile.

"And I'm Ace."

"Nice to meet you properly, Ace. No last name?"

"What would be the point?"

Nina shrugged, he was still being stubborn, if the short sentences and hard glare were, anything to go by.

"Well," she looked around as though seeing the place for the first time. "We've got two," she listed. "Probably one and a half nights to get better acquainted before I go home."

"Home, being?"

She noticed how he'd avoided her reference to getting better acquainted. But she'd leave that for now. "Oh, come on. I know you're a Brit and I know you know I am."

He smiled. A proper smile that went to his eyes. Nina wished she knew what colour they were.

"Now that was a helluva sentence, wasn't it?" She mused.

"It was." His lips twitched, trying to keep up. She was so full of sunshine and bubbling vitality. He really shouldn't encourage her. "What gave me away?" He asked reluctantly, needing to satisfy his curiosity.

"This morning, you said the magic word."

He frowned and Nina could see he was turning over their brief conversation in his head.

"You got me. What did I say?"

"Bonnet."

The rich sound of deep laughter filled the air, transforming his face. Nina wasn't surprised by how much she liked the sound of his voice or how young and approachable his features had become.

"Guilty." He put his hands up, admitting defeat, and relaxed into his chair. He could be her friend, for a night, he decided charitably. He wasn't a complete ass-hole.

"Well?" Nina prompted, with a slight nod.

"My family moved to the States when I was thirteen."

"From London? Chelsea perhaps?"

His eyebrows snapped down into a tight frown. "How did you know?" He demanded.

"I like languages; accents, the whole British English, American English, to-mar-toe to-may-toe thing." She explained, lapsing into her fascination with words and languages.

To give him his due, he did listen and accepted his bottled water with barely a glance at the waitress.

"So, all your family are here, in America?" She asked a bit later.

"Yeah, you've met my cousin Kyle—"

"Kyle?" Nina frowned, "Oh, you mean Cuteness!"

Ace didn't like that. "If you mean the guy you were feeling up this morning, then yes, Kyle." He gritted, as he remembered.

"I was not feeling him up!"

"It looked like it from where I was sitting."

They stared at each other, Ace realising, in dismay, that he had inadvertently said way too much.

Nina took a swig of the water he'd ordered for her and carefully put the bottle down as she tried to keep from smiling. The music had changed in tempo, and some Latin beat was playing, but it faded into the background as she observed him.

"The only person I want to touch now is you." She revealed, with honest softness, her dark eyes reflecting her vulnerability.

They looked at each other and Nina held her breath, waiting for his response.

Just as he opened his mouth, about to say something, Andy came up to the table.

"Hiya," she greeted them with a bounce.

"Hey Andy," Nina would have done anything to know what Ace had been about to say. "Pull up a chair." Nina invited, watching her friend sit down before making the introductions.

"I'm ready to head off."

"So early?" Nina said.

"It's after one, and I want to email Gareth before I go to bed. I just don't understand why we can't get internet service in our suite for crap's sake!" Andy lamented.

Nina stood up to leave, unable to hide her dismay.

"You can stay," Andy said, catching the look and touching Nina's arm to stop her from moving. "And I'll take a taxi."

Nina looked at Ace, who was listening to the exchange but giving nothing away. Nina didn't want the night to end.

"Okay, but we'll walk you out," she looked at Ace and, with a cheeky wink, added. "Although hot wheels here will wheel out beside us." She walked off, not daring to see how he'd reacted to her little joke.

Outside, Andy hugged her close. "You sure you're okay? I can stay a little longer if you like. It's just that Gareth wants me—"

"No, go ahead." Nina interrupted. "Text me when you get there."

"And you be sure to text me if you leave here to go anyplace else," Andy ordered right back, sending Nina a knowing look and nodding towards Ace.

They grinned, hugged and kissed each other's cheeks.

"I will," Nina confirmed, and she watched as Andy stepped out into the road and raised her arm to signal a yellow cab like a native. She waved as her friend disappeared.

Nina held the door open for Ace as they went back inside and to his table. Someone had cleared it while they'd been gone. It smelled of pine disinfectant.

They sat down and looked at each other. Nina didn't know him well enough to know what he was thinking; yet, she added to her thoughts.

"So, do you come here often?" Nina teased, to fill the silence. She needed to lighten the mood after the bombshell she'd dropped earlier, but at least he was still here which was encouraging, she thought, dashing away her anxiety.

"You and your friend are close?" He asked, ignoring her

question.

"Oh yeah, we're sisters."

"Sisters?"

"Not blood related," she explained. "We've known each other since primary school."

"Tell me about your life Nina Mae." Ace invited.

"I'm a golden child. Very much a daddy's girl and a mummy's darling." She began conversationally, not the least bit embarrassed by her admission. "Spoilt. An only child of only children. There's just my mum and my dad and little ole me, but I'm not a brat." She told him. "I'm an Essex girl. Do you know what that is?"

"No,"

She smiled at him. "You'll have to visit me in England to find out." She went on. "Are you going to dance with me?"

He scowled. "No."

"Why not?" She pressed.

He crossed his arms over his chest and frowned at her again, Nina realised it was his way of telling her to shut the hell up.

"Let's play a game," she said instead, determined to get her way. "If I win, we dance and if you win you get to ask whatever you want."

Ace pulled in a deep breath and let it out in a noisy whoosh. Why was he still here, he thought, but already knowing the answer. She wanted him, had made it damn obvious with all the nervous chatter and hair flicking. She was desperate enough to keep him guessing, and he was curious enough, egotistical enough, to want to know how this would play out. "What's the game?"

"Things that go together," she explained. "But as pairs."

"Pairs?"

"Yeah. For example, I have to say something that is always referred to in a pair, like Kings and Queens and bricks and mortar, things like that."

Ace shook his head; he'd never come across anyone so complex and playful in his life. But he was game. The pub was emptying, and if he lost, it would be no hardship to wheel around by the table pretending to dance. Jesus Christ, this is what his life had become, playing fucking party games to get his ego stroked.

"You start," he ordered. "Wait," he held up his hand. "How many pairs to win?"

"How about until one of us stops?"

"Cool."

"Left and right. Your turn.

This was going to be so easy, he thought. "Brush and comb."

They played for almost fifteen minutes; Ace was getting into it but knew he was going to lose. She was just too good and too fast. He eventually faltered, and she clapped her hands, declaring herself the winner, of course. His lips twitched into a smile.

"Come on." She stood quickly, eagerly heading over to the dance floor, but turned back when she saw that he hadn't moved.

"Not out there," he said. "Here."

"Okay." Nina agreed, grabbing the back of his chair because it didn't have any handles and, without asking, positioned him so that his back was to the bar and he was facing the wall, where a large mural depicting fields of heather gave the impression, they were in County Tipperary. It was a beautiful focal point.

His wheelchair wasn't bulky at all and was easy to manoeuvre. She'd never seen one like this before, it was compact, with large thin wheels. Then again, had she ever really looked at a wheelchair? Or the person in it? She shook away her dismal thoughts and rolled her shoulders as she stood in front of him, her legs shoulder-width apart as she waited for him to look into her eyes.

She would have preferred softer music but didn't want to chance breaking the mood by asking for a request from the DJ, 50 Cents' *Candy Shop* would have to do.

She picked up the beat and moved around him, undulating slowly as she danced for him, stretching and moving her body to the music. Strippers and pole dancers had nothing on her, she thought confidently, as she lifted her leg to her head, holding the pose as his eyes fed on her legs and her privates, hidden away by her velvet shorts. With another twirl, she placed her leg on his right shoulder before leaning closer, hooking it around his neck. She watched him swallow, before re-releasing him and twirling away, smoothing the backs of her hands down the sides of her body as she danced for him.

Ace was transfixed and as hard as he'd ever been in his life. Some part of him computed the fact that his pipes worked. She danced so close, barely touching him, but he could feel her heat and smell her arousal. He wanted to reach out and smooth his hands up and down her legs. He wanted to lean forward and bury his face in her thighs. She was a tease, and she knew exactly what she was doing to him—the little minx.

"Do you like it?" She asked in his ear, touching her tongue to his lobe with the earring.

He didn't reply. He was too busy enjoying his first full-blown hard-on in months. He wanted to grab her hips and press her down onto it in case it went soft, never to come back.

"Closer," he growled, when she turned her back, pushing her ass nearer, her legs on either side of his. Her dexterity was amazing; she was folding herself around him, without needing to hold on to anything for balance.

Nina looked over her shoulder at him, then turned to face him again. She angled closer and picked up his hands to place them on her hips. Finally, he was touching her. She flicked her hair to one side and ran her tongue up his neck. The saltiness of his skin was a massive turn on.

He turned his head slightly, and their lips met. Their first kiss wasn't tentative or delicate. They didn't ponder their newness. No, with another deep growl Ace grabbed the back of her neck with one hand and her waist with the other and took control.

Nina had been kissed before. Many times. She enjoyed kissing, but this? This was like something she had never felt before. She felt as though she was now his, as though they were now a couple. His lips were familiar and comfortable, as though they'd already shared a lifetime of stories and intimacies.

She knew she wanted to keep on kissing him. Never mind that they had just met, that was irrelevant, her parents had met and married within two months of meeting each other. Nina knew Ace was already a part of her; she felt it.

Wanting to be even closer to him, she bravely sat on his lap and looped her arms around his thick neck, matching his aggression. His erection seared her bottom, and she rocked into it.

Someone dropped a load of glasses or bottles because the loud crash was enough to jolt them both and Nina shot off his knee in surprise. The room fell silent, and the music stopped.

"Sorry!" Someone called out and after a few seconds, the music resumed. *We belong together* by Mariah Carey.

Ace and Nina looked at each other and Nina, not knowing why grinned down at him and waited.

It took ten long seconds to come, but he eventually smiled, and she flung herself onto his knees again, wrapped her arms around his neck and buried her face in the curve of his neck, squeezing him tight, but his entire body went stiff, and she heard his breath catch.

"Oh my God, did I hurt you?" She asked, leaning back. His mouth was tight, and even in the dim light, she could see that his skin had paled. Alarmed, Nina scrambled off him.

"Oh my God," she said again, watching him rub his right thigh and close his eyes. "I hurt you. What should I do?" She asked, worrying her bottom lip in distress.

"It's okay, just give me a minute," he breathed. The pain up his right leg, hip and lower back sliced through him in waves. How could he forget his injuries like that? Fuck!

"I'll call an ambulance,"

"No!" He grabbed her wrist as she made to leave. "It'll pass. It's going already," he lied. "Just give me a minute."

Stricken by guilt, Nina pulled out a chair and sat beside him.

She had no idea why he was in a wheelchair. Hadn't wanted to seem too forward and insensitive by asking. She'd just assumed he didn't have any feelings from the waist down because his legs were held in place by two wide Velcro straps over his jeans.

"I'm sorry," she said, reaching for the hand closest to her that was in a tight fist on his leg. She rubbed her thumb over the white knuckles trying to give him what little comfort she could. "I'm really sorry," she repeated, in a small shaky voice.

Ace opened his eyes to see tears pooling in hers.

"Come here, baby," he ordered softly, as he laced his fingers through hers, pulling her closer so that he could open her hand and kiss her palm. "There's nothing to be sorry about okay?" He captured her chin, forcing her to look at him, and he gave her a reassuring smile. "Want to get some air?" He asked.

She nodded.

"Where are you staying?" He asked, to distract her. Seeing her in tears brought out a tenderness he didn't know he had. Nina named the hotel. "It's just a few blocks from here. Come on." He held out his hand and smiled when she took it.

***

"You called me hot wheels." He said when they'd walked a few feet in silence. New York was never quiet, no matter what time it was and even now, the roads were busy with theatregoers, mixing with people going to and from nightclubs and whatever other social events people went to. They were all vying for the attention of the stream of yellow cabs that snaked up and down the street as though it were midday.

Nina giggled. "So I did,"

"Yet you called me rude."

"It's my term of endearment for you."

"So we have terms of endearments now?" He asked with a smirk.

"Of course. You've seen me naked."

"You weren't naked."

"But very close."

"Hmm," he moved off again, remembering the acres of brown skin on display before she'd pulled her T-shirt on this morning.

They moved on in silence.

They'd only just met, but Ace knew she had something on her mind as she was unusually quiet, and her stride had lost its bounce. She hadn't been this quiet since they met.

He wheeled a little faster then stopped in front of her, blocking her path. "What is it?"

She shrugged and tried to step around him. He blocked her again.

This wasn't good, he thought, realising how much she had come to mean to him in just a few hours. He wanted to hear her non-stop chatter. She made him forget the decisions he had to make.

"Peanut butter and jelly."

"What?" She glanced at him confusion evident in her gaze.

"Moon and stars."

Nina grinned at him and put her hand on his shoulder as they walked. "Nuts and bolts."

"Bows and Arrows."

"Cops and robbers."

"Good one," he praised chuckling. "Ben and Jerry's."

"I won that round I think," Ace said, after a little pause.

Her tinkle of laughter lightened his heart. "I'll tell you what I want later," he said, winking at her as he zigzagged his chair playfully on the sidewalk.

Later, she thought. They had a *later*. She smiled as she rushed to catch up with him with a renewed spring in her step.

CHAPTER FIVE

"This is it," Nina said as she spied the black and gold décor of her hotel. They'd covered the seven blocks without really noticing; talking and laughing all the way.

She learned that he came from a large, blended family with one biological brother and four stepsisters, and he had a raft of cousins. He loved the outdoors, and when she finally asked him what he did for a living, he said, 'nothing at the moment', but that he used to be a stunt man. He didn't say why he was in a wheelchair. But it obviously had to do with his past job.

"Will you come with me to check my emails?" She asked, as the uniformed doorman opened the door with a flourish and a tip to his cap and they entered the decadent interior. An enormous chandelier dominated the lobby, casting soft, twinkling light over the dark marble floors like tiny stars.

"Sure."

Music and laughter were coming from behind a set of double doors to their left. A large black and white portrait of a young Asian couple stood beside them with the words 'Forever loved' and today's date underneath.

"I think a wedding reception is going on," Nina said, seeing his look as they moved past. She skipped ahead to open the door for him. He smiled his gratitude as they went into the empty internet room, set up with two long tables and seven terminals on each.

"What did we used to do before emails?" Ace asked conversationally as he pushed a cream leather office chair out of the way and wheeled himself in front of a computer.

"Waited for days for a little bit of news," Nina mused, going to the terminal beside him and switching it on. "Or had a phone call."

"Yeah, this technology thing has taken off in the last five years.

A laptop in every household will be the norm in a couple of years. You got a digital camera?" He asked, but she wasn't listening, he noticed. Instead, she was biting her pinky fingernail and staring at the monitor. "Nina?"

"Hmm?"

"What is it?" He looked over at her screen, seeing rows of unopened emails. "Bad news?"

"I don't know yet."

"What do you mean?"

"I can't open it."

"Open the email?" He asked, confused, then shot her a quick and concerned glance. She was worrying her bottom lip. "Why not?"

She turned to him. "I applied to Oxford University, and the email is here."

"That's great!"

"What if I didn't get in?"

"Then you go to someplace else."

"I don't want to go someplace else. I need to go to Oxford. It's been my secret dream for years. Now I've told you, and I've told Andy and probably jinxed it." She gabbled, winding herself up. "I shouldn't have said anything," she worried. "I won't get in."

"Nina?" Ace said, then waited until she looked at him. "Open the fucking email."

"Your lack of manners is clearly showing." She scolded as she turned to him.

"Yeah," he agreed, knowing she was stalling. "Now open the fucking thing."

"And your language is appalling."

"If you don't click on it in three seconds, I'll delete it."

"You wouldn't!" She gasped.

"Lady, you have no idea what I'm capable of."

Nina turned to the monitor, moved the mouse over to the open button, closed her eyes and clicked.

"Ace?" She whispered.

"Yes, baby,"

"Can you look for me?"

"I did already."

She kept her eyes closed but turned towards him, her hand valiantly seeking his knee for reassurance.

"What does it say?"

He didn't say anything.

"Ace?"

No answer. Then his lips touched hers.

"Congratulations Nina Mae. You're going to Oxford."

She screamed and wrapped her arms around his neck. "Really?"

"You did it, babes!" The endearment fell from his lips. He'd never been one to give affectionate names to anyone. Hell, he barely remembered a woman's first name, now he was giving out pet names like a fucking pro. He'd only just met her. They hadn't even spent a day together, but already he was emotionally invested in her life. Her happiness meant something to him.

"Oh my God, Ace!"

He laughed. "Are you going to read it?"

She finally opened her eyes, kissed him on the cheek, turned to the screen then just as quickly turned back to him. Her eyes wide.

"What?" He asked puzzled, capturing her gaze.

"Whiskey."

"You want some whiskey?"

She shook her head. "No, your eyes are the colour of my dad's prized bottle of forty-year-old whisky."

Nina had been so caught up in the email and exciting news it hadn't even occurred to her to look at him properly in the fluorescent lighting.

His eyes were a clear, uninterrupted whisky brown, and his hair had strands of auburn.

"Your beard is reddish-blond." She reached up and touched his face as though seeing him for the first time. Yet, in some distant part of her mind, she really was seeing him properly for the first time she acknowledged.

"You have a problem with my red beard?" The scowl he tried to do didn't quite make it.

She laughed, "No, not at all," she replied, rubbing it with both hands, then kissing him quickly. She'd noted earlier how familiar he was to be around. She didn't know him, yet she knew him. It was a peculiar feeling. She felt safe.

"I'll read the rest of this later. Let's celebrate."

"It's three o'clock in the morning!"

"So? You have somewhere you need to be?" She placed her hand on his knee again. "Life is too short as it is. You have to grab it and live it without apology!" She ordered. "How old are you, anyway?"

"Twenty-two," he answered. "How old are you?"

She turned away. "Turning twenty-two in a couple of months."

"Finish up, then let's get out of here." He said. If one thing today had shown him, it was that being around Nina Mae was the distraction he'd needed.

Just then his phone rang, and he fished it out from where he'd stashed it beside his leg. He looked at the number and sighed.

"What?!" He said to Kyle and listened.

Nina, read the Oxford email twice, before checking her other mail and logging out of her account and turning off the computer.

Ace was busy reassuring his cousin that he was fine, and no he didn't need a lift, and yes, he would call him if he needed anything and yes, he was with Nina. He rang off without saying goodbye.

"You and Kyle are close?"

"He's a pain in the ass."

"But you love him?"

Ace grinned. "He's my boy!" He grabbed her hand. "Where to?"

"The wedding reception."

"We can't go in there." Ace stopped just outside the door.

"Why not?"

"Hello. Invitation?"

"Who in their right mind would stop and ask a guy in a

wheelchair if he was invited?"

She had a point, but before he could agree, she looked down at herself and told him to wait there. She would be right back.

Ace watched her walk across the marble floor. She looked out of place in her velvet shorts, bare legs and calf-high boots, yet she walked with a confidence of belonging, that only class and money could bring. Then she turned and came back to him, holding her hand out, palm up.

"Forgot something?" He asked.

"Can I have your phone please?"

He frowned up at her, but pulled it from the side of his chair, although holding onto it. "Why?"

Ace could see the indecision and vulnerability in the look she sent his way, then her chin went up, and she folded her arms across her chest as though ready to fight him for it.

"Will you be here when I come back?"

Ah, Ace thought tenderly as he reached for her hand, swinging it between them. "You don't need my phone, Nina."

Nina gave him a bright smile and let him kiss her knuckles before walking to the elevators again.

What the hell was happening to him, Ace thought, as he pointed to the bar opposite the bank of lifts, letting her know where he'd be. She made a thumbs-up sign just as the elevator door closed and she disappeared from view.

Ace ordered a beer, it was draft, he didn't like draft beer but paid for it and a glass of Cabernet for Nina and wheeled himself to the darkest corner, away from a loud group of men who looked like they were part of the wedding party, as the colour of their suits, shirts and bow ties were all the same.

He still wasn't used to being looked at as though he was some kind of freak, people avoiding his gaze, or being overly friendly just to assuage their own warped feelings of guilt for being normal.

When he'd finally gotten out of the hospital, the hardest thing he'd had to do was adjust his mindset to being that man in a wheelchair and being the shortest in the room.

It had been a stunt gone wrong. He jumped from rooftop to rooftop, filling in for the 'A' list actor who was too precious to do it himself. Someone had left a wrench on a wall. Ace had stepped on it as he leapt, which caused him to skid and lose height and speed. He fell seven stories, hitting the concrete below. He could have died. He should have died. Some days, especially those early days, he wished he'd died.

He'd been laid up in hospital practically all of the previous year. The fall shattering most of the bones in his body. His spine and right hip were so messed up he'd been in surgery for hours over a period of weeks. They didn't think he would ever walk again, but the feelings eventually crept back into his toes, slowly moving upwards and he could feel sensations all over his legs. His hard-on tonight was another milestone in his slow recovery. All thanks to Nina.

He smiled to himself, picking up his drink and taking a long swallow before wiping his mouth with the back of his hand. For saying the hotel was up there in the ranks, the beer was warm and flat.

Now he had a decision to make, Ace knew. Tuesday was the day he was supposed to go back into the hospital. He couldn't cancel again; spinal surgery, the one operation that could maybe decide his entire future.

He'd lived five months in a wheelchair; he had some feelings in his legs. Was it so bad? He was managing, adapting his life. He could go and work in the family business and learn to drive. Nina didn't mind him being in a wheelchair. The fact that she wanted him, even though he was in a wheelchair and clearly a burden, was testament to her commitment to them both. He didn't need to risk never walking again to have her. She accepted him as he was.

***

A lull in the conversation all around made Ace glance up to see what the distraction was. Everyone had turned to the door.

Nina had paused in the doorway, searching through the ultra-dim lighting for him, and Ace felt himself swell with pride. This beautiful woman was looking for him. Him, the man. Not the man everyone noticed for all the wrong reasons. Him.

He wheeled a little to the left, into the aisle, and felt his heart skip a beat as she smiled brightly and walked over to him.

Ace felt his throat close and reached unseeingly for his beer mug. She was so fucking beautiful with her hair swept to one side like that.

She was wearing a long, skin-tight black dress. The straps went to the very edge of her shoulders, as though about to fall down. Her throat and shoulders were bare, and a long split to her thigh played peek-a-boo with her left leg every time she moved. Her body was fucking amazing, and right on cue, he got his second stiffy for the night.

There was a new sass in the swing of her hips too, and Ace looked at her feet and almost choked. Her feet were naked but for a thin metal strap at her toes and another one-inch strap with diamonds on them around her ankles like a cuff. Her toenails were painted in a dark colour.

"Hi," she said shyly.

"You look beautiful," Ace said, wishing he could stand up and pull her chair out for her.

"Thank you." She sat down and looked at the glass of wine. "Is this for me?"

"Of course."

He watched her take a sip and then touch her tongue to the wet spot left behind on her bottom lip, before placing the glass down.

Without words, they looked at each other for long moments, only the laughter of the crowd at the bar interrupting their individual thoughts.

"Andy was awake," she chatted conversationally when his stare was becoming too unnerving.

Ace looked around to signal for another beer, but the bartender was busy.

"Oh yeah."

"On the phone with her new boyfriend."

"I guess you don't like him."

"There's just something about him Ace," she picked up her glass again. "We met him at the same time, although I was a little worse for wear in Marbella—"

"Worse for wear?" He interrupted.

"Tipsy," she evaded, she didn't know why she was now ashamed of her past behaviour. When her dad had shouted at her about it, she'd gladly told him she'd passed out, had practically bragged about it in fact.

Ace raised a brow, his disapproval was clear.

"It won't happen again. Or only if I'm with you." She promised with a wink. "Well, anyway. He was in Marbella by himself. Who goes to Marbella, the party capital of the Costa-Del-Sol by themselves?" She didn't expect him to answer and went on talking, telling him how Gareth had spent the night in Andy's room and travelled back to England with them the next day. That in itself was creepy. How he lives in London and that his family owns some sort of biscuit factory and that he's rich.

"I'm rich Ace, and I don't go around telling strangers that I am."

Ace smiled knowingly.

"You're different," she defended bashfully.

He nodded and let her talk. She was very animated, he thought, watching her delicate hands fly this way and that as she talked passionately about her friend and how she thinks there is something wrong with this Gareth person.

Ace tried to signal for another glass of wine for her, but again the bartender ignored him. Feeling his temper rising, Ace tried valiantly to calm down. This time last year he would have pulled the asshole over the bar and given him one, he thought in frustration.

"I'll just go and get us another round," Nina said, looking at his glass sometime later. "Same again?"

"I'll get it," Ace said, moving his chair, but ending up bouncing the table, making her glass fall over. Luckily, it was practically empty. "Sorry."

"Never mind," Nina used a paper napkin and mopped up the small puddle of wine. "Stay here."

Before he could move, she'd already gone to the bar and was leaning over it waiting to get the bartender's attention.

Ace gripped his hands into hard fists. He should be able to get his woman a fucking drink, he thought bitterly, as he watched the bartender casually walk over and take her order.

A man from the wedding party stumbled over to Nina and put his arm around her shoulders and began whispering in her ear.

Nina pushed him away, but he grabbed her ass.

"What the fuck, man?!" Ace growled, coming over to where Nina was standing.

The man turned with red-rimmed eyes and focused on Ace. He put his hands up.

"I'm just playing man," he slurred. "No harm done was there, honey?" He turned to Nina and stroked her arm.

Nina flung her arm away and moved closer to Ace, but the man followed, grabbing her arm again.

"Get the fuck off her man, or I swear to God."

"Ace, it's okay," Nina started.

"Yeah, Ace," the drunk mimicked. "The lady said it's okay,"

"You have five seconds to get your hands off my woman," Ace threatened.

Ace placed his chair between Nina and the man.

The drunk laughed.

"Come on, Ace, let's go." Nina urged, trying to de-escalate the confrontation. "He's not worth it."

"Or what Ace?" The drunk slurred in a high pitched baby voice.

Ace growled.

Taking matters into her own hands, Nina quickly grabbed what she could of his chair and wheeled him away with the drunkard's laughter ringing out behind them.

Nina wheeled them straight across the lobby and into the privacy of the internet room.

"Don't you *ever* do that again." Ace snarled as soon as he

regained control of his chair and spun around to face her.

"What?"

"What the fuck Nina?! You don't think I can fight my own battles?"

Nina crossed her arms over her chest and leaned against the door.

"It didn't even cross my mind,"

"Then what the hell was that? You pull me out of there like I'm a fucking wimpy shit!"

Nina shrugged, which seemed to incense him even more as his golden eyes blazed at her.

"I'm sorry Ace," she said quickly, walking towards him and pulling out a chair to be at his level.

Ace scrubbed his hands over his face, groaned and then looked at her. "What are we doing, Nina?" He asked warily.

"What do you mean?"

"This? Me and you. What are we doing?"

She reached for his hand and laced her fingers through his. "To be honest Ace," she looked at him, ready to catch his reaction to her next words. "I don't know. I live my life by the moment. The only thing I've ever reached out for is Oxford. I'm a party girl back home. I shop and spend too much money. But," she revealed. "I saw you this morning," she chuckled. "Well, yesterday morning and knew we hadn't finished our conversation."

"We said not even ten words Nina,"

"But it's what we didn't say Ace," she released his hand. Why wasn't he getting it? "For the first time in my life, I wanted to continue a conversation with a stranger who made me feel things by just looking in my direction. I couldn't even see your eyes. Was I wrong, Ace? Was I wrong to plan more than an hour ahead?"

When the seconds dragged without him acknowledging her words, she got up and moved to the door.

"I'm sorry, Ace." She turned to go. "Maybe I was wrong." She whispered past the lump in her throat and hesitated, waiting for

him to tell her to stay.
He didn't.

CHAPTER SIX

"He just let me go, Andy!" Nina wailed into Andy's neck.

"He's a wanker, Nina, and doesn't deserve you."

"Yes, he is Andy."

"Here," Andy passed her the last brownie from the gift basket.

Nina laughed. "You're such a nut," Nina said through her tears, as she bit into the rectangular piece of heaven.

"I'm not the one crying over a lad I just met yesterday." Andy amended, going over to the minibar. "How about we get on it?"

"Good idea!" Nina put two thumbs up. "And tomorrow we go to Macy's, with huge sunglasses on to hide our hangovers."

Andy came back with two heavy tumblers filled with ice.

"What are we drinking, Andy?" Nina asked as she slid to the floor.

"We're going for a quick buzz," Andy clarified, opening two miniature bottles and waving them under Nina's nose. "Whiskey."

Andy didn't know what she had said, but Nina burst into fresh tears, gulped everything down and held her hand out for another drink. "Keep 'em coming Andy, keep 'em coming."

Andy didn't keep them coming though. Gareth rang, and she went into her bedroom to take the call and, after waiting ten minutes, Nina gave up and went to help herself.

Not in the least bit tired, even though she'd been awake practically twenty-four hours straight, Nina was about to go to bed when with the glass in her hand she decided to go downstairs to the ballroom.

She wrenched opened the door and almost fell on top of, Ace.

"You weren't wrong, Nina." Ace said quietly as she focused on him. He looked at the glass in her hand and raised a questioning brow. "You broke your promise."

"What?"

"You said you'd only get shit faced if I'm with you." He reminded her. "Can I come in?"

"I was about to go out."

"It's five-thirty."

"So? I'm back to living for the moment."

He chuckled, then reversed easily to let her pass. "Where were you going?"

"To dance in the ballroom."

"Dance?"

"Yes. I dance when I'm emotional."

"I made you emotional?"

"Don't flatter yourself. I'm not opening myself up to you anymore."

He tipped his head to the side. "I did something I never thought I would do in my life a moment ago."

She looked at him curiously and took the bait. "Oh yeah, what?"

Ace looked up and down the hallway, then back at her.

Nina sighed dramatically. "Okay, you can come in."

He went in.

Nina took off her shoes and, as he watched, said. "They look good but are murder on the feet."

"So why wear them?"

"To see the look on your face."

"I thought you weren't going to flatter me?"

"That was then." She locked the door. "Didn't you have something to say to me?" Nina asked as she put her glass down on a side table, her buzz completely gone, then turned to look at him.

Andy had turned off all but two side lamps in the living room, and Ace was cast in a delicate, pale, golden light that picked out the red strands in his hair.

He sighed and moved to her side, pulled her over to the couch and pushed at her narrow hips to make her sit.

"You could have just told me to sit down, Ace." She said as she bounced against the cushions before making herself comfortable.

"Yeah, well this was more fun." He winked, then reached for her hand. "This wheelchair shit is new to me, Nina," he started softly. "Not so long ago, if any sonofabitch were to put his hands on what was mine, I'd fuck him up. Real good." He paused and looked at her fingers, *piano fingers,* that's what his mother would say; long and elegant. He looked at her again. "So, when you pulled me away, it pissed me off. It made me remember who I was. Just a guy in a fucking wheelchair who can't even defend the person he's with."

Nina leaned forward and rubbed his knee. "I liked it better when you called me your woman," she whispered candidly.

"You can't be yet Nina." He replied, holding her gaze.

When she was about to say something, he cut her off with the look she was beginning to recognise and kept quiet.

"I told you I'm a stunt man," he began again. "Up until my accident, it was me doing most of the stunts around Hollywood. Every blockbuster, jumping out of helicopters, running on top of trains and cars, going over bridges and driving through flames. You name it, I've done it, and I loved every damn minute of it," he reminisced, looking past her to the floaty curtains that hid the view of a small park. "Then I had the accident," he looked at her, pinning her in place with his golden stare. "I fell from a building and busted every fucking bone in my body."

Nina gasped, quickly moved her hand from his knee in case she was hurting him.

"Put it back," Ace ordered, picking up her hand and placing it on his knee himself. "It doesn't hurt." He confirmed. "Where was I?"

"You broke every bone…"

"Yeah. I can't allow you to think of us passed the time you get on that plane and go back to your rich girl party life."

"Fuck you, Ace," she swore. "You can't tell me how to think."

He laced their fingers together.

"You know why it took me so long to get up here?"

"No, I was too busy calling you every name under the sun and trying to drink myself into a stupor."

He chuckled before continuing.

"I had to go to the front desk and beg the receptionist for your room number," he brought her hand to his lips. "I played the invalid."

"I'm sorry."

"Yeah, it wasn't my finest hour."

"But you're here now."

His lips twitched into a small smile. "Yeah, I'm here now." He smoothed his fingers over her hand again. Her hand was so small he thought, her skin so soft he mused.

"Want to go to bed?" She offered suddenly, moving to stretch out the kinks in her shoulders by rolling her head back and forth.

"Nina, I—"

"It's okay, Ace. I just want you to lie with me. Will you?"

"Sure. But—"

"I know you have things to say, but no more tonight, okay?"

"Okay."

Nina led Ace into her bedroom. "If you would like to have a wash, there're towels and stuff in there," she indicated the bathroom, mentally thanking God the doorway was wide and wheelchair friendly. Strange how she'd never had to think this way before and now she was doing it naturally.

"I'm going to use Andy's room for a shower. There's a chaise lounge just there," she pointed to the far end of her room, "I think the bed might be too high for you to get on." She finished without realising that she was biting the nail on her little finger.

Ace noticed.

They both looked at the massive four-poster bed.

"The chaise is cool."

With a nod, Nina walked over to the bed and pulled off the top layers and spread them over the chaise. She did the same with the pillows.

At his questioning look, she made a production of yawning and stretching her arms over her head, then went around her room collecting her night things as he watched.

With the T-shirt she liked to sleep in, hotel robe and her

toiletry bag she hadn't unpacked in her arms, Nina, feigning calmness, walked casually towards him when in fact her insides were a bundle of nerves. He had yet to enter the room properly.

She leaned over him, kissed him on the cheek before whispering. "I'm glad you gave us a chance." She touched his cheek, and he captured her hand, turned it over and kissed her palm.

Nothing else was said, they didn't need words and Nina went to use the bathroom in Andy's room.

***

"He's here!" Nina screeched excitedly as soon as she closed the door behind her and jumped on the lump under the covers that was Andy. Andy was a burrower.

"Huh?" Andy sat up slowly and reached for the bedside lamp, turning it on, then grabbing her friend's ankle to stop her from bouncing.

"Ace! He came upstairs. Oh my God, Andy, I can't breathe!" Nina clutched her chest and fell onto her back with a muffled scream.

Andy grinned. "I'm happy for you. I really am, but I've only just got to sleep."

Nina sat up, pushed her hair out of her face and looked at her friend, "You've been on the phone all this time?"

Andy yawned looking slightly embarrassed.

"I've never known you to be like this. You really like him, Andy?" Nina asked.

Andy smiled weakly.

Andy looked at her phone and Nina followed her gaze realising the phone was open.

"Is he still on the phone?" Nina whispered.

Andy nodded again.

Frowning, Nina slid off her bed, "I'm just going to use your bathroom okay? I wanted to give Ace some privacy." She backed away from the bed. "Erm, tell Gareth I said, hey."

Nina turned and went into the opulent bathroom that

had everything on the opposite side to her own. Slightly disorientated, she pulled off her dress and barely there knickers, brushed her teeth then pulled on a shower cap, before running the water for her shower.

Something wasn't right with the relationship between Andy and Gareth, Nina thought, she knew her friend. Andy was smiling and saying all the right things, but her smile didn't reach her eyes.

Nina had a feeling of foreboding when she thought of Gareth. He was a little shorter than herself, slightly built with brown hair. He wasn't what Andy usually went for. Andy liked what Nina called the British Bulldog type of man. Bald, brawny and rough around the edges. Nina didn't know what it was, but as soon as they got back to England, she'd look closer at their relationship. Something wasn't right with Gareth.

Squirting her favourite vanilla and lotus flower shower gel into her loofah, she quickly washed and rinsed, patted herself dry, smoothed lotion over herself and finished off with a liberal mist of vanilla and lotus flower-scented body spray.

She looked at her reflection, grinned at herself and resprayed herself. She had never done anything like this before. Andy, yes. She no. She partied hard, snogged anyone she felt like, but have a man stay over on the first night? No. This was new, but this was right. This was Ace.

Opening the door, she crept passed Andy, who was murmuring into her phone. Nina blew her a kiss and wished her goodnight, before padding softly over to her own room.

***

She tapped on her door then pushed the door open. Ace had turned off all but one of the lights.

"Hi," she said shyly, as she avoided looking directly at him lying in the chaise and went instead to her bathroom to put down her toiletry bag.

The mirror was still steamed up, and the moister in the air

smelled of five-star generic hotel soap.

"Was it okay in here? Did you manage all right?" She asked, as she finally went into the bedroom and stood in the centre of the room swinging the belt of her hotel robe around and around as though she was whisking eggs.

"Are you sleepy, Nina?" Ace asked instead.

She looked at him. He had on his jeans the top button was undone. His shirt was open, and Nina was able to drink in the pale strip of his chest. His wheelchair was within reaching distance.

"Erm, not really." She replied honestly.

"Then come and talk to me. We don't have much time."

She threw off her robe. "Ah, so you believe me now when I say we have to move now." She tipped her head to the side. "That was a terrible sentence." She said, more to herself.

"I never disbelieved you."

"Then why all the drama, Ace?"

"I'm not used to this pace."

"What do you mean?"

"You've been in charge of the pace," Ace admitted. "If you hadn't walked over to me tonight, I wouldn't have talked to you."

"You're just saying that,"

"No, Nina, I'm not." He stated. "This isn't a good time for me. If I met you last year, if I wasn't in this," he hit one of the wheels with the side of his fist in frustration. "I'd have hauled you over my shoulder and taken you home and made love to you all night."

At that visual, Nina felt a tingle slide to her privates and closed her eyes as she pictured him making love to her.

"Don't," Ace said, on a tortured whisper. "Please."

Nina opened passion-filled eyes and tried to focus on him. His dark gold eyes were filled with yearning.

"I'd like nothing more than for you to make love to me, Ace,"

"No!" he yelled. "Nina," he scrubbed his hands over his face twice, before he looked at her again. "I can't."

"But I can wait," she finished lightly, as though they were

waiting on a pizza order.

He chuckled. "You're something? Do you know that?"

"I'm your something." She confirmed cheekily.

He shook his head and then rubbed his chin. "Are you going to stand in the middle of the room all night?"

Nina walked towards him, seeing his eyes on her bare legs. He patted the space beside him.

She lay down, curling on her side. "Am I hurting you?" She asked.

"You're not even touching me."

Nina turned onto her back and looked up at him. This was the first time she was looking up at him.

"Tell me about your injuries."

"Tomorrow."

Nina edged closer to him. "Am I hurting you?" She asked again, feeling the heat of his body at her back and wishing she was naked.

Nina felt herself hauled around the waist into the curve of his upper body.

"I'm not made of glass babes," he left his hand on the curve of her waist. "Is this okay?"

"This is perfect."

"You're easy to please Nina Mae,"

"Thank you,"

They lay in silence for a moment, Nina cataloguing every part of her body that was touching his. She loved the feel of him, his large hand now on her stomach, his fingers spread out wide. She felt safe and cherished and dare she even think it; she felt loved.

"Ace?"

"Nina," he replied in her ear.

"I'm glad I met you."

She felt his smile behind her head, and his hand pressed into her lightly.

"Go to sleep, baby. You've had a long day."

"Are you comfortable? Do you need anything?"

"Just you in front of me so I don't fall off this fucking chair." He said, with a chuckle.

"Oh, Ace, I didn't think?"

"I was joking baby."

"Do you have any feelings in your legs?"

He sighed. "You're not going to let up, are you?"

"No,"

"I have tingly feelings. Some days it feels like hot pins and needles and hurts like fuck."

She turned to him and skimmed her hand lightly over his thigh. "Can you feel this?"

"Yes."

She walked two fingers up to his groin and over his hip. "This?"

When she'd danced for him at the club, she'd known he'd gotten hard.

"Yes."

"When was the last time you made love, Ace?"

"Nina," he groaned.

"I want to know."

"The day of the accident."

"Was it with someone you cared about?"

Ace thought back to Cleo, another stunt double. They had sex whenever they were on set together. Did he care about her? No.

"Not really."

"Oh."

"That's it?"

"What do you want me to say?"

"I don't know, maybe have some form of feminine outrage that I could have sex with someone I didn't even care about."

She shrugged.

Ace found that he didn't like what she wasn't saying.

"Have you?" He ground out. "No, don't tell me," he rushed before she could answer. "I don't want to know."

She giggled.

"Ace?"

"Nina."

"Today has been the most perfect day."

She felt his lips at the back of her neck and smiled. "It has. Now go to sleep."

CHAPTER SEVEN

Ace had slept the best sleep he'd had in fucking months. Nina had managed to wrap herself all around him, and he'd pulled her in close, anchoring her to him.

He could hear her talking with her friend Andy, and Ace used the opportunity to haul himself into his chair. Nina had put it right beside him and, appreciating her thoughtfulness, went to the bathroom.

The space between the toilet and the basin was too tight so, like last night, he pissed in the open shower, squirted shower gel around the drain and turned on the water to clean it.

He washed, brushed his teeth and rubbed his hands over his hair and tied it back because he couldn't find her brush or comb.

"Hiya," Nina said, as she knocked and walked into the bedroom.

"Hey, babe."

"Andy ordered a load of food for us, want to come out?"

"No,"

"Huh," she paused mid-stride and turned back to him.

"Not until you say good morning properly."

The smile she bestowed on him set him on fire, and her walk made his heart combust. What the hell was happening to him?

"I can do that."

Nina placed her legs on either side of his and leaned down to kiss him. This was their first proper kiss since the pub, and it was just as emotionally powerful as their first. Nina gave all that she got. A meeting and exploration of tongues as Ace cupped the back of her head, taking charge of their movements. He was running this show.

Her groan set him off, and he released her mouth, only to glide his tongue down her throat, behind her ear and back to her mouth again.

Her breath fractured, and her hands went to his shoulders for support as, with uncanny navigation, he swept one hand up and over her breast to sweep across her nipple.

"Good morning Nina Mae." Ace smiled, against her lips before going in for another kiss and releasing her.

"Good morning, Ace,"

"You said something about breakfast?" He reminded her, as he watched with a satisfied smile, the way she touched her tongue to her bottom lip.

She was wearing a simple pair of blue jeans and a white V-necked T-shirt. Her hair was caught over one shoulder. She looked young, fresh, and happy.

"Follow me, hot wheels," she joked, walking ahead of him and screamed as his hand tapped her backside as he wheeled past her and went to the table where Andy was already sitting.

Nina had purchased fresh underwear and a shirt for Ace from the hotel shop, saying they only had a limited time together and that he wasn't going home to change.

They'd jokingly argued, him calling her a jailer and she telling him she'd gladly lock him in her bedroom.

It was midday by the time they got themselves together. If Andy hadn't already planned their shopping trip and sightseeing tour, Nina would have gladly stayed holed up with Ace, but her friend had flown thousands of miles to be with her, and she wasn't going to let her down.

They went to Macy's, although Andy was texting or talking on her phone as they perused the aisles. Nina would have minded if she wasn't having so much fun just walking beside Ace, with her hand on his shoulder. With agreement from all, they voted to forego the sightseeing and headed back for an early dinner.

"I'm off to my room," Andy announced when they entered their suite after a quick meal in one of the hotel restaurants. "And I won't be coming out." She winked at Ace. Then she went into her room.

"She's really discreet," Ace chuckled.

Nina laughed.

"Film?"

"Sure,"

Nina turned on the TV and gave him the remote. "You choose while I go have a quick shower. I need to get this New York grime off me."

"Hey, you insulting my city?"

"I might be," she teased. "What are you going to do about it?"

"Come here, and I might just show you."

She stalked playfully towards him then stopped when his phone rang.

"Whatsup," Ace answered, watching as Nina changed direction and walked to her room, giving him a glimpse of her slender back as she pulled off her T-shirt along her way, sending him a look over her shoulder. The minx.

***

With Kyle's call, reality had intruded. Ace pondered the phone he was still holding, wanting to throw it at the damn wall. His family loved him, he knew, and this past year and a half had been hard on all of them. But they had to realise he was a grown-ass man. He could stay out all night if he fucking wanted too. If he were walking, they wouldn't even be concerned.

So okay, the hospital had called his mom to confirm times and what he shouldn't be doing in the next twenty-four hours but fuck that shit. He planned on spending every fucking moment with Nina. When she left, then he would think about how fucked up his life was going to become, but right now, he was doing what she'd said yesterday, grabbing his life and doing it his way without fucking apology!

***

"Everything okay?" Nina asked, when she stepped out of the bathroom, seeing Ace exactly where she had left him in the living room, looking down at his phone as though it were a grenade or something.

He looked over at her, his frown clearing as his eyes skimmed her T-shirt and bare legs.

"You look beautiful,"

"I'm wearing what I wore last night," she clarified, looking down at herself.

"And you wear it well."

He wheeled into the room and stopped.

"I had them change the bed," she told him nervously, walking over to the king-sized bed and smoothing a non-existent wrinkle out of the Bengal striped white and gold duvet. "Is the height, okay?" She asked anxiously, walking around to him.

"It's great." He moved to the bed. Her thoughtfulness touched another piece of his heart. She'd been doing that all day. Opening doors for him, scouting out the elevators, *lifts*, as she insisted on calling them and she'd even quietly pointed out the disabled toilets for him in the hotel lobby before they came upstairs. As he said, her considerations touched his heart.

"I want you comfortable, Ace,"

"Come here, babes and let me kiss you."

She skipped over to him and let him kiss her. She had never been so happy in her life.

"Do you need help in the shower? I got them to bring a chair type thingy for you."

"I'll be fine," he pulled on her arm, and she came down to his level. "Thank you." He smoothed his lips over hers.

With a heart like he'd never felt before and all thoughts of Kyle, his mom and hospital pushed firmly to the back of his mind, he took a shower and changed into the grey sweats and T-shirt she'd laid out for him.

***

"Ace?"

"Nina."

They were in bed, not bothering with the film, her head resting on his shoulder, one of her legs laying comfortably over the two of his, once she'd established, she wasn't hurting him, that is.

"Are you going to tell me why Kyle keeps ringing?"

The hand that had been stroking her arm stopped.

"What time is your flight tomorrow?" He asked, instead.

"No, no, no, Ace, you are going to tell me what's going on before I get on that plane un'all."

"Un'all?"

"It's Essex speak," she explained, nudging his arm. "Now tell me!"

"Fucking God woman I'm delicate!"

"Last night you told me you weren't made of glass!" She reminded him and moved to look down at him, ready to tell him off. But she was caught in his golden gaze and smoothed her hand over his right eyebrow instead.

"Ace?" She said as she continued to stroke his eyebrow.

"Nina."

She didn't say what she was going to say, but kissed him instead. Long and deep.

He stroked her back, his large hand going under her T-shirt to smooth her skin. Nina felt as though a trail of fire was touching her. If he could make her this hot with just a touch, what could he do if he were inside her?

Carefully, she rearranged herself closer, keeping all her weight on her knees as she smoothed one hand down his arm to his wrist and back again.

She was surprised he hadn't stopped her yet, as, with feminine cunning, she ran her tongue over his ear and down towards the neckline of his white T-shirt. She would do anything to have him take off the damn thing but knew if she stopped now, he just might not let her start again.

She kissed him long and hard. Loving the feel of both his hands now under her shirt, skimming her lower back, playing with the shallow dimples she knew were there before his hands moved to cup and massage her bottom. She'd put on the sexiest knickers she had with her—a sheer black number with a nineties style cut which did amazing things to her legs and hips.

She leaned back onto her thighs, still careful with her weight.

He said he wasn't made of glass, but he was still healing, and she couldn't bear to hurt him as she did last night in the pub.

She moved back and forth, kissing his throat and his lips, encouraged by the harshness of his breath, and when his hands went high enough to cup her breasts, she went to heaven.

"Oh Ace," she whispered against his neck as he pinched her nipples. She'd needed this all day. She'd needed this her entire life, she thought, and she rose to her knees again, making it easier for him to touch her.

"Take it off, Nina," he ordered, fisting the front of her shirt.

"Gladly." She hauled it off and threw it on the floor, raised above him and let him have his fill of her.

"God, you're beautiful," he said reverently, cupping his hands so that her breasts overflowed into his palms. He massaged them like dough and rolled and pinched her nipples, all the while watching her closely through eyes half-hidden.

"Closer," he growled, deep in his throat, as she moved so that her breasts were within tongue reaching distance from his mouth. He flicked first one nipple and then the other with his tongue. He pushed them together and feasted on her body.

They made love, touching and caressing, sucking, nipping and exploring.

Nina felt Ace boldly sweep over her hip to skim the lacy edge of her knickers. She held her breath and looked at him.

His eyes had turned to a burnished dark golden colour, and his face was flushed a deep sensual red.

"Do it," Nina ordered, feeling his fingers dance around her crotch, one finger sliding back and forth across the damp fabric.

In the inner recesses of her mind, Nina knew Ace must have been an amazing lover before his accident, as what he was doing to her now, without using any other part of his body was amazing. She'd never been this aroused in her life and had never wanted a man inside her as badly as she wanted him.

She was unable to keep her eyes open when he slid one finger into her, slowing moving in and out and rubbing her hard nub as she tried to still the natural rhythm of her hips.

"Are you coming, baby?" He asked, adding another finger and pumping harder.

Nina threw back her head, riding his hand, not the least bit embarrassed that she was completely open to him. Her emotions were on show, open and honest and with a scream she rolled into the biggest, longest orgasm she'd ever had in her life.

He continued to slowly pump in and out of her, calming her and then stroking her softly as, with her eyes now on him, he sucked his wet fingers into his mouth.

She didn't give him a moment to consider what she was about to do and quickly moved onto her side and slid her hands under the elasticated waistband of his cotton sweats.

"Nina baby," Ace groaned, as she pulled his swollen penis free.

He was beautiful, long and with a wide girth. Nina ran her tongue over the smooth head and then traced the thick dark vein that meandered underneath, sucking it gently as it disappeared into his balls.

"Let me Ace, please," she begged, taking him into her mouth as far as he could go, swallowing and tickling him with her tongue.

She watched him closely, looking for any signs she might be hurting him. All her weight was on her right elbow and hip; only her mouth and hair were touching him.

He grabbed her hair into his fist and tried to take charge, but she shook him away.

"This is my show." She told him and watched as he leaned back against the pillows and let her have her way.

But his eyes snapped open when he felt her move over him.

"Nina," he warned.

"Shh," she leaned up to him and kissed him. "I won't hurt you."

"I know, but—"

"Please Ace, I know what I'm doing."

Ace watched as she moved over him, unable to stop her as she placed her knees on either side of his hips.

Ever so slowly, she lowered her body onto him.

"Shh, I just need to feel you inside me, Ace," she whispered. "I just need to take the feel of you here," she squeezed her inner muscles around him. "Home with me." She confessed huskily as she tensed and released around him, once then twice, stamping his image onto her walls.

She knew she wouldn't be able to keep from jarring his fragile body, so with all that she had, she slid off him, quickly turned around and used her mouth and her tongue to encourage the drops of pre-cum to give more.

She'd never allowed a man to cum in her mouth before, but she captured and drank every last drop of Ace.

They fell asleep for a moment, Nina wrapped around him, Ace sliding the backs of his fingers up and down her back.

His phone ringing woke them, and Nina reached it for him, noticing that it was Kyle calling again.

"Yo bro," Ace said, and unlike any other time he'd been on the phone, Nina stayed precisely where she was and listened.

"I'll be there." Ace gritted.

Kyle obviously said something more as Ace lost all patience and yelled. "I'll be there all right! If you blow up this phone one more fucking time, I will personally drape your balls over a fucking washing line!" He snapped his phone shut and threw it on the floor.

"Are you going to tell me now?"

He sighed.

"Tomorrow, I need to check into Mercy General for major spinal surgery that will define whether I'll ever be able to walk again. It's high risk. I could lose what little feeling and mobility I have, or I could be off skiing in Colorado and jumping freestyle over buildings next year." He stated matter-of-factly in one breath.

Nina gasped. "Tomorrow?"

"Yeah."

"So," she raised onto her elbow, cradling her head with her hand. "Shouldn't you be prepped or something?"

"It can wait until tomorrow."

"No Ace, I'm all for you having your little dalliance, but this is serious,"

"Dalliance?" He scoffed at the word. "For your information,

even standing upright I would never have a *dalliance* with you, you mean more to me than that!" He yelled. "I wanted to be here. I know what I'm doing. I'm not a fucking kid."

"I never said you were and don't you take your anger out on me. You are being deliberately obtuse when I know you should be in the hospital right now."

They had a stare-off. Ace was the first to break.

"Look," he started on a sigh. "I didn't have anything to eat after ten o'clock. I stopped the alcohol yesterday. The only thing they need to prep is probably shaving my fucking balls. I'll get there when I'm good and ready, and that will be when I've seen you on that fucking plane."

"You're that eager to get rid of me, Ace?" She said, softening after his passionate little outburst. There wasn't any point arguing, it was gone midnight after all. He wouldn't be able to go to the hospital to be prepped now anyway.

"Never."

"Good."

She lay down again, her head on his shoulder in what was fast becoming her all-time favourite place to be.

"Ace?"

"Nina?"

"My flight is at six o'clock. What time is your surgery?"

She didn't like the pause before his answer and gathered herself.

"Two."

"So, what had you planned to do?" She asked. "Tell me you had to nip out for a bit and never come back?"

"No. I hadn't thought that far ahead."

"You are so full of it."

"Seriously, I don't have a plan."

"Were you going to tell me?"

His silence told her his answer.

After a while, he said quietly. "Nina, I told you last night, this is the wrong time for you and me. Any other year and I'd be on that plane with you. I wouldn't let you out of my sight. You mean something to me."

"You mean something to me too."

"We'll deal with it tomorrow."

"I'll come with you to the hospital. At least until your family comes to be with you."

"You'll need to check-in three hours before your flight."

"So, we pack in the morning, and I take my stuff with me. Andy won't mind checking out early," she said. "Please."

"We'll figure it out." He hugged her close and kissed her forehead. "We'd better get some sleep."

***

Breakfast was a light affair, Nina feeling guilty for her All-American breakfast as Ace looked longingly at her turkey bacon.

"None for you mister," she teased.

"One of these days..."

"Promises promises,"

They'd told Andy the change of plans and Andy being Andy checked them out early and arranged for a limo to pick them up and take them straight to the hospital.

***

As they arrived at Mercy General, Ace was whisked away, and Nina and Andy sat around surrounded by their luggage, as they awaited any news.

"We never thought our New York trip would be like this huh Nina?" Andy said as she bit into a chocolate bar.

"I have never in my whole life been with someone who makes me feel like this Andy."

"But what if he doesn't walk again?"

Nina shrugged. "It really doesn't matter to me. I met him like this."

"But to never walk? Never have kids? I know for a fact you want a big family. It's all you've ever talked about."

"Then we adopt or whatever Andy, I don't care. I just want the man."

Andy continued to look at her and Nina was relieved when her phone rang, and Andy walked off to talk to Gareth.

They were there hours, waiting and hearing little tit-bits. Yes, he had his pre-operative bloods taken. His blood pressure was fine, he'd had a special shower, and although sedated, he was now able to see her.

Nina excitedly flapped her hands, signalling Andy to watch their bags as she ran to his room, only to stumble to a stop in the doorway.

"Hey babes," she said tentatively, stuffing her hands into the pockets of her black and yellow University of Maryland hoodie she was travelling in.

"Hey beautiful, you coming in or making love to the door jamb?"

She laughed, walking into his room. He was wearing standard hospital robes, and his long hair was pulled into a knot on top of his head. On any other man, the style would look ridiculous, but on Ace, it just made him look edgy and sexy as hell.

"How are you feeling?"

"Fine. They poked this and pulled that, turned me over, drew some shit on my spine and now we wait. How are you doing?"

"Wishing I didn't have to fly away. I might just cancel my flight." It hadn't been the first time she'd made that offer.

"No fucking way. You have Oxford to sort out."

"Yeah, Oxford." She said, without enthusiasm.

"Hey, take pity on me and come closer," he reached out his hand, being careful not to tug on the cannula in his vein and clasped her small hand into his.

"Oxford is your dream. Follow it."

"But—"

"No buts, if things go well, it will take me months to even get on my feet. With you over there carousing with all those yuppy highbrow English boys, I've got the motivation to knock 'em out and go get my woman."

She smiled at him, and he pulled her closer until he could kiss her. "Thank you for being here."

"Thank you for being all pervy and winding down your window to tell me you've been pervy or we would never have met."

Their eyes met and held and, seeing her getting all teary-eyed again, Ace pulled his small gold stud out of his ear and gave it to her. "Here."

Nina took it and placed it in the spare hole she had in her left ear. On her seventeenth birthday, in Toronto, she'd got an extra piercing for no other reason than to be different.

They laughed and, looking at the clock above the door, knew they had a little over an hour before his family came. Nina stayed, clutching his hand, committing every word he said, every movement he made and every flicker of emotion he showed to memory.

A tentative knock on the door sometime later interrupted their argument over whether or not tea and lemon was a rightful pair.

"Nina, your mum is on my phone."

"My mum?" She asked, alarmed, standing up to hurry to her friend. She had switched off her phone at the behest of all the warnings plastered around the ward.

"I'll be right back," she told Ace, as she walked with her friend out of the room and to the waiting area.

"Mummy?" Nina said, grasping the phone with trembling fingers. Her mother didn't like telephones and only ever used them when she deemed it absolutely necessary. Her dad was the talker. Nina had already talked to her parents today, telling them about Oxford and confirming their flight. "Mummy, what is it?"

"I need you to come home. I've already told Andy the change of plans. The driver will meet you at the airport and drive you straight home."

"Why? What's going on?"

"I need you home now Sabrina." Her mother rang off.

"What's going on, Andy?" Nina said, frightened even more. No one called her Sabrina. Something terrible had happened. "Did she say anything to you?"

"Only to get you on that flight. We have to leave now Nina." Andy was looking at the time on her phone.

"Now?"

Andy shook her. "We have to go."

"But Ace…." Nina whispered, on the verge of tears.

"His family will be here soon. You were planning on being gone before they came, anyway. Let's go. Something has happened."

Torn, but knowing she had no choice, Nina went into Ace's room. The sedative they'd given him was kicking in with a vengeance now that he wasn't fighting it; she walked up to him and touched his face.

"Ace, I need to go. My mother called."

"Okay baby." He slurred, turning his face to kiss her palm. "See you soon."

"See you soon, Ace." She whispered, letting her tears fall.

"Ace?"

"Nina?"

"I love you."

His smile was sleepy, his eyes had already closed, but his lips tugged up to one side.

"I love you too."

***

Andy had called a taxi and was already loading their bags. With tears streaming down her face, Nina tried to help but was told to sit in the back seat as she was more of a hindrance.

"It'll be okay, Nina." Andy soothed as she closed her door, and the taxi pulled away from the kerb.

"Wait!" Nina yelled, banging the back of the driver's seat. "Stop!"

"What is it? What's the matter?" Andy asked.

"Paper Andy, I need paper!"

Andy scrambled around in her bag and pulled out a small

notepad and pen.

Nina grabbed it and took off, running into the hospital, taking the stairs to his floor and rushing to the nurses' station.

"Can you give this to Ace for me?" She tore off a piece of paper, drew a large heart and wrote Dandelion and Burdock, hugs and kisses, then the words Me and You. She wrote her mobile telephone number underneath, folded it and held it out to the nurse. "He's in room two three one, about to have spinal surgery. Please give it to him." She handed the paper over.

"I sure will, darling." The nurse promised, standing up to do just that.

"Nina!" Andy had come up behind her and took her arm to drag her away. "We've got to go!"

Nina looked over her shoulder, seeing the nurse enter Ace's room, only then did she move.

***

By keeping the gate open an additional ten minutes, they were able to make the flight. Andy slept the entire eight hours while Nina became an emotional wreck.

She went from missing Ace and wanting to be with him, to wondering what would be waiting for her when they landed. It was going to be bad. It could only be bad. Her mother, usually a calm and serene woman, floated through life being pampered and adored by her husband. She didn't give orders.

Nina didn't eat, and she didn't sleep. She was watching the clock and praying everything would be okay with Ace.

They were met by the driver that was permanently on call for the family and whisked, not to the family home, but the flat in central London. Her mother met them at the door looking bedraggled and broken, her eyes swollen with tears, no make-up and no pearls.

The rest of Nina's day was a haze, as she tried to come to grips with her dad hanging himself in his office. Her mother had found him.

Over the next few days, funeral arrangements were made. Being a popular, likeable man, her father's send-off was an elaborate affair and, only once he was laid to rest, and the visitors had left, was Nina able to breathe for the first time since her mother's phone call seventeen days ago.

She'd rung Mercy General several times, but as she wasn't a relative and unable to give his full name, they refused to bestow any information to her.

That's when it hit.

She only knew him as Ace. What was his given name? What was his surname? They'd been so caught up in the here and now, cramming being together in the few hours they had, that neither of them had asked the right questions, not wanting reality to intrude in their brief moments of bliss.

Now she was paying for it. It was worse not knowing if he was all right, how the surgery went, was it a success? Could he walk? She felt as though she had abandoned him. But then, why hadn't he called her or sent her a text message? It had been seventeen days. He could have had Kyle ring her, or send a text?

Not knowing what to do, Nina made plans to fly back for a few days after the Will was read and her mother safely ensconced in the new house in Cornwall, the one her dad had told her about.

Nina expected the Will reading to be quick, and it was. Only the news they received wasn't what they'd expected. There was no money.

Nina cancelled her flight to be with her mother, who had a complete breakdown in the office.

CHAPTER EIGHT

"Alister, why has it taken you so long to visit your mother?!" Ace found himself engulfed in the tiny arms of his stepmother, then having his cheeks pulled as though he were a chubby youngster.

"You saw me last month, Mom." For that reminder, he got himself slapped upside the head and then kissed on both cheeks.

"A month, a year, it doesn't matter to a mother, I need to see my children regularly." She chastised.

Ace loved the little fireball who had captured his father's heart all those years ago. She had been a tourist in London with her then little daughters, recently widowed, but she fell in love with her Englishman and his two sons.

"If you tell me you've been climbing mountains again, without a rope, I will likely faint and hit my head, and you will be at fault for my death. Charles! Charles," she yelled for her husband. "Charles," she said, as Ace's father walked into the room with an indulgent smile on his face. "Tell this son of ours that he is going to be the death of me."

"Alister, I don't want to be mopping up any blood tonight." He commented, used to his wife's emotional dramas. Then he met his son halfway across the hallway and hugged him tightly. They used to be the same height, but Ace had lost an inch from his surgeries. He was now six foot two.

"Hi, Dad,"

"Hi, son. How long are you in the city for?" Charles Edwards asked, in the British accent Ace had lost years ago.

Ace shrugged. He'd never been able to stay in one place for too long and, since the accident, his need for freedom and open space had increased tenfold. New York felt like a chokehold most of the time.

"A few days," he shrugged.

"You brought a girlfriend home with you this time?" His mother asked, at least this time he'd managed to get his coat off before the question arrived.

"Not today."

"Seeing anyone? Any grandbabies for me to hold?"

"Mom, anyone would think you don't have any grandbabies. Didn't we have two christenings this year already?"

She tutted and went to the kitchen, knowing that he would follow.

"Alister, you break my heart. I want to see you married, not jumping out of planes. I want to see you laughing." She looked at him.

Ace had heard the lecture countless times over the years. It had been almost seven years since his last surgery, and apparently, he hadn't laughed since if his mother was right.

He laughed, but only at all the superficial stuff that didn't touch him, he mused.

"Charles? Alister said he would come with me tonight,"

"Hold on, what?" Ace jumped, in realising a little too late that he had done the dangerous thing by tuning out when his mother was talking. Now she was looking at him expectantly, and his dad was telling her that was a great idea. "Hey!"

"You raising your voice in my house, young man?"

"No, ma'am."

She grinned. "I didn't think so." She patted his cheek. "We're heading into the city; I'm going to see my favourite author. She's never in town but doing a one night only reading at an independent bookstore. Your brother managed to get me and your sisters' tickets."

"So why aren't you going with them?"

"We're meeting Kelly and Charlene." She turned to the stove and dished out a plate for him. "Here, eat this while I go make myself look beautiful."

"You're already beautiful Mom,"

"Ah, look at you," she patted his face. "I raised you right." He chuckled as she went off.

Ace shook his head fondly after the little dynamo that was his mother. She was five foot one, if that, chubby with straight black hair with a wide streak of silver at the front. She dressed for comfort rather than style but loved costume jewellery and wore lots of it.

His own mom had died when he was a baby, and his dad had raised him and his brother alone for years and then Greta came along and literally moved them to America overnight. They went from a family of three men to a household of Italian American women times five. It was chaotic and loud. Ace loved it.

Sitting down at the large family table, he tucked into his Cacciucco and rolled his eyes at how fantastic the fish stew was. His mother was the greatest cook on earth. No one could tell him otherwise.

Ace reached for the paperback book that was on the table and looked at the cover. Dark grey, with a pink rose, tipped over into a small pool of water. *The Beloved* spelt out in red. He shook his head.

His mother made no bones about the fact that she read every romance that came out. This particular author, S. M. Forrester, was her all-time favourite though, as he himself had bought her the Italian version in hardback while in Florence one year.

There wasn't an author photograph on the back, which was odd. Most authors were egotistical enough to want to be known and recognised in the street for their work. But not the elusive S. M. Forrester.

Ace put the book down when his father sat beside him, knowing what was coming next.

"How are you feeling son?"

"Fine."

"When are you going to stop?"

"When it stops hurting Dad." Ace replied honestly. He could manage the odd little twinge in his back, but it was his heart he couldn't handle.

Charles touched his youngest son's shoulder and squeezed,

knowing all that had gone on that weekend seven years ago, and the search ever since.

"It will never stop hurting Alister. It will only feel different."

"Is that how it is with you? You still love my mother?"

Charles nodded. "Always, but my situation was different. With her death, I got closure. But over the years the loneliness set in. You boys were getting older and didn't need me as much. I needed someone to love and slam, there she was, walked right out into the street without looking." Charles remembered fondly the day Greta had walked into the street as she'd looked right first, instead of left, being an American, and him mowing her down on his bicycle.

"All this riding of motorcycles at high speeds and jumping out of planes you're doing is because you have no one to come home to. You need to open your heart and find someone you want to come home to, or your life will be wasted."

Ace nodded. He'd heard it all before. Kyle, his brother Matthew, his gaggle of sisters all trying to set him up with their friends. He'd dated, he had needs after all. He'd even dated one woman for four whole months, but she wasn't Nina, and that was the crux of it. None of them was Nina.

***

His mother hadn't told him he would be meeting his sisters for dessert, before the book thing, so Ace found himself the only male with three women, all telling him how thin he was and how they didn't like what he was doing for a living. It was only when he threatened to leave that they calmed down and he allowed himself to enjoy their company. It had been a while since they were together like this, and he sipped his beer as he listened to them discuss the book. When something Kelly, the baby of the family said, caught his attention.

"Say that again?"

"What?"

"You said something about a game they played. What game?"

"This thing of pairs. Greg and I have started playing it. It's great fun."

The blood in Ace's ears began to roar.

"You okay Ace?"

"Didn't I tell you not to call him by that ridiculous name?" Their mom told Charlene off. Ace knew it was because it reminded her of the time he nearly died.

"Sorry, Mom,"

"Let me see the book?"

"I've not got my copy with me," Kelly turned to her sister. "You have yours?"

Charlene pulled it out of her bag. Kelly grabbed it from her. "Have you even read it?" She asked, turning over the pristine copy.

"This will be for her to sign. It'll be worth something years from now."

Her sister scoffed at her. "Yeah, alongside the other hundred million that were printed. This book is still number one. Sixteen weeks and counting."

"Can I have it?" Ace asked, losing patience. He'd held his mother's copy just a few hours ago. He'd leafed through it, but he hadn't read any of it.

Kelly passed it over.

"Why so curious, big bro?"

"No reason. Just want to read the blurb and author bio," he said vaguely.

"Careful you don't crease the pages and actually, wipe your hands before you open it. Alister!" Too late he'd already thumbed through and was reading the bio.

There was nothing deeper than the usual bits about lives in England and gardens. He flicked to the back cover and read.

***

Dessert over, and with his mother's arm tucked into the crook of his, they walked casually to the book shop, laughing and talking along the way.

It was good to be around family, Ace thought as he listened to his youngest sister Kelly, the one born from both parents, lament about her husband and his lack of cooking skills and why should she have to do all the cooking. She's a modern woman!

His mother patted his arm at that announcement, and he smiled. Yes, it was nice being around family.

When they stopped, Ace stepped back and looked up and down the street. No, it can't be, he thought, taking in the modern façade.

Both windows were predominantly filled with towers of the guest authors latest book, *The Beholden*. Her other titles sprinkled artfully around. There was a sign announcing her appearance and today's date.

He shook his head at his mother's troubled look and opened the door for them. The entrance was different, no longer a narrow door painted dark mottled green, but now double doors made of natural wood and glass, the handles made of brass.

"What is it, Alister?" His mother asked as they sat down in padded chairs in the second to last row. There were about forty or so people already seated in front of two chairs on a small, makeshift platform.

"I'm not sure." He answered, honestly.

"You're not hurting?" She asked, her already lined face creasing with concern. "Your back is okay?"

He smiled, his whole stance softening as he looked down at her. "My back is fine Mom."

"You wouldn't lie to an old lady?"

He chuckled, about to answer, when a woman in a sharply tailored black suit, white shirt and thin red satin tie walked out from behind a curtain at the back. Her hair was blue-black and cut in a severe bob to her ears. She was the epitome of a publicist.

"Thank you for coming everyone, and a special welcome to our Radio one five nine New York FM winners."

There were whoop whoops and excited clapping from a group of about seven women in the front row.

Ace tuned out to look around. It was the same place and, looking to his left, the large mural of purple heather confirmed it.

"As you know, this is the last night for the American leg of *The Beholden* book tour. Ms Forrester particularly wanted New York to be her last stop because, as some of you may know, New York holds fond memories for the author and is where she set that special weekend in *The Beholden*."

Ace made a mental note to read the book. He didn't realise he was rubbing his leg until his mother touched his hand, and she folded her be-ringed fingers around his.

"So, without further ado," the publicist said, enthusiastically. "I'd like to introduce bestselling author and my friend, S.M. Forrester!"

Everyone stood up and started clapping.

Ace's first thought was that she was thinner, much thinner. Where seven years ago, her cheeks were full, now her cheekbones were sharper, giving her a haunting beauty. Her eyebrows were narrower and arched differently, and her hair was in one, two, three... he counted twelve plaits, flat on her head, in what he thought was called cornrows or something to do with corn anyway, and the long ends went over her right shoulder to rest on the slope of her breast.

Everyone sat down, and there was a shuffle as people made themselves comfortable.

She smiled.

Ace gulped; her smile was the same.

She was wearing a silky chequered shirt in green and black, with the top two buttons undone. Then, mesmerised, he watched her put on a pair of red-rimmed glasses that made her look both sophisticated and cute at the same time. She'd grown into a beautiful woman, he thought, drinking in everything she did and said; and just like it did back then, his body reacted to her.

She read from the book, Ace hearing her words, remembering how she liked words and wondered if she was a linguist. Her accent was slightly different, more clear cut and upper class with none of the Essex slang words she'd liked to use back then. Then again, she was reading, he mused, and she was older.

She read for about twenty minutes, and Ace felt as though he hadn't breathed in that time. His mother was still clutching his hand and Ace thanked God for her support. It kept him anchored in his seat when what he really wanted to do was charge up there, pick her up and make love to her as he'd never had the chance to do seven years ago. Then they would talk.

The publicist stood to announce a question-and-answer segment. There were the usual questions, and Ace was beginning to lose his patience, who gave a fuck when the writing started anyway?! She was a writer and made it in an industry where so many failed. Ace was so proud of her.

Ace whispered in his mother's ear. She nodded and put up her hand.

"Yes? Lady at the back," the publicist said.

Greta stood up. "Have you ever been in love?" She asked the author.

Ace watched Nina closely and noticed the subtle jarring of her body at the unexpected question, and she stroked her ear before replying.

"Yes, briefly. Unfortunately, it didn't work out, and I make up my own heroes nowadays, it's easier on my heart." She touched her heart dramatically and smiled. The smile didn't reach her eyes, he noticed.

There was a ripple of laughter.

Another question and then another. Before long, the publicist stood up to close. Ace spoke to his mother, who looked at him as though he'd gone mad.

"Can I ask one last question, please?"

The publicist pulled back her sleeve to look at her man-sized silver watch then at Nina, who nodded. The people in the front turned expectantly.

"Do you think tea and lemons are a rightful pair?"

The audience ooh'd then turned back to see what the author

was about to say.

Ace watched as she put her hand to her ear again and now that he could see, she was touching an earring. He couldn't see if it was his, but he had a feeling it was.

She was panicking, Ace could tell, she didn't know what to say, and Ace wanted to help her, but she looked at the publicist who said something about it depending which country you were in and closed the session.

There was a round of applause, then a scramble to a long table, off to the right, stacked with books.

Book signings came after. And Ace, with his hat pulled low, moved out of the light and into one of the aisles. The romance section.

"So?"

He should have known she would follow him.

"It's her Mom."

"The one from..."

He nodded, overcome by emotion and was grateful when she pulled him down into a hug.

He was floundering, and she knew it.

"You listen to me?" Greta said sternly, turning his head to look into his eyes. "You go and talk to her, no scaring her off." She told him. "It's been a long time and a lot of things could have happened. Talk."

Ace heard the warning. A lot had happened in seven years, but one thing he knew for sure was that he hadn't stopped searching for her.

"Kelly will take me home," Greta confirmed before he could ask and, patting his face affectionately, turned away.

Ace watched as his mom and sisters, who were one of the last groups to leave, gave him the thumbs up before closing the door behind them.

He moved to the back row and sat at the aisle seat, disappointed to see that she wasn't behind the signing desk.

Alarmed that she may have left through the back entrance and he could have missed her, he was about to walk to the back, when the publicist came out again with keys in her hand and, oblivious to his presence, loudly declared over her shoulder that the circus was now over, and the real Sabrina could stand up.

Ace heard a tinkle of laughter and chastisement from the back and then she walked through.

He hadn't been able to see her lower half all night. She was wearing black pants that skimmed her hips but didn't cling to her legs, and heels in a bright green colour. Then with one hand on the desk, she pulled off each shoe rolling her eyes in relief.

"Have you—," she stopped, looking up with one hand still massaging her toes when she addressed him. "I'm sorry we've finished."

A disappointment like no other lanced through him. She didn't recognise him.

***

"Natalia?" Sabrina turned to address her friend and publicist and nodded towards the man sitting in the back row.

She'd noticed him earlier while she was reading and had been aware of him all evening until he'd disappeared. She didn't know why she was cognisant of him, there were other men in the audience, but there was a particular—she couldn't think of the word—hmm, essence maybe? Yes, there was an essence around him with his New York Yankees hat pulled low on his head, as though he didn't want to be seen at her signing and his broad shoulders in a dark coloured shirt and black jacket.

"Excuse me, sir, we've finished for the evening," Natalia said, in her no-nonsense voice that made everyone jump to do her bidding.

Ace stood, pulled off his hat and looked expectantly over at Nina and waited.

"Ace?" She whispered, reaching once more for the table.

***

"Alister Charles Edwards. Ace. Date of birth, eleventh of May nineteen eighty-three. No current address as I got lost seven years ago and have been trying to find my way home ever since. The last three digits of my social security number are seven three eight, and I love Nutella on my bagels and hate spaghetti but don't tell my mom. I'm not allergic to anything and," his face creased into a frown. "I can't think of anything else to tell you."

He'd walked towards her slowly with every word he'd spoken. Her lovely dark eyes were wide and bright, first in shock and then with tears. One droplet fell onto her cheek, and he stopped its slow descent with his thumb, then he cupped her face with both hands as he watched closely.

"Ace?"

"Nina." He said, with a tender smile and, moving his hands to her shoulders, pulled her into his arms.

CHAPTER NINE

Sabrina held onto him. Wrapping her arms under his jacket and around his waist as she buried her face into his shirt and cried.

Seven years ago, their goodbyes had been rushed, he'd barely been cognisant, and she'd been out of her mind with worry for him and herself. Now feeling his solid arms around her, squeezing her, was somehow giving her all that she needed. She felt secure enough to finally let go of seven years of pain and sorrow.

She cried as she'd never been able to do from the moment her mother had met her at the front door to tell her that her father was dead.

She cried for the nights she held her mother, completely broken for the man she'd loved. Sabrina cried now as her mother had cried then. Gut-wrenching sobs, that if she thought about it, she would never have done, but this was Ace. Her promise.

The memories of their time together had kept her going.

She sobbed, remembering the cruel, grief-stricken words her mother had said. It was Sabrina's fault her husband was dead. Sabrina, who always selfishly got what she wanted. Sabrina, who had no idea of the price of her selfishness. It was Sabrina's fault. Everything was Sabrina's fault, spending and spending and spending. Sabrina's fault, Sabrina's fault!

Sabrina relived the shell-shocked moment and feelings of hurt as her mother spat those ugly words at her, then turning and calmly walking up the stairs, saying she didn't want to be disturbed.

Sabrina hadn't cried that night but had gone straight into her father's office, where she'd started to plan.

Taking her mother breakfast, the next morning, a pink rose on the breakfast tray, a mushroom omelette, orange juice and a pot of Lapsang Souchong brewed precisely as she liked it. Sabrina had opened the bedroom door, squinting against the harsh early morning sunlight, and smiling at her mother, who was dressed immaculately in a white suit and gold low-heeled sandals, laying on top of the floral duvet. Only she hadn't replied to Sabrina's cheery good morning. She'd been dead.

Sabrina hadn't cried for the friends she'd lost. They all bailed like rats on a sinking ship. Andy, who, days after the second less elaborate funeral, had told Sabrina she and Gareth were getting married and that Gareth had said she couldn't be around someone who was so spoiled and selfish as Sabrina was. Andy had looked her dead in the eye and told her she wasn't a nice person.

The one person, the only person Sabrina had ever confided in, had betrayed her the most and with her head held high Sabrina had opened the front door and watched Andy, her lifelong friend, walking out without a backward glance.

The worst of it, though, was the credit card bills Sabrina received weeks after her parents' deaths. Andy didn't want her friendship anymore, but she still spent her money.

No, Sabrina hadn't cried then either. She'd breathed in deep and carried on.

Sabrina felt Ace's hand at the back of her neck, rubbing the base with his thumb and a fresh round of tears caroused down her face as she remembered everything through a narrow tunnel of emotion. If she hadn't told her dad about Oxford over the phone, she knew, without a doubt that he would be here now. Her mother would have been here.

She was moving, Ace sat down and pulled her onto his knee, her head now buried in his neck as she held on tight, she didn't ever want to let him go. His smell was different. His long hair was gone, but his arms around her felt like the safest place to be. It had been so long, so very long since she'd been able to feel. So long since she'd been held like this.

He pulled back to cup her face. Those whisky coloured eyes of his looking at her with concern. She remembered sitting on the floor, her dad's prized bottle beside her, now halved. She remembered holding her glass up to the light and remembering Ace's eyes. She'd been right when she'd told him his eyes reminded her of her daddy's whiskey. She'd missed them both like crazy. She'd gotten drunk. But she hadn't cried.

"I'm sorry," Sabrina mumbled, as Ace used tissues to gently wipe her eyes. He held one to her nose, and she sniffed loudly, then laughed self-consciously. "I'm not blowing my nose,"

He smiled. "I won't look, I promise." He said, holding the bundle of tissues under her nose. She took it from him, turned away slightly and blew her nose.

"I'm sorry, I don't know what came over me," she apologised after another hiccup as she tried to get her emotions under control. She went to move off his lap, but he held her down, tucking her head under his chin and rocking her as though a child.

They didn't speak, and as the hiccupping of her body settled to the odd tremor, Sabrina became aware of her surroundings. It was quiet. The lights were dim, and they were sat away from the front windows in total privacy.

"Where's Natalia?" She asked.

She felt his low rumble of laughter through his shirt. "I think you bursting into tears scared her off," he clarified. "She left the keys on the table and left you in my capable hands."

"She isn't a girly girl," Sabrina giggled. "I'd have loved to see her face when I started crying like that," Sabrina said, imagining how appalled Natalia would have been, before taking off. "But she just left me with a stranger like that? I'll need to have words."

Ace stroked her back and cuddled her even closer. He couldn't get enough of the feel of her in his arms.

"I think you crying all over me, was a sure sign that we knew each other Nina."

Sabrina giggled and again tried to get up, but his arms tightened around her waist, and she eventually relaxed against him.

It wasn't until the lull of sleep startled her out of her reverie that she scooted off Ace, who wasn't expecting the sudden movement and let her go.

Sabrina rubbed her hand across her face and under her eyes, knowing not even the highest standard of waterproof mascara could have withstood her flood of tears and as she suspected, her fingers came away with smears of YSL mascara.

"I'm just going to wash my face," she told him softly, utterly embarrassed by her melt-down.

He smiled, watching her closely. "You sure you're okay?" He asked.

She nodded, backing away, turning and heading to the back room, where a small office, kitchenette, storeroom and the bathroom were situated. She splashed cold water on her face, patted it dry with a paper towel and reapplied a little make-up.

Her eyes were slightly puffy, but the redness was clearing. Breathing in deep, she got ready to face the next chapter of her life.

***

Ace was standing by the signing table when she came out, and she stopped to look at him.

"You're really tall." She said self-consciously, watching his grin as she stared at him, seeing him for the first time, towering over her like this.

She started at his feet, taking in the rugged black boots that looked broken in, stylish yet comfortable, his black jeans that teased her senses as they skimmed his long muscular legs. She took in his sedate leather belt, navy blue shirt with a large damp patch she'd made with her tears and looked at his jacket; sporty but tasteful. He had an excellent sense of style. But then again, when they'd met at the pub years ago, he'd looked nice then too.

He looked so familiar to her even without the trendy beard and long hair. He still had an earring; in fact, he now had one in each ear.

Then a feeling of shyness came over her as she caught him

looking at her in much the same way she had him a moment ago.

"Hi," she said, to break the silence. "My full name is Sabrina Mavis Forrester. I live in Derbyshire, England, and my birthday is May nineteenth. I love apple pie and custard and Moroccan food, especially lamb tagine." She listed. "I can't stand okra," she shivered, thinking about the slimy vegetable. "And I'm learning to ride horses." She went on. "Oh, and I sleep with a night light. Always."

Ace stepped forward, but she held up her hands to stop him. "If you come any closer, I'm likely to start crying again," she warned on a wobble. "Would you like some tea, or a coffee maybe?"

"Coffee would be nice." He didn't want a coffee but was aware they both needed some normality and stayed where he was.

Her smile was over bright as she asked him how he liked it, before disappearing once more to the back of the building.

Ace sighed. Of all the seeing-her-for-the-first-time scenarios that he'd had over the years, this was not it.

Not being able to follow his own advice, Ace walked to the back to see her bent over the counter, her head low, her shoulders hunched. The kettle was on but not yet boiling. Two mugs were laid out to the side beside a bottle of instant coffee.

Ace turned her gently around by the shoulders and because he had to, bent down slightly to kiss her.

Her mouth trembled under his, but he slipped his tongue over her lips ever so gently, soothingly, reacquainting himself with the feel of her and giving her the chance to do the same.

Her arms crept up and over his chest to his neck, and he pulled her in closer as he plunged into her mouth.

He remembered her taste. He remembered how she felt, the softness and feel of her tongue as he sucked and played with it.

He shifted, stroking her body and palming her ass to curve her body into his. His erection was powerful, hard and heavy between them and the slight rocking of her hips made him groan and pull her shirt out of her pants to sweep his hands beneath, urgently smoothing her soft skin, as he lavished kiss after kiss under her chin, the back of her ear and her throat as one hand anchored her to him, and the other roughly moulded her breast, rolling and tugging her nipple.

"Ah Ace," she breathed, opening herself to him. She couldn't get enough of the feel of him. He was so hard, his muscles bulging and trembling under her fingers. She pushed at his jacket and clamping her lips to his helped him shrug it off.

Ace roughly pulled open her shirt, her buttons pinging against the tiled floor and pulled down her black bra to cup and lift her breasts like an offering, up to his mouth.

"God, you're so beautiful," he whispered reverently, as he sucked first one and then the other hard tip into his mouth.

She grasped his hair, remembering the softness, mourning the loss of his long waves, but still enjoying the silky texture skimming through her fingers, she grabbed a handful and pulled his mouth back to hers.

Their kisses were long and deep, her hands went to his belt buckle, and he moved slightly, urgently, to let her open it. She couldn't manage, so on a deep-throated growl, he helped, the two of them struggling with the button and then the zip and then, thank God, her hands were on him.

Ace roared on the inside. The feel of her hands on him. Squeezing him, pulling his length. He couldn't take much more of it. He was going to explode.

Some part of him, the sane part, knew they shouldn't be doing this just yet. But this was Nina, he'd dreamed about it, stamped her image on his brain as he fucked someone else. The thought should have sobered him, made him feel guilty, but it didn't. Roughly, he shoved her pants and underwear down in one urgent tug.

The kettle was boiling, steaming up the room, and he jerked the cord sharply to pop the plug out of the socket. Then he was on his knees in front of her. Kissing and sucking her hidden nub to play with his tongue. Her scent was how he'd imagine it to be. He'd desperately wanted to taste her that night all those years ago. But he couldn't linger, couldn't savour. Not now.

Ace surged to his feet, spun her around and took her from

behind.

One arm clamped around her waist, the other on the counter, he surged in and out of her. Fast and hard. It was quick. He heard her scream. He felt her convulse around him and only then did he let himself go.

It was unbelievable. More than he imagined it would be. More than he ever remembered. He leaned against her back as he tried to bring his breathing under control.

She pushed against him, and he moved back, slipping out of her to pull up his pants.

With her back still turned to his, she fixed her clothing then waited with her head bent and hands gripping the edge of the counter.

The guilt came swiftly. This was not how it should have been for their first time, Ace thought and was about to open his mouth and beg forgiveness when his heart stopped.

"What the fuck is that?"

CHAPTER TEN

Shocked by his aggression, Sabrina turned around to ask what he was talking about. He made it seem as though she'd grown a tail or something and she, mug that she was, actually looked.

"What?"

He grabbed her left hand and brought it to her face.

"This. I mean, what the fuck Nina? You're engaged?!"

Sabrina looked at the ring. She'd forgotten she was wearing it and slipped it off and threw it in the bin. It hit the metal bottom with a loud ping.

Ace looked at the bin and then at her.

"It's fake," she explained. "When I'm on tour, it helps to keep the creepy guys away."

"Creepy guys?"

"Yeah, the ones who think, because I write romance, with quite a bit of sex, that I am what I write." She shrugged. "It keeps them away."

"Does that happen often?"

She cocked her head to one side. "Now and again. Do you think I would do what we just did if I were engaged?"

There were two answers to her question Ace knew, but he risked going with neither.

"Have you eaten?"

She shook her head, looking down at her ruined shirt. "I was going to get something at my hotel. Your language is still appalling, I see."

"Yeah, go figure," he smirked. "When are you going back?"

"Day after tomorrow," she looked at him, knowing he remembered too. "Some things never change, huh?"

He shoved his hands into his front pockets and smiled at the similarities to the past. "Not much time. Same flight?"

She smiled. "Yes."

"Daddy picking you up?"

"My dad is dead." She told him quietly, trying to close her shirt, but there wasn't enough material to tuck it in securely, and she held the two ends as though they held the secrets of the universe.

Ace took off his jacket and handed it to her.

"I'm sorry," he watched her put it on, liking the feeling of her wearing his clothes. "When?"

"The day you went into the hospital. He killed himself, and my mother killed herself twenty-two days later." She walked out, leaving him stunned.

"Nina?" He grabbed her arm as she moved to the chairs and started to stack them.

"Not now Ace. We'll talk later."

Ace helped her stack the chairs and watched as she went to the back, coming back with her handbag. She turned off all, but one of the lights then looked around.

"I love this place," she whispered, almost to herself.

"I recognised it."

"You did?"

That seemed to have pleased her, he thought, going up beside her as they both looked at the mural of heather. The things she did to him in front of that picture. Fucking wow!

"As soon as I walked through the door with my mother and sisters."

Nina bit the corner of her nail in concentration, for some reason it pleased him that she still had the habit.

"She asked about being in love," he prompted at her puzzled look.

"And about the tea and lemon pairing," Sabrina confirmed, smiling, as she remembered the tiny lady with rings on all of her fingers and a white streak in her hair.

"That's her. My stepmother."

They moved to the door, and Sabrina locked up, Ace waiting behind her.

"Same hotel?" He asked.

"Yep, more for convenience really, and they give me seventy-five per cent off for being such a loyal customer."

They walked in silence, retracing their steps. Their hands touched once, then twice, before Ace captured her fingers on the third brush of her knuckles and weaved their fingers together.

"Tell me what happened to your parents, Nina." He urged quietly.

She told him, methodically, from the phone call to burying her mother.

"Why didn't you come to me?" He asked. All these years he thought she'd continued her life in the security of wealth, forgetting him.

"I couldn't," she stopped. "All I knew was your nickname Ace," she laughed at herself. "And even that was bogus." She accused.

"I'm sorry. We were so young, Nina, thinking we had all the time in the world to talk about ourselves."

"I know."

They walked on.

"Do you live in New York?"

"Not really, I have a place here, and I want to take you to it, but if I do that, I won't let you leave," he volunteered without a trace of apology. "I'd make love to you as I should have." He confessed. "I'm sorry about earlier. Did I hurt you?"

"No."

They walked several metres in silence. It was a warm night.

"What do you do for a living?" Sabrina asked.

He smirked down at her and started to swing their hands back and forth. "I got a huge pay-out from the movie company, but no more stunts. For some reason, I couldn't get a job after my accident." He joked. "Much to my family's distress, I test racing cars and motorbikes. I work for Formula One and any other racing body that needs a live crash tester."

"Isn't that dangerous?"

"I know what I'm doing."

"But you could get hurt again."

"I could, but then I could walk in front of a bus."

"And that's how you justify yourself?" She jeered, pulling her hand away. "Don't you think you're being irresponsible?"

He looked at her sharply. "What happened to the 'Living your life' motto you used to live by?"

The sound she made didn't make it into a laugh. "I grew up."

"Meaning I haven't?"

"I didn't say that," she retaliated. "I just think you dice with death. You like the adrenaline rush that you get without thinking about the people who love you and what you put them through every time you do something stupid."

"I'm careful."

"You know what I think, Ace?"

Her hotel was in sight, and he held her arm to pull her to a stop and face him.

"What do you think?" He knew he wasn't going to like what she was going to say next.

"It doesn't matter." She shrugged him off and walked on.

Ace watched her, feeling as though he'd disappointed her somehow, and the Nina from seven years ago would not have just walked off. Where was her fire?

"I'm careful, Nina." He said again, catching her up.

"It doesn't matter Ace."

They reached the hotel, and she turned to him awkwardly, warily as though she was ready to say goodbye.

"Dinner?" He suggested quickly. He wasn't letting her go. He couldn't let her go. "Just dinner Nina." He coaxed. "We have a lot to talk about."

Her smile didn't reach her eyes. "I'll go and change."

He watched her walk away, remembering last time when she'd marched back to him, making him promise he'd stay. He held his breath, hoping she would at least turn around. She didn't.

The bar that used to be there was gone, replaced by some sort of seating area with lots of leafy foliage, he opted to stay a little off to the side to wait.

She was back within minutes and had changed into a pair of black jeans, a white shirt and a plain black blazer. She looked as though she was about to chair a Saturday meeting at the office, Ace thought.

"Lead the way?" He suggested and stepped behind her as she led the way to a bistro where she was greeted by her first name. When they sat down, Ace asked for her phone.

"I'm not losing you again, Nina." He said simply, as he demanded her phone number and e-mail address, put them into his phone and then rang her. "Save my number," he ordered and watched as she manipulated her smart-phone.

Dinner was quiet. They talked about everything but themselves as they both had a simple steak salad.

"Are you involved with anyone?" He asked later when she'd scooped the last of her ice-cream into her mouth.

"No time."

"How so?"

"I write and have a small business in Morocco."

"Morocco?" He asked. "What business?"

"Morocco is practically my second home."

"How so?" He asked again and listened when she told him about the land her father had purchased years ago. She'd only discovered it after his death and had planned to sell it unseen, but something made her look at it, and from there she set up her argan oil business. The local women picked and ground the nuts. She supplied oil for the beauty industry and had her own line of bath soaps and oils.

"You've been busy."

"But?" She invited, hearing a touch of resentment coming from him.

"But what Nina? I've been searching for you for years, and you just carried on. Did you even look for me?"

She gasped, hurt at his accusation. "Oh, I looked for you, Ace, but remember all I had was Ace. A guy in a wheelchair who may or may not be walking. Oh, and he used to do stunts and have sex with people he didn't care about!"

"Keep your voice down," he gritted, looking over her shoulder at the other guests.

"No, I won't. I was lost, Ace. I'd lost everything. Everything! I waited for you. But you never called me. I still have that number just in case," she laughed at herself. "How corny and pathetic is that! And remember this was all before every bit of our lives could be Googled, so I waited, then got on with it. It wasn't just me I had to think about. So yes, I moved on and forgot about you. I did my degree at night, and I worked my arse off with two jobs until I was too tired to even sleep. So yes, I stopped looking." She threw down her napkin and moved as though to get up.

"We're not done."

"I know we're not."

She pinned him with a look he'd never seen from her before. Hurt.

"Why didn't *you* ring me?"

Before he could answer, she went on.

"You know why you didn't ring me?" She asked, then answered her own question. "You didn't ring me because I was the distraction. You weren't even going to tell me about your surgery, any of it." She threw at him. "I selfishly rail-roaded you into being with me. I had to fight for every crumb of your attention. Hell," she scoffed at herself. "You even said it yourself. It was the wrong time. Don't even bother to deny it!"

"I won't."

She felt the tingling in her eyes and knew the tears were coming.

"But that doesn't mean I didn't want to be with you, Nina. The timing was wrong, but I didn't do anything I didn't want to do. I wanted to be with you, but I was broken, Nina, literally."

She wiped away a tear. "But why didn't you—"

Ace shook his head, and she watched as he pulled his wallet from his back pocket, opened it in front of her and slipped his finger behind a picture of someone smiling. He unfolded a bit of paper, smoothed it out on the table and then gave it to her.

Sabrina looked at it, puzzled until she recognised her handwriting.

"My note," she said softly, seeing the faded heart, the words *dandelion, her* and two of her seven-digit mobile phone number. The rest was indiscernible. Through her tears, she asked. "What happened?"

"I think someone put it under my water jug for safekeeping and it got wet and smudged."

Sabrina wiped at her damp eyes. "You couldn't ring me."

"I *couldn't* call you. My cousin even took it to this forensic scientist guy he knew, but we couldn't get anything. Five days after my surgery, I was moved to DC for physio, and I was there for months. In my cockiness, I figured I knew it all. We lived in the moment back then Nina. We shouldn't have. I thought you were at Oxford and had forgotten about me. But I came to England as soon as I could."

"You did?"

"I went looking for Nina Mae, but she wasn't anywhere, not at Oxford, or anywhere else studying linguistics. I couldn't find you. Then I thought that maybe you didn't want to be found." His eyes held so much promise. "We had something then Nina and we have something now."

"We can't Ace."

"Why not?" He sat forward and captured her hand that was fiddling with the base of her wine glass. "We need to give us a chance."

"I don't live how I used to. I can't watch you dive off cliffs and race cars and be okay with it. You were broken when we met, but I can't allow myself to be with someone who is so careless with their life,"

"Nina—"

"My name is Sabrina!" She shouted. "Nina died years ago. I need stability Ace. You had a glimpse of my past life, and it's nothing like that anymore. I'm not exciting. I live in a tiny village, where everyone knows everyone else. I have a routine. I needed a routine to survive. I can't have you disrupting it with the attitude that you have! I just can't."

"Ni—Sabrina, we're still young. We'll figure it out." He coaxed.

"You don't understand Ace. It's not just about—"

"Then tell me!"

"I have a daughter!"

"What?!"

"I have a daughter. We have a daughter."

Sabrina watched him as he sat frozen.

"We—" Sabrina began nervously, wanting to fill the silence when he didn't react.

"Shut up."

Ace suddenly grabbed her arm and pulled her from the table, leading her out of the restaurant, across the lobby with the same chandelier of years past and straight to the lifts. He pressed the button in silence. When Sabrina tried to pull away, he held her tighter.

When the lift came, he marched her inside.

"Which floor?" He asked quietly.

She didn't reply fast enough because he rapidly stabbed all eighteen buttons. Sabrina sneaked a look at him. He was looking straight ahead, the tension evident in his shoulders and the tick in his cheek.

"It's this one," she said quietly, on the eighth floor and led the way to her one-bedroomed suite.

Sabrina kicked off her shoes by the door.

"Would you like a drink?" She offered, dreading the upcoming conversation.

"No, I do not want a drink, Sabrina," he seethed, walking around her. "I want you to explain."

"It was that night."

He frowned. "We didn't have sex."

She moved away from him and looked out of the window.

"It depends on your definition of sex though, doesn't it Ace?" Sabrina said, over her shoulder. "Are you going to make me give you a blow by blow?" She challenged. She didn't want to relive that night. "You were there, remember?"

"Yes, Sabrina, you will give me a blow by blow," he ordered darkly. "We did not have sex. I would have remembered coming inside you, believe me."

She turned to him then, his words igniting the feel of him inside her not two hours ago. Well, if he needed to be reminded, she was going to bloody well tell him!

"My mouth was on you, and I just wanted to feel you inside me, just the once. Remember?" She prompted. "I put you inside me, and you told me not too. But I did it anyway because that's how I was back then. I did it knowing there was a chance I'd get pregnant. But I didn't care. I was as selfish as my mother and Andy accused me of being. I stole from you."

He glowered over at her from where he was standing in the middle of the room with his hands on his hips. "That makes no sense."

"There was a tiny drop of life, and I took it," Sabrina stated flatly.

"Jesus fucking Christ, Nina," he ran his hands through his hair in frustration, trying to take it all in. He had a daughter. All these years he had a daughter. "Where is she?" When she went to her handbag, he stopped her. "No." The look he sent her was tortured, his eyes unusually dark. Then he turned and walked out—the door closing with a soft thud.

Sabrina stood there, stunned. One minute he was here, the next gone. What if he didn't come back, was her first thought and then dismissed it, he just needed a moment to himself.

Sabrina had taken a shower and changed into her floral pyjamas when there was a light knock at the door. She opened it.

"That's it? You just open the damn door!" He blazed, walking past her. "You yourself said you have creepy guys following you."

"It could only be you coming back Ace." She replied softly, noticing his mood hadn't improved.

"What's her name?"

"Heather,"

He smiled at the significance of it.

"Show me,"

Sabrina had already taken out her tablet and had the photo album app ready.

"She's almost seven and the brightest thing ever," Sabrina

gushed, about to take the tablet to him, then stopped and looked anxiously over at him as he sat on the sofa looking at her, waiting expectantly.

"What?" He asked, catching her biting her nail. "You've already given me the biggest surprise of my life, so unless you're about to tell me you're a man, let's have it!"

"She has a disability."

"What kind of disability?

"She's deaf."

He nodded. "Let me see her." He patted the seat beside him, and Sabrina sat with him swiping through the pictures of Heather as a baby sucking her fingers, Heather playing in the mud, Heather holding a worm, picture after picture of Heather right through to last week where she was dressed in jeans and sandals and a white T-shirt. She did not look happy.

"We were going to the church fête, and I wanted her to wear a dress, the sandals were the closest I could get to something feminine," Sabrina explained, with an indulgent smile. "She's very headstrong."

"She's beautiful," he told her past the thick lump in his throat. "She has my eyes."

"I know."

"Where is she now?"

"Boarding school," she explained. "It's for children with special needs. She's normally a day student but wanted to stay while I did this quick tour instead of our usual arrangements."

"I'll travel back with you. I want to meet her and don't you fucking dare tell me no Sabrina or I swear to God."

"Stop jumping to conclusions Ace," Sabrina warned. "I wasn't going to, and you can stop with the attitude and swearing I will not have you swearing around her. She's impressionable."

The look he threw at her could have wilted trees, but she held his stare until he gave her a small nod.

They made the travel arrangements, Ace giving her his credit card to book his seat on the same flight as her, day after tomorrow.

"Tell me about her," he urged, ignoring Sabrina's yawn.

She put the tablet on the low glass coffee table in front of them and curled her feet beneath her.

"I didn't know I was pregnant until I was almost five months. I put my missed periods down to the turmoil in my life at the time. It was a shock. I didn't know what to do."

"Thank you for having her." Ace said gently, reaching over and patting her knee.

"I'd always wanted lots and lots of children."

"Yeah well, you just might get your wish." He said sardonically.

"What?"

"I didn't use anything when we had sex in the bookshop." He replied. "I'm sorry I just couldn't stop."

He didn't look the least bit sorry, Sabrina noticed. "Bollocks," she swore. "You can go around taking risks with your own life, but not mine. How dare you put me at risk like that. Who knows what you could have given me!"

"Now you hold the fuck on." He yelled right back. "The only person I've *never* used a condom with is you! And you're one to talk. You stole from me!"

CHAPTER ELEVEN

Sabrina gasped and coiled away from him.

"I'm sorry," Ace said, immediately contrite. What the hell was wrong with him? He scolded himself. "I'm sorry, Sabrina."

"You're right," she sniffed. "And I paid the price."

"I have a clean bill of health," he rushed, hoping to stave off her tears. "I recently did a physical before they let me test drive the Ferrari for Formula One," he explained. "You gave me my daughter, and I will be forever grateful to you."

"Oh yeah, will you be grateful to me knowing I'm the one who caused her deafness? I drank hard and even smoked weed!" She yelled back at him. "Are you grateful to me now? I caused it. It was my punishment for being such a selfish, spoiled brat, just like Andy said. I take things without thought to the consequences. If I hadn't passed out in the street and bashed my head, I would have continued drinking and smoking just to get me through the day!" She was in tears now. "So, you see, your gratitude is misplaced. I've been a bad mother from the moment I stole from you!" Sabrina wailed, before running into her bedroom and slamming the door.

Ace stayed where he was and picked up the tablet again. A picture of his little girl was smiling back at him. He swiped through them again, taking in her hair that was a little lighter than his and with his family red streaking through it. Her curls were loose and to her shoulders. Her eyebrows were dark and straight, and she had the cutest little pudgy nose like her mothers. That's all she had of Ni-Sabrina, the rest was all him, and if she was anything like he was as a kid, she was a handful.

He smiled, looking through the pictures of Heather up a tree and another playing football with other children, then he took out his phone and took a photograph of one of her looking directly at the camera with a frown, it was so like his that he to laugh. A handful would be an understatement. She was, no doubt, a little terror. He sent the photograph to his mother and managed to count to six before his phone rang, and his parents were on the line.

***

Sabrina didn't bother to go back into the living room and went straight to bed instead. At first wondering what Ace was doing and then settling in to sleep, when she heard him on the phone, talking and laughing as though he hadn't a care in the damn world. She was angry at herself. It had been a long and emotional day, and she hadn't handled being with Ace at all well. Crying all over him like that before she'd even said a proper sentence to him! And the sex! What was she thinking? She sat up suddenly and reached for her phone, pulling up the calendar app, looking at the date, before skimming her phone onto the nightstand and lying back against the pillows. She just might be okay.

***

Sabrina woke to Ace lying beside her on top of the covers looking down at her. It was unnerving.

"What are you doing?" She asked, mindful of her morning breath.

"Want to go down to City Hall and get married?" He asked, instead.

His breath was all fresh and minty, she noticed. But he did need a shave, and she curled her fingers into the sheets to keep from stroking the red hair peeking through.

"No Ace, I do not."

He grinned. "Just thought I'd ask." He stood up and stretched his arms over his head, then rotated his hips. He looked happy and younger than he'd been seven years ago.

"I really can't get used to you walking around," she admitted, watching him walk around her room and then back to the bed. "Is that weird of me?"

He laughed. "Nah, when I could stand properly, it was weird for me too." Then he tugged at her sheet. "Come on, we have a busy day ahead."

"Okay," she made a shooing motion with her hands. She hadn't planned on doing anything today other than a walk and to catch up on some sleep. She was happy enough for him to take over and plan her day.

"What?" He asked.

"Get out. I need to get changed."

He smirked down at her, his lips curving into a knowing smile.

"The Sabrina I used to know would have left the bed naked and danced in front of me."

"Yeah well, this Sabrina has a little bit of something about her nowadays. I don't dance, especially naked, for you or anyone else."

"Don't talk about anyone else. I don't like it." He glowered. "But one day you *will* dance for me."

"Get out, Ace. I need to make some telephone calls."

"You've got half an hour."

***

Ace sprawled on the sofa as he waited for Ni-Sabrina to get ready.

The night had been emotional. He'd rung just about everyone in his phone book last night and talked to Kyle for hours.

He was so fucking happy. Ace had always chased after that feeling of euphoria, but what he was feeling right now had magnified every bone-ass stunt he'd ever done in his life. He had a daughter. He kept rolling her name over and over in his head and smiling to himself. God, a daughter. He'd never thought about having kids before, and of course, there was a time when he thought he'd never have any. If the surgery had gone wrong, and he'd ended up in a wheelchair for the rest of his life, he still would have had his little girl. Sabrina may have thought she'd stolen from him, but she'd given him the greatest gift anyone could ever give him.

The shower had stopped running, and he listened acutely to the movements in Sabrina's bedroom. She'd be naked, her brown skin all glistening and wet. God! Why was he torturing himself like this? He got hard just thinking about her and last night when she described her mouth being on him, he'd just about came in his pants! She didn't know the memory of that night was forever scorched in his brain anyway, but he'd wanted her to describe it. Masochistic asshole that he was.

Ace looked up when he heard her bedroom door open, and he all but drooled. Sabrina was wearing grey skinny jeans, black ankle boots with a small heel and an oversized white jumper that slid off her shoulder. Fucking Christ, where was her bra strap?! Her hair was loose with wiggly waves to her shoulders, and she had small gold hoops in her ears.

He stood up as she stepped closer and he could see the subtle make-up she was wearing; she'd added gold stuff to her eyes, and her eyelashes were thicker. Her mouth, God her mouth, looked extra ripe with the shimmer of lipstick on her lips.

"You look amazing." Ace said as she walked past, but he reached out and captured her arm to pull her into his embrace.

"Thank you," she said, tipping her head to look at him and then dipping it quickly when he went to kiss her. "We shouldn't, Ace," Sabrina told him shyly.

"I disagree." He rearranged her in his arms, tipping her back and off-balance. She had to hold on to his shoulders to keep from falling.

"What are you doing?!"

"I want to make love to your mouth."

She gasped, inflamed by his words.

"I want to make love to your body too," he went on casually.

"Ace,"

"Yes, Sabrina?"

"I—"

"Exactly," he ran his tongue up her neck to nip at her ear. Her perfume was light, vanilla and something flowery came to mind as he bent her even further backwards and cupped her backside, tucking her into his legs.

"Let me up please," she urged. "I'm getting dizzy."

"Seriously?"

"The ceiling is spinning."

Ace looked at her closely, her eyes were closed tight, and he chuckled, kissing her once, twice on the mouth before pulling her back up.

She even swayed on her feet.

"How are you with heights?" He asked.

"Not very good."

"Roller-coasters?"

"Will never go back on one in this lifetime."

"Deep-sea fishing?"

"No way in hell."

"Skiing?"

"I have no desire to put planks of wood on my feet."

"So, what are we going to do for fun?"

"I like crosswords puzzles and word searches."

He laughed, throwing back his head as he thought of himself sitting down doing a crossword. He'd never completed one in his life.

He kissed her hand. "Come on. Let's get some pancakes. And if you tell me you don't like pancakes, we will fall out."

"I prefer the British recipe nowadays."

He looked at her wide-eyed. "You're kidding me, right?"

"Why would you have stacks of stodgy cake for breakfast when a lovely light and fluffy British pancakes is so divine?"

"Woman, if we didn't have a kid together, I swear I'd dump you in the river."

Sabrina giggled as she picked up her bag and walked to the door. "You coming?"

Not the type of coming I want to do, Ace thought, looking at her ass as they walked to the elevators. Her body had changed over the years, but she was still curvy where he liked curves to be.

They were walking across the lobby when Sabrina's name was called, and the desk clerk rushed over to her, all flushed and excited, with a long white box in her hand.

"This just came for you, Miss Forrester." The young clerk gushed and waited eagerly as Sabrina took the box.

Sabrina had met Marisola last year when she was in training at the hotel. She was a fan of her books and had asked if she could sign her copies for her. Sabrina had done one better and invited her to a private book club reading that night too.

For Marisola's benefit, Sabrina played the role of the eager recipient, when inside she was feeling anything but. She was aware of Ace standing behind her. "Thank you." She told Marisola, opening the box to see a perfect single pale pink rose lying on a bed of white tissue paper. She picked up the small gold envelope and opened it. It simply said *I'm Sorry.*

"Who's it from?" Ace asked, glowering down at the box.

"No one important," Sabrina answered. "Would you like it, Marisola?"

"Oh no, I couldn't!" The desk clerk exclaimed, putting her hands to her chest.

"Please, my gift to you." Sabrina pushed the box into the girl's arms, giving her no choice but to take the box. Then Sabrina walked off.

She knew she'd been rude, but she needed to get out of there. She was being watched again.

"Hey," Ace caught up to her and swung her around to him. "I thought you told me you weren't involved with anyone?"

"I'm not."

He wanted to punch a wall.

"It's a fan."

"Fan?"

"Yes, can we go now?" She looked around, suddenly feeling cold and vulnerable, and she stepped towards him close enough to wrap her arms around his waist. She didn't breathe again until she felt his strong arms around her.

"Come on. I'm hungry for American pancakes!" He joked, a

moment later when he felt her trembling stop. She'd been scared, brave to his face, but she'd been scared, and he wanted to know what the hell was going on.

***

They had breakfast. Ace had his pancakes and Sabrina her pot of tea and two slices of toast. He'd teased her for being so British, and she berated him for forgetting his roots and that he was no longer her Englishman in New York. Then he started singing Sting's famous song, bringing her to tears of laughter as he couldn't sing for the life of him. Bless him!

Ace talked about the places he'd been to as they walked to his apartment, a beautiful modern building with a uniformed doorman.

"You live here?" She gasped as she tipped her head to look at the modern building. "Just how much was your pay-out, anyway?" She asked as they walked inside.

"I'm rarely here and maybe only for a night or two. As for my pay-out? I never have to work again, and neither do you."

She shook her head at him. "You're too funny Ace," was all she said in the face of his seriousness.

His apartment was beautiful, but the view stole the show. Sabrina went straight to the floor to ceiling windows that framed Central Park perfectly.

"Oh my God, I could stay here forever." She whispered.

Ace heard and, smiling, he walked up behind her and wrapped his arms around her waist.

"I'd like nothing better than having you stay here forever." He whispered in her hair, as he slipped his hands under her sweater to touch her skin, then he turned her and kissed her hard. Pushing her up against the glass as he sank his whole body against hers.

"If my parents weren't expecting us, I'd be carrying you to my bed." He said, with regret against her lips.

"I'd have stopped you."

He touched his forehead to hers. "Against my powers of persuasion?" He tapped the tip of her nose, before pulling reluctantly away. "I doubt it." He turned his back but said over his shoulder. "Make yourself at home. I'm just going to shower and shave."

Sabrina looked around. This was her first time in Ace's space. Seven years ago, he hadn't shared anything with her. They didn't have time. Now he was rapping, rapping? Drake's *The Motto* as he showered. He kept telling her how much he wanted her around, and he kept touching some part of her every chance he got. He was doing everything she had done seven years ago. The only problem was she wasn't sure about him or their future. She was happy as she was. She was meeting his parents because Heather needed to know who her relatives were. That was all.

Sabrina picked up a magazine called He Man Him and, leafing through it, saw Ace in yet another dimension. He'd been featured in a four-page spread, climbing Chachacomani in Bolivia, Sabrina read, skimming the article. He'd lived amongst the local people for months. There was a photograph of him white water rafting and others sitting talking with tribesmen and getting his body painted. He was like the American version of Bear Grylls, she mused.

Ace was a He Man, and she? Well, she liked the security of village life now, Sunday afternoons down at the cricket green. Essex and the Spanish Costas were a distant, distant memory. She preferred the person she was today.

Ace's flat, or apartment as they say in America, was in tonal shades of grey, from an earthy clay to deep cloudy grey. She was expecting to see quite a few artefacts from all his travels dotted around, but all she saw was a Mexican rug in shades of blue that looked entirely out of place on one wall and a large mahogany dancer with one leg up in the air, very much in a pose Sabrina had been able to do when she'd been younger, was on a glass side table.

She walked around, appreciating the wooden floors as she went to his kitchen, which was of the expected stainless steel and marble variety, very clinical, suiting the building more than the man. She opened the fridge; eggs and a six-pack occupied the top shelf; the rest were empty but for bottles of water. Closing it, she nosied in the cupboards that were practically bare but for some packets of seasoning, a jar of Nutella—she smiled at that—and more water. Americans really liked their bottled water, she mused, leaving the kitchen to go to the open living room space.

One of those vast American sofas in a soft suede dominated the room and faced a massive TV on the wall. Sabrina shook her head at the size of it. You'd never need to go to the cinema if you had that thing in your house she thought, shaking her head and walking to the short corridor Ace had disappeared down.

She found a bathroom in natural stones, another one in white and yet another in a combination of both. A linen cupboard, a bedroom without a bed, another bedroom naked but for the double bed and a stack of paintings in one corner, a smaller room and then, standing a little before the open doorway, she knew had to be Ace's room.

She turned around, not daring to go any further.

"Why d'ya stop?" He asked from behind her, towelling his hair.

She turned at his question. Oh wow.

Sabrina knew she was staring, but oh double wow, he was beautiful. With just a towel around his waist, she had an almost unobstructed view of his tall, lean body.

Where seven years ago his skin had been a blank canvas and pale, today he'd tattooed most of his chest and shoulders. She wanted to look closer, but her eyes decided, all on their own, to travel downwards and check out the long thick promise hidden behind the black towel. As she stared, it twitched in response, and she took a step back and hid her hands behind her back.

"Don't stop now Sabrina," he taunted, stepping closer, smiling at her embarrassment and arousal. Her skin was a deep toasty brown, but he was able to see a faint tide of red scorch her cheeks, and she touched the single gold knob in her ear.

"I—I better go and check my messages," she stammered, bolting down the hall to his laugh.

Ace finished dressing with a smile on his face. Tonight, she was going to be his. In his bedroom, in his bed; he glanced at his massive bed. He'd dreamed of having her in this bed and if his parents weren't expecting him in—he glanced at his phone— in fifteen minutes he would be chasing after her right now and asking her about the earring. It was his. He knew it was.

Sabrina went through her phone messages, checked in with Natalia, who lived in New York anyway and then waited. Ace came out wearing a pair of blue jeans that skimmed and moulded and a thin navy jumper with three buttons at the neck. Two were undone. He'd also pushed up the sleeves. If she hadn't seen the myriad of tattoos on his body, she would not have known he'd sported any.

He walked up to her and cupped her face in his big hands to kiss her lightly. He was very tactile, she realised.

"I'm so glad I found you, Sabrina," he said, almost reverently, and watched with a subtle frown as she dipped her head to hide her face from him. He didn't like that, what was she hiding? He had no time to unravel that puzzle today, but tomorrow he'd probe a little deeper.

He drove his red, custom-built for him, Ferrari 458 to his parents' house. It didn't come out very often, and he'd even toyed with the idea of selling it. A Saudi friend of his had offered him cash and increased the offer by a hundred thousand every time he saw him. But for Ferrari to call you directly to offer you one of the few built, you held on to it.

"Do your parents know about us?" Sabrina asked as he drove them through the traffic.

"Yeah, my dad was with me the first time I came to England as they didn't trust me to look after myself."

"And why is that then?"

Ace chuckled. "You sounded very British just then," he said, before continuing. "I was barely out of the hospital, just graduated from a walking frame to crutches when I flew there."

"I'm sorry Ace,"

"What have you got to be sorry about?" He said, touching

her denim-clad knee briefly. "It's not like you intentionally disappeared. It was one of those crazy flukes that happen for no fucking reason other than to screw with our lives."

"I wonder what would have happened if you could have rung me?" She said softly. She'd always wondered in those early days when she'd found out she was pregnant.

"That's easy. We'd be married. I would have seen you swollen with my baby and we'd be living the white picket fence dream."

She laughed. "I can't picture you and a white picket fence."

"Why not?"

"You are, or were, a stunt man. You're an adrenaline junkie and have a spread in He Man Him. You would never drive a people carrier on principle."

"Don't judge Ni-Sabrina. I'd do anything for you." He clarified, with a dip in his tone.

She gasped at the conviction in his words. "You barely know me,"

"But what I know I like."

"We spent barely thirty-six hours together seven years ago. I've changed."

"So, you keep fucking saying." He flashed her a scathing look.

"Why are you even getting mad?"

"Because you want me to."

"No, I don't. I just don't want you to be disappointed," she said softly, turning as far as her seatbelt would allow to face him. "I'm not a party girl anymore. I don't do crazy impulsive things. I don't drink, I—"

"Do you dance?" He interrupted.

"Sometimes."

"But I'm guessing not on bars?" He joked.

"No, Ace," she puckered her lips. "Not on bars."

"Whatever happened to your friend who was always on the phone? What was her name?"

"Andy,"

"Yeah, her."

"We fell out."

"How come?"

"Her new boyfriend thought I was a bad influence."

"Asshole."

"Exactly."

"When was this?"

"Right after my mum died."

"Fuck me,"

"Exactly," she repeated.

"You had it pretty rough, hey babes?"

"Since when have you been the prince of the understatement?"

He laughed, remembering all she used to talk about was her love for words. "What happened to the linguistic degree you were so eager to take?" He asked, instead.

"Heather. I needed to be able to support us, and the best thing was to do an all-rounder degree. I chose business. I didn't go to Oxford."

"I'm sorry,"

"Not your fault. I just got on with it."

"Now who's being the prince of the understatement?"

"Princess. But I left my crown behind years ago. It's all reality and hard work for me now. I have my daughter to think of."

"I'm here now."

"I know."

"You don't have to work so hard."

"I have my own money, Ace. We live well. Heather wants for nothing."

"That's great, but I intend to look after the two of you from now on."

"That's very noble of you, but we're fine."

"I wasn't asking Sabrina."

"I don't need your money Ace. We don't need your money."

"Why are you being so difficult?"

Sabrina decided she wasn't going to answer him. He needed to understand on his own. They were too different now.

Ace drove on in silence, but boy was he mad. Why was she so stubborn about it? Was she planning on letting him see Heather

106

a few times a year for hourly visits? Not on his fucking life! He was going to be in their lives forever. He was going to marry Sabrina even if he had to tie her to a tree to do it and he was *not* going to miss another day of his daughter's life.

"Sugar and Spice."

Sabrina looked at him puzzled.

"Sugar and spice," he prompted.

"Erm, bat and ball?"

They played pairs until he pulled up into the driveway of a modest white, all American looking, clapboard house with moss green shutters. He was cursing under his breath and gripping the steering wheel until his knuckles were white.

"What is it?" Sabrina asked, alarmed. They'd been laughing and playing, and now he was glowering at the double front door. Within seconds the door was flung open, and adults and children of various ages came flooding out surrounding the car. Sabrina's car door was yanked open by the lady with the rings, his mother, and she was pulled out of the car and engulfed by hugs from all around.

"Hi, I'm Greta," she greeted, stepping back to make a little space. "Welcome to our home Sabrina." She said, before looking guiltily across the roof at Ace. "She hugged me back Alister." She said brightly, hoping to wipe the frown from his face as she'd gone against his wishes and invited the entire family over.

***

Sabrina was introduced to his whole family, and she managed to remember everyone's names as they had a light lunch of spinach ricotta gnocchi with various antipasti salads and crusty breads. Everyone was milling around, laughing and chatting. They were a noisy but loving bunch with affectionate teasing and passionate debates.

Ace was like his father, Charles, in appearance, Sabrina noticed and spent a good few minutes sneaking glances at the older man, knowing Ace was going to look just like him in years to come.

She got her tablet out, and one of Ace's teenaged nephews hooked it up to the flat-screen TV in the family room, and they all looked at picture after picture of Heather.

Sabrina hadn't known so much love. They were a great family.

She was helping Greta and Charlene tidy the kitchen when Ace walked into the room and hugged Sabrina from behind, kissing her neck.

"She's a beautiful and brave woman, Alister," Greta told him in Italian, as she handed him a dishtowel. They didn't have a dishwasher as Greta had said she had children and enough grandchildren, and they needed to learn to look after themselves without all the mod cons.

"She speaks Italian Mom." Ace told his mother.

Sabrina gasped. How did he know?

"How do you know?" She asked him in English.

"You talk in your sleep."

If the ground could open up, Sabrina would have gladly jumped through it, she thought in embarrassment. "I do not!"

"Yeah, you do," he smirked. "Seven years ago, you said. 'I think I love him,' in Italian, so of course I asked who, and you said, Ace. Then you rolled over and went to sleep with a smile on your face."

"I did not!"

He laughed and patted her on her backside. "No, you didn't, but you told me you knew several languages at the pub that first night. I'd said something in Italian, and you answered without hesitation."

"Ooh, you are something else!" She whacked him with her tea towel.

Greta was laughing and then clapped her hands when the front door slammed, announcing the arrival of another family member if the tidal wave of people into the hallway was anything to go by.

Sabrina watched from the side-lines to see who it was. After several minutes, a tall man with dark red hair came into view. He was wearing a black suit and carried a laptop bag across his body.

It was Charles, Ace's dad, who introduced him to her.

"Sabrina? This is my eldest son Matthew. He drove down from DC to meet you."

Matthew walked towards her. His eyes weren't as golden as Ace's, and a more hazel green Sabrina noticed. His smile was just like his brothers. Warm and welcoming. Sabrina put out her hand. He took it and dragged her into an embrace, squeezing her lightly.

As they moved apart, he welcomed her to the family in sign language.

Sabrina gasped and signed thank you, then asked stupidly–because she wasn't thinking–if he knew sign language, and with a grin and speech he said yes, he's deaf.

***

It was late afternoon, and Sabrina was out in the back garden, a pretty cobbled space, with every type of rose plant in containers and bushes. The air was scented by the graceful flowers of every colour now in full bloom. Sabrina used to like roses, but not anymore.

She sat alone on a weathered wooden bench that was against the side of the house, placed there because it obviously caught the late afternoon rays. She was content but wholly overwhelmed and ready to go home to England.

Seeing Ace with his family, the rough and tumble uncle, wrestling his nephews and chasing his nieces around the house as they screamed and ignoring his mother's shouts to be careful, was a revelation. She'd never seen him like this, all carefree and happy. Seven years ago, she really was the distraction. He'd barely smiled back then, and she remembered working so hard to get any kind of response from him that wasn't a frown.

"Hey, there you are." It was Matthew. He handed her a glass of home-made iced tea and a cannoli. He'd bought two large boxes from some famous bakery that apparently had its own reality

TV show. "Can I join you?" He asked, but it was a rhetorical question as he'd already sat down and was stretching his legs out in front of him crossing them at the ankles. He'd changed into a pair of jeans and a T-shirt.

"Tell me about Heather's deafness." He said.

Matthew worked for the government. She wasn't sure what he did, but it was high up, and Sabrina felt slightly intimidated by him.

"You tell me about yours first." She countered and caught his eyes widening slightly in surprise, but then he flashed her a grin that knocked years off his face.

"Hereditary deafness. I was born deaf." He explained, telling her about his early years and diagnosis.

Sabrina couldn't help the tears that fell. Heather was just like him, the exact disease. Her deafness wasn't caused by Sabrina's binge on alcohol and the one night she'd smoked weed. It was hereditary. It was no wonder Ace hadn't even flinched when she told him about her disability. It was no wonder he hadn't even questioned her paternity. Heather carried his family gene.

"Why are you making my woman cry, Matthew?" Ace asked, coming outside and seeing the redness in Sabrina's eyes before she turned away from him. He pulled her up beside him and wrapped her in his arms.

She could feel Ace signing to his brother, wondering why they didn't just talk as Matthew was a pro lip reader, he'd said so himself.

Ace kissed her head then let her go. She sat down again when Ace pulled up a chair to join their conversation.

"You sign with an accent," Sabrina said, lightening the mood as they talked about the differences in sign language between the two countries.

It was sometime later when one of their nieces came outside with Sabrina's handbag, telling her, her phone was ringing.

Recognising the tune that was playing, Sabrina thanked her, and rummaged in her bag to find her phone, trying not to panic.

That lasted all of twenty seconds with what she was told.

"I have to go." She stood up, turning to Matthew and Ace, beginning to shake. "Heather is missing."

CHAPTER TWELVE

Ace called in every favour that he could, to get them in the air within two hours.

It had been frantic, but they'd managed it.

Natalia had met them at Sabrina's hotel, with her passport and bag, then they went to his place, picked up his passport and his travel bag that was always packed at the ready for his whimsical transient lifestyle anyway, and then they were off.

A friend of a friend was heading over to London and, yes, they could hitch a ride. A small aircraft would then be waiting to take them on to Manchester airport. Then a car would be waiting to get them to Heather's school in Derbyshire.

He closed his eyes; he'd yet to meet his little girl, but the terror he felt was as real as the one Sabrina felt, if not more so. He was a father; it was his job to look after his family.

When Sabrina got that phone call and was talking to the Headteacher, a Mr Pratt, she'd gone to pieces. Heather had last been seen at dinner time, three hours ago. Three fucking hours. Ace still couldn't believe a school could lose a kid. She was only seven!

When Sabrina all but dropped the phone, Ace had taken over, introducing himself as Heather's father and the asswipe had said in his uppity fucking cock sucking voice, that Heather didn't have a father and that he refused to speak to anyone other than Sabrina. That's when Ace saw red. He knew the little fucker was power tripping when his little girl was missing, and calling Sabrina by her first name? What was that about? It was not Ace's finest hour.

Matthew had brought their dad out, and Charles had taken over, explaining, with the calmness of a man who was used to giving orders, that they were currently in America, they were getting the first flight out. Then he'd asked all the questions neither Sabrina nor himself had got a chance to ask as they'd both been rolling with their emotions. But when the Headteacher had said no, they had not yet called the police; Ace had gone ballistic.

Sabrina was in the bathroom, the A-list actor Graham Murphy, who they had hitched a ride with, was, ironically, the one Ace had done his last stunt for. He'd murmured an uncomfortable hello, asked how he was, then taken himself off to his bedroom with his model girlfriend.

Sabrina came out having changed into a pair of leggings, and she'd put her hair up.

"How ya doing?" He asked. She'd barely spoken to him on the way here. Now it was time for her to answer some questions.

"As I should be. Where could she be Ace?" Fresh tears threatened.

"We'll find her. My dad has got his old pals scouting the area. She can't have gone far."

They'd ascertained that the school was pretty isolated in the Peak District of Derbyshire, a picturesque place of fields upon fields and tiny villages dotted around. The school itself was pretty secure, set far back from the road, gated and walled through much of it. She had to be on the grounds.

"She's done this before," Sabrina revealed reluctantly, sitting across from him. The plane seated about forty people comfortably and had two bedrooms, a kitchen, and a small office area that doubled as a dining space.

"When?"

"About six months ago. She'd decided she wanted to walk along the wall that surrounded the fields and had taken her friend George with her. He'd fallen off and hurt his leg, and she stayed with him and set up camp. It wasn't until the end of the school day that they discovered them missing as it was sports day."

"And you took her back there?!" Ace bellowed, completely incensed that the school had lost his baby twice and Sabrina had still enrolled her there.

"The year before she was excluded from another school for

being a distraction."

Ace mulled this over. He'd been excluded from more than one school. But Sabrina didn't need to know that.

"Tell me about her and her hearing."

"She doesn't have much hearing. She's just like Matthew."

"Does she sign?"

"When she feels like it."

"What do you mean when she feels like it?" He leaned forward in his seat, pinning her with his stare.

"Heather is headstrong and stubborn. She *likes* not being able to hear!"

"What?" Ace was utterly flummoxed.

"Yes, that's right Ace, she lives in her own little world, shutting me out and everyone else for that matter, whenever she feels like it. She's too bright for her age, bored with school and hates confinement. Heather would rather live in a tent in the woods sleeping under the stars than live in a house."

Ace decided now was not the time to tell Sabrina he had been just like that too. *Like father like daughter* took on a whole new meaning to him.

"I've tried so hard to keep her safe. The village we live in is tiny. Everyone knows everyone else. It's good for her. They look out for her."

"Then why go to that school, and why doesn't she have a cochlear implant?"

"Because she's not considered a good candidate," Sabrina explained. "She'd strip off and go swimming in the local river whenever the mood suits. She has no interest in communicating with me, or anyone else unless it affects her directly sometimes."

"What about her speech? She's seven. She must talk to a degree."

"Not really."

"What the hell, Sabrina?" Ace swore at her. "She's supposed to be living as normal a life as she can. Deafness is not a disability that affects day to day living when you've been educated right!"

"Are you accusing me of not being a good parent, Ace?" Sabrina challenged quietly.

"You're over here on a fucking book tour enjoying yourself, and she's thousands of miles away in a boarding school where they'd already lost her once. You tell me?!"

Sabrina gasped with hurt.

"I'm on tour so that I can sell some books so that I can support my daughter! It was only for five days!"

"Why didn't you bring her with you?"

"She didn't want to come. She said she wanted to stay at the school and be with her best friend George."

"You're her parent you should have taken better care of her!"

"Fuck you Ace."

They had a stare-off, then Sabrina closed her eyes, she felt guilty enough. Heather was only seven, but she'd pleaded and cried and begged to be able to stay at school. She wanted to be with George, her best friend. It was a treat to stay overnight in the dorms. Being a day student, she left at three o'clock and thought she was missing out.

The school had a good reputation, was up there in the league tables and Heather was comfortable there. She was learning, if not in the conventional sense. Heather danced to her own drum and made everyone else dance to it too. She was seven, but she was intelligent beyond her years.

"I'm sorry." Ace said, into the silence.

Sabrina had finished talking, unbuckling her seatbelt she went into the bathroom that was so much larger than a commercial flight, washed away her tears and then sat across from Matthew who was reading and Charles, who was sleeping.

When Matthew looked at her with a question in his hazel gaze, she shook her head, buckled herself in and closed her eyes. Wiping away another tear that had slid past her closed eyes.

***

The rest of the trip was uneventful, Sabrina refused to speak to Ace, childish she knew, but she was still smarting from his accusations, she was a good parent. At least she wasn't diving off cliffs and hang gliding off mountains just for the thrill of it without a thought for the people who cared about her.

She was here for her daughter with two feet firmly on the ground. Heather was cared for and loved. Everything Sabrina did was for her daughter; it was beyond awful of Ace to think she would jeopardise Heather's safety in any way.

They already knew that Heather still hadn't been found as Sabrina had been talking to Jonathan Pratt, the headteacher, from the moment they touched British soil.

The police had been called and were on site, teachers and also friends of Charles had arrived two hours ago and were scouting out the area. Sabrina didn't know much about these friends, but Charles did say they worked for the government. When she asked if it was Scotland Yard, he simply replied 'something like that'.

The school was made of local grey Derbyshire gritstone, a menacing building over three floors. It was sprawling on one side with multiple sloping roofs and chimneys. A long high wall with a wooden gate was to the right. It was one of those English buildings you just knew had a long story to tell.

"Any news Jonathan?" Sabrina asked, leaving the group of men to talk to the headteacher.

Jonathan was in his forties but looked younger than his years. Tall and nice-looking, in a lean no chin kind of way. She'd known him for several months as he'd lived locally before becoming the headteacher. She'd even had dinner with him on one occasion but thought it best to leave their relationship as a parent-teacher one when Heather had started his school.

"No luck Sabs," he touched her arm and led her inside.

Ace smouldered. She hadn't spoken to him in hours, anything she did say was directed at his dad or Matthew, and now she just walked off as though he didn't matter! He marched in behind them and followed them into an office to stand behind the chair Sabrina had sat on. His hand on her shoulder.

"This is Alister Edwards, Jonathan, Heather's father." She

introduced.

"Where's my daughter?" Ace asked instead.

Jonathan ignored him and looked at Sabrina.

What the fuck? Ace tried and failed to keep his temper in check.

"You have five seconds to answer my fucking question or so help me God I'll throw you out the fucking window!"

"Ace!" Sabrina yelled, standing up to face him.

"It's all right Sabs, I'll answer the–" Jonathan looked him up and then down. "Heather's dad." Everyone in the room knew he'd wanted to say something else but held himself in check.

"Have you spoken to George?"

"Yes, but he doesn't know anything."

"Can I speak to him?" Sabrina asked.

"It's very unusual Sabrina. I can't just pull him out of bed."

"But—"

"You get that boy out of fucking bed right now, or I'll wake everyone up then go to the papers first thing in the morning and tell them how you lost my daughter. Twice!" Ace yelled, losing all patience. Time was ticking. Heather had been lost for almost ten hours. It was getting dark. Didn't anyone give a shit? Sabrina was sat there all prim and fucking proper being all fucking British, and polite and nothing was happening!

"I'll go and get him," Jonathan said, leaving the room.

Sabrina swung around to Ace as soon as Jonathan closed the door. "Did you have to be so rude?"

"Did you have to sit in here as though you were about to have a nice little chat when my daughter was missing!?"

"There is a way to handle Jonathan,"

"Why the hell are you on a first-name basis with the man?"

"What?"

"You heard. He calls you Sabs!" Ace seethed, furious just thinking about it. "Are you fucking him?" He asked quietly, unable to stop the question that had been on his mind the minute the asswipe had put his hand on her arm with a familiarity that spoke volumes.

"You are out of your mind if you think I'm even going to answer you. You have no right!"

"Oh yeah," Ace, was in her face now. His control gone to fuck. "I have every right. As you have been cavorting around the world, my daughter is missing. So yeah, I have a fucking right!"

"I wish to God you had never found me." Sabrina breathed, meaning every word.

"I'm sure that you do and don't think I'm going to let you cavort with any and anybody. Your days of being single and playing around are over!"

"Screw you Ace. You don't own me."

"That is where you are wrong, Sabrina. *You* are mine.

The door opened, and 'Jonathan' came in.

"I've got George for you, Sabs."

"Her name is Sabrina." Ace charged darkly.

Sabrina sent Ace a dirty look. "Sabs is fine, Jonathan." She smiled at the other man and turned her back on Ace. "Where is he?"

"Follow me."

Jonathan led the way to an empty classroom.

"Can I talk to him alone?" Sabrina asked.

"It's not normal policy."

"Please, you can look through the window in the door."

"Fine," he replied. "But don't be too long. I really need his parents' permission for him to be talking to you."

She smiled her thanks.

"Hey George," she signed to the freckled face little dark-haired boy who was her daughter's best friend.

"Hello."

"How've you been?"

"Fine."

"Do you know that film Stardust with the cowboy and the horse that can run really really fast?"

"Yeah," he replied moodily. He was in his pyjamas and was shuffling his slippers back and forth under his chair.

"Well, guess what?"

"What?"

"I was just on a plane with the cowboy in that film."

His eyes rounded. "Really?"

"Really," she smiled. "You see, he let me fly in his plane with him all the way from America because we can't find Heather. Do you know where she is?"

The shuffling stopped. "No."

"Any ideas?"

"Not really."

"What was the last thing you did together? Do you remember?"

"Looked at the roof," he signed rapidly. "Heather thought she saw a bald eagle landing, but I told her that was silly because we don't have bald eagles in England. They're in America."

"That's right. You are so clever."

He grinned at her, and the shuffling started again.

"Did you guys have something to eat at dinner?"

"Yeah, burgers, but Heather," he looked around and leaned in close. "She put my cob and her cob in her pocket and some stuff for a picnic she said."

"Why'd she do that?" Sabrina whispered, mimicking his actions.

"Not sure. She told me not to tell, or she'd tell Mr Pratt about the time I broke the shed window," he clapped his hands over his mouth. "You won't tell?"

"I won't tell," Sabrina promised. "Do you remember where Heather saw the so-called eagles?"

"Yeah, above the teachers' bedrooms. She said the teachers were too stupid to even know what they are. I told her teachers know everything and are proper smart and she said her mummy, that's you, is smarter than everybody, and I said—"

"You've been a super help, George," Sabrina interrupted quickly. "Thank you,"

"You're welcome." He replied. "Can I go back to bed now?"

"Course you can treasure. You've been a star."

He grinned at her and went off.

"Any help?" Jonathan asked, coming into the classroom with

Ace on his heels.

"She's on the roof."

"Roof!"

"Which roof?" Ace asked.

"The teachers' roof. She's gone to feed the bald eagles."

"We don't have bald eagles in England," Jonathan said, in his superior tone.

"She thinks they're eagles," Sabrina replied. "Which is the quickest way to the teacher's wing?"

"This way." Jonathan led the way down a corridor, up a shallow flight of stairs, down another dimly lit corridor, down a flight of stairs until they got to a set of double doors. "This is the teachers' entrance, but there is another way."

"Let's just go with this route."

He led them past several flats and then at the very end a door which led to the roof.

"I'll go first, shall I?" Jonathan suggested.

"No," Sabrina said. "I'll go."

Both men watched as Sabrina navigated the narrow hall then a flight of stairs before disappearing from view. Ace pushed Jonathan out of the way to follow.

***

Sabrina pushed open the heavy wooden door that was typical for the seventeenth-century building and walked on to the slate roof. It was sloped precariously, and she felt better once she was crawling on her hands and knees.

She searched the shadows and closed her eyes when she forgot she didn't like heights that left her open and vulnerable to the elements like this. After a moment she went on. She knew her daughter. If Heather wasn't on this roof, she was in a tree, probably with a pair of binoculars looking for the so-called eagles.

Sabrina spied a trainered foot covered in dried mud, and white socks, also covered in dried mud, and she crawled towards it with relief.

So as not to alarm her, Sabrina stroked her daughter's shin and sat beside her a little distance away. Heather was leaning against the slope, one foot stretched out, the other bent at the knee. There was orange peel, an empty packet of prawn cocktail crisps, chocolate bar wrappers, cheese stick wrappers and a bottle of purple Fruit Shoot beside her. Heather had come prepared, Sabrina thought. At least that was something.

Heather looked at her, then smiled. She had a tooth missing on the bottom, Sabrina noticed sadly, missing the event.

"Hey, baby."

Heather scrambled to her and flung her skinny little arms around Sabrina's neck then curled into her lap. At least she had her coat on, Sabrina thought, making herself comfortable as she snuggled her daughter close.

"Okay?" She signed.

Heather nodded.

"She's here!" Sabrina called out. She heard Ace relay the news.

Moving a little to look into her daughter's eyes, eyes that were so like Ace's, she touched her face.

"I was worried," she said. "Why didn't you tell anyone where you were going?"

"Because they wouldn't let me come see the mummy bird."

"But I was scared, baby. When they couldn't find you, they rang me in America, and I flew straight here."

"That's okay. You were coming home tomorrow."

Sabrina sighed, Heather and her logic.

"I have a surprise for you?"

Heather looked at her.

"I saw your daddy."

Heather shrugged her shoulders.

"He's here."

She shrugged her narrow shoulders again and stuck her thumb in her mouth. She only ever did that when she was at home and tired.

"Can we go down now?"

Heather shook her head, pointing to a dark corner.

"What's over there?" Sabrina asked. As much as she could, she encouraged Heather to speak.

Heather pointed again.

"No, what's over there?" Sabrina repeated.

"Baby birds," Heather said, her words were slow and slurred, but you could pick up the gist of what she was saying if you listened carefully.

"Mummy bird won't come and feed her babies if you stay here Heather,"

"Why?"

"Well err," she heard someone stepping onto the roof and turned to see Ace. "She's okay." She told him.

"Can I come up?"

"Yeah, on your knees though, it's very narrow." She explained, putting her malice with him to one side for the sake of their daughter. She turned back to Heather. "Because mummy birds like to see their babies all by themselves." She answered Heather's question before adding. "Your daddy has come to say hello."

Heather didn't look the least bit impressed; in fact, she cuddled closer to her mother.

"Over here Ace," Sabrina instructed and watched as he came closer, his eyes glued to Heather as he sat beside them on the other side of Sabrina. He roped his arms across his knees and turned to look at them.

Heather was watching him.

"Sweetheart?" Sabrina touched Heather's arm to get her attention and waited for her to look at her in the dim evening light. "This is your dad," she introduced. "What do you say?"

Ace looked at his daughter. She was so like him. He felt his heart swell in his chest and for the first time in his life, he wanted to cry, yeah, him, the man who would climb mountains and endure tribal initiations without grimacing.

"Hello," he stuck out his hand and waited.

Heather looked at him beneath her lashes then took his hand.

"What are you doing on the roof?" he croaked, he wanted to hold her, cuddle her close, breathe her in. He'd made her. She was part of him. He was so overwhelmed he wanted to give in and bawl like a baby.

She pointed again to the corner of the roof that was in deep shadows.

"You came to feed the birds?" He signed.

She nodded.

"You gave them chicken nuggets?"

She grinned and shook her head, then held out the bread she'd been holding for hours. It had curled up and moulded to the shape of her little fist.

"You gave them bread?"

She nodded.

"I bet the mummy bird is watching from the trees and wants to tell her babies goodnight. Shall we go so she can read them a story and put them to bed?"

Heather nodded and quickly shifted off her mother's lap.

"Would you like to hold my hand so we can go down together?"

Heather looked at his hand, then looked at her mother for permission. At Sabrina's encouraging nod, she ignored his hand and held out her own to her mothers' instead.

"Thank you, baby," Sabrina said, letting herself be pulled to her knees and then led from the roof. She felt Ace's pain at the rejection, but there was nothing she could do about it on the roof. He had to build his relationship with his daughter, she would help, of course, help smooth the way, but ultimately it was up to the two of them.

They picked themselves off the roof slowly, Heather chatting about the baby birds. They all blinked when they reached inside, with the harsh overhead lights.

"Well, what do you have to say for yourself, young lady? Detention for you!" Jonathan blazed down at Heather who walked past him without a care in the world "Sabs, that child is in need of—"

"Be very careful my friend," Ace said conversationally, fighting the urge to smash the asswipe in his throat. But he was too busy watching his daughter walk off with her hand folded in her mothers. One of the Velcro straps on her sneakers was flapping each time she walked, and she had grass stains down the legs of her jeans. "I'm sure you'll appreciate that she will not be returning to this school." Ace supplied, just in case the idiot asswipe had other ideas.

Sabrina was relieved to see the legions of police and unmarked cars had left, and only her own blue Ford Focus stood in the driveway.

She didn't even ask how it got there, she was just glad to see it, and so was Heather, it seemed, as she skipped to it and was already opening the passenger door and sliding in.

"Where's Charles and Matthew?"

"Gone to a hotel. They'll catch up with us tomorrow." He glanced at Heather, who was already in the front seat. "She okay?"

"Fine, not the least bit perturbed by all she put us through. She had enough food to last for days."

"Lucky her," he charged coldly. "Let's go,"

"Aren't you going to the hotel?" She asked. "There's only the one. It's more of a B and B, but it's clean."

"I'm staying with you."

"I don't have room for you."

"Get in the car, Sabrina." His high-handed tone brokered no arguments.

She got into the driver's seat but not before slicing him a dirty look as he got into the back. It took forty minutes to get to her little cottage in Frecknor Green, it really was a storybook cottage, but instead of being called the proverbial Rose Cottage it was called Lilac's Way. A gritstone two-bedroom, one-bathroom house with a tiny walled garden at the back and a single patch of grass cut in half by a narrow pathway at the front.

Heather skipped out as soon as the car stopped, hopping on one foot as she went to the door.

CHAPTER THIRTEEN

Sabrina's house was not what he'd been expecting. It was small, which was okay, but all the floral prints and netting at the windows would have suited his grandmother, make that his great grandmother, he thought, peering around.

"I'm going to sort Heather out." She told him, switching on the lights as she walked around. "You can do what you want."

He looked at her, a smart comeback on the tip of his tongue, but he held it in. It had been a long day. They were both stressed out and tired, and he'd said some pretty unforgivable things to her.

Watching her now, as she knelt in front of his daughter, taking off her coat and giving her a tickle before pulling her in for a tight hug, Ace felt the stirrings of guilt. She was doing the best that she could. He kept forgetting she was on her own, a single mother with a deaf child. She didn't have the love and support of a family as he did.

"I'm sorry, Sabrina." He said simply, and she looked at him under her lashes then nodded.

"I'm going to run a bath for Heather." She told him over her shoulder as she led his little girl out of the room and up a flight of stairs.

"Are you hungry, sweetheart?" Ace could hear her asking Heather as they climbed the stairs.

Ace sat wearily on the floral sofa of pinks and creams, the flowers on it the size of dinner plates. It was horrible. Comfortable, but horrible. He scrubbed his hands over his face, feeling the bristles. He was tired, and when he was tired his back ached.

"Ace?" Sabrina called sometime later from upstairs. "Would you like to come and wish Heather goodnight?"

"Sure." He felt that lump in his throat again. He was a dad.

He had a daughter. He climbed the very narrow and very steep stairs, that actually creaked, for crap's sake. They weren't safe.

"Hey there sunshine," he told his daughter as she lay looking up at him from her single bed. Her room was tiny. He'd been expecting a lot of pinks, frilly stuff and maybe stuffed toys all over the bed like every single one of his nieces. This room resembled a hotel but with a single poster of Wayne Rooney facing the bed. Her duvet was in brown and cream geometrics, nice, but very grown-up.

Heather looked up at him with eyes already heavy with sleep. He wanted to maybe give her a kiss or something but remembered he was still a stranger to her. She looked over his shoulder to her mother, who was behind him.

Sabrina must have signed something to her as Heather, with her thumb in her mouth, sat up and opened one arm out to him for a hug.

Ace held her close and breathed in her scent. She smelled of cherries.

"Goodnight sunshine," he said, as he laid her down and cupped her face to graze his thumb over her cheek.

"Sunshine is boring," she signed at him. "I'm a storm cloud."

He grinned at her, smoothing her reddish curls away from her brow. "Okay, Storm Cloud. See you in the morning?"

She nodded and closed her eyes. He watched her for a moment, smoothed her hair again, kissed her on the forehead and left the room to go downstairs.

He'd heard Sabrina in the bathroom, so went into the galley kitchen and put the kettle on. He was in dire need of a stiff drink, but coffee would have to do.

She came downstairs just as the kettle began to boil and he was remembering what they'd been doing the last time a kettle had been boiling. Rewind thirty-six hours.

"What would you like?" She asked, moving past him to pull out two mugs. "I haven't got any milk so either herbal tea or black coffee."

Ace was busy looking at her legs. She'd changed into this long

T-shirt type dress that could have originally been black but had faded to grey or was just dark grey. It covered her from neck to floor but had long splits at the sides.

"Ace?" She prompted.

"Coffee. Black. Two sugars."

"Please."

"Please."

"Are you hungry?"

"A little. Are you?"

"I'll make some toast," she said, turning to the cream enamel bread bin, then stopped with her hand on the wooden lid. "No bread."

"I'll go to the store." Ace offered.

"Nowhere is open. I'm sorry."

"Don't worry about it. We'll sort it out tomorrow." He led the way back into the living room, holding his coffee. There wasn't a TV, he noticed.

Sabrina sat down in a small chair opposite him. She was strangling the mug she was holding and looking everywhere, but at him, he saw.

The split on her dress fell to the side and Ace watched, distracted for a moment by the shape of her slender thigh.

"How soon can you pack up the house?"

"Huh, what?" She asked.

"How soon can you pack up the house? You're moving in with me."

"I'm not going anywhere." She told him, taking a sip of her drink. "We are not going anywhere."

"You'll go where I tell you to go."

"Have you lost your marbles Ace? I don't even know you."

"You know me, Sabrina."

"Another thirty-six hours amounts to what? Three days of togetherness? I'm not packing up my house and moving countries to be with a man I hardly know." She countered. "No. Forget it."

"What have you got here? You live in the back of beyond. I've

already told asswipe, Heather will not be attending that school
—"

"What?"

"You heard. She won't be going back there, Sabrina."

"You had no right!"

"I had every right!"

"You don't understand. There isn't anywhere else that will take her around here. That school did."

"That school lost her."

Sabrina shook her head. He didn't understand. Heather was special, she had Pervasive Development Disorder Not Otherwise Specified or PDDNOS, her social skills could go either way. It was imperative at this stage in her development that she be around other kids and her care worker, Hazel. They had the next four years mapped out for her.

"We're not moving," she clarified. "But just curious? Where exactly would we live Ace? In New York where she could wander off and then someone simply walks off with her. She'd be overwhelmed by the place. She needs space."

"Then we find someplace else."

"No, we're fine here. Everyone knows her. We're a community. Everyone looks out for her."

"You mean like how shitface did?"

"Will you stop calling him names? I agree the security was a little lax tonight and I'll have words."

"You will not have words, as you will not be going anywhere near him again!" Ace growled.

She looked at him, finally understanding. "You're doing this because you're jealous?"

"I'm not fucking jealous! I don't like the man."

"Whatever Ace." She dismissed with a wave of her hand. "I think you should go now."

"Not until we've sorted this shit out."

Sabrina stood up to put her mug in the sink when there was a knock at the door, she walked past him, ignoring his glower as she opened the front door.

"Hiya Stewart, come on in." She welcomed.

Stewart Harding was her closest neighbour and landlord, a widower in his fifties. "I saw the lights on like and thought I'd stop by. I brought this." He gave her a basket covered with a tea towel. "Heard our little Heather decided to wander off again. She's a little Miss is our Heather, but no worries at least she's safe like."

Sabrina wasn't surprised everyone knew what had happened and walked into the living room. Ace was now standing by the unlit gas fire.

"Stewart, this is her dad Ace."

"Ay up, nice to meet you mate," Stewart said in his broad Derbyshire accent, holding out his hand.

"You too."

They shook hands.

"Bless you Stewart, bread, milk and eggs. I'm dying for some toast."

"Not to worry Sabrina, let me know if you need anything else. I'm here for you and our Heather."

"Aww thank you, Stewart. We'll pop round tomorrow. Has the cat had her kittens yet?"

"Two days ago. I know the one our Heather will choose. Cute little thing it is, all ginger and white." They were walking to the door.

"Thanks again for the goodies, Stewart."

Sabrina hugged him and watched him leave for longer than she would typically stand at the door, as she could feel Ace's anger rolling off him.

"Just how many men do you have around my daughter Sabrina?"

"You are so stupid; I'm not even going to answer you." She walked to the kitchen, suddenly starving and pulled the loaf of bread from the basket Stewart had brought her. She wanted toast.

Ace crowded up beside her and pulled her around to him.

"You will answer my question."

"Or what?"

"Don't mess with me, Sabrina. I'm not in a good mood."

"Move off me Ace." She could feel his body heat, his breath fanning her neck as he bent over her, his arousal pressing into her thigh. She needed to turn him off. "Stewart is my neighbour and landlord." She pushed at his chest.

"And why couldn't you just say so?"

"I don't answer to you."

"You are the mother of my child."

"But not your wife or girlfriend."

"That is going to be easily rectified believe me."

"Was that a proposal Ace?"

"What if it was?"

"You can forget it." The toast popped up, and she squeezed past him to her under the counter fridge for the butter. It was made locally and was the ultimate in creaminess.

Ace watched her bend over and gritted his teeth. He'd like nothing better than to have sex right now, he was so fucking frustrated, but his daughter was upstairs, and they had things to work out first.

"Would you like some toast?" She asked, buttering her own.

"No."

"Thank you."

"I do not want any fucking toast! I want you to understand that I want you both close to me. In America, living under my roof."

"You are so full of shit Ace; you don't have a proper roof. You don't live anywhere." She walked into the living room again.

"I will for you and Heather." He said, trailing behind her like a fucking puppy. He was no damn dog, he thought, coming to a stop in the middle of the room.

She shook her head, then bit into her toast. With the slice in her hand, she opened her laptop that was on the small table to the back of the room.

"So, I'm supposed to pack up, leave everything I've worked for to live with a man I barely know and stole his sperm from?"

"Will you stop saying that. Your foresight was a blessing."

"Is that what you've decided to call it, my foresight?"

"What the fuck is wrong with you?" He was losing all patience. "We have something Sabrina, always have."

"Yeah, well that was before things changed. I'm not the same free spirit I used to be. I rely on no one but myself. I can't afford too. Everything and I mean, *everything,* I do is for my daughter."

"She's my daughter too."

"And I will never stop you from seeing her."

"Seeing her?" He frowned. "What are you saying?"

She looked at him while she waited for her laptop to start up. "I'm not moving to America with you. You are as selfish as I was, if not more so." She put in her password. "You do things without a care in the world. As a mother, every scrape on Heather's knee, I feel in my own heart. What you put Greta and Charles through, and everyone else who loves you, is selfish and for what Ace?" She pinned him with a look. "The thrill of it? Ten seconds of adrenaline that leaves your heart racing but has your mother in tears as she watches you zip-line across Nepal, or free climb Shanghai Tower without safety rope and then break your collarbone on the way down!" She listed, passionately. "I'm not putting myself through that! You were given a second chance with your life, and what do you do? Flirt with death!"

Ace looked at her, something she'd said playing over in his head. "How did you know I broke my collarbone?" He asked suspiciously.

She turned her laptop to him. "The same way I know every selfish, unnecessary act you've ever done!" She spat. "I may not have found you when Heather was born, but by the time she was three, I knew everything about you."

"You *knew* where I was?"

"That's right. I didn't need to look for you. I already knew where you were."

Ace walked over to her to see the file marked Ace. She opened it, and there was every article ever written about him.

"You bitch."

Sabrina stood her ground at the insult.

"So, you see, I am not allowing someone like you to destabilise my life or my daughter's life." She folded her arms across her chest as she stood to face him. "We will not be moving to America with you. I will not be marrying you. I will look after my daughter my way, so she won't get hurt or see her daddy break another bone or wind up dead at the bottom of a canyon he had no business being in!"

She grabbed her handbag from the table.

"Here are my car keys. Drive straight down to the intersection and turn left. The B and B where your dad and Matthew are staying is the fourth house on the right." She instructed, pushing the keys into his hand. "Now get out."

"I'm not going anywhere." Ace ignored her hand, holding out the keys. "What the fuck Sabrina? You knew where I was?" Ace said again, walking closer and grabbing the back of the chair as she looked over at him with dark eyes filled with hurt and accusation.

"A simple Google search and voilà!" Sabrina sat down again and did just that, selecting the images option, where it revealed Ace had millions and millions of hits in less than a second.

Ace leaned over her shoulder. He'd never Googled himself. He didn't have a Facebook page or Twitter account or any other social platform. Life was too short for such social fuckery, he thought. But now that same social fuckery had condemned him.

There was picture after picture of him climbing, diving and racing. There were professional photos of him from magazine spreads and fundraisers. There were pictures of him and Kyle before the stunt accident, partying hard. There were even more photographs of him after the accident. Then there were the women. Hell, there were photographs of him with some women he didn't even remember, some he'd hooked up with for a night or two and some photos of women who just happened to be standing beside him and grabbing the opportunity of a photograph.

There were tears in Sabrina's eyes now, and Ace felt a deep shame as his life was laid out to her in candid fucking colour. It wasn't pretty. Fuck me. There was even a paparazzi shot of him with his hand on the breast of a blonde, taken a month ago.

"Those women meant nothing to me, Sabrina." He said earnestly.

She shook her head. "I was struggling Ace," she revealed, dashing the tears away. "I couldn't cope. I had a baby who cried whenever I picked her up. I had no help from the state because there were still assets to get rid of, but nobody was buying. This was all smack bang in the recession!" The tears were pouring now. "I almost, for a tiny second, thought about giving my baby up." She revealed. "Can you imagine? I thought about giving my beautiful, loving baby girl up for adoption."

Ace stepped closer, his hand going to her shoulder.

"No, don't touch me!" She threw herself away from him. "I held on to you and the memory of you for so long Ace, it got me through those dark days, and then I went to the library."

He frowned, puzzled at her reference. "The library?"

"Yes, the library. I didn't have a computer. I was desperate. I had no money to take care of Heather, and I was still living in Essex. So, I Googled you, and that's what I found." She flung a shaky hand at her laptop. "It sorted me out like nothing else. I moved from Essex and made a life for my baby and me without you."

"You can't blame me, Sabrina, you saw the note."

"But I didn't know that at the time, did I?" She said. "To me, it looked like you'd just got on with it, Ace and forgotten me."

"Never!" Ace held out his arms to her, his golden gaze pleading for her to understand. "I never forgot about you."

She shook her head. "You didn't try hard enough to find me." She turned to her computer again. "Exhibit number two." She said, on a self-deprecating laugh. "Nina Mae's Facebook page." She turned it for him to see. There was a picture of her as he knew her back then. Full make-up, long hair, revealing clothes. "I did this for you seven years ago."

"I—"

"So, in words, you can understand, fuck you, Ace. I could be found, but you just didn't look hard enough. You didn't care."

"Sabrina—"

"I need you to leave. We'll sort out something with Heather but take me out of the equation. I'm happy as I am. I don't want you in my life."

"If you think I'm going to let you go, *ever*, you have another fucking think coming!" He roared, completely incensed at her words. "You are mine!"

"Screw you Ace. I don't need love from any man. "

His laugh was short and harsh. "That's rich coming from a romance author."

"I'd rather live it in my head. Romance isn't all it's cracked up to be, and I'd rather be free and single and see whoever I want."

"You will not be seeing or sleeping with anyone but me!" He leaned over her. The thought of another man touching what was his was like a fucking choke-hold on him. He literally couldn't breathe. "Did you hear what I said?" He asked at her scathing look, then added darkly. "Do you need reminding how it is with us?"

"You stop right there," she held up her hand. "Is this the part where you come on all He Man Him on me and lift my skirt and have me over the table."

He smirked, his golden eyes shimmering at the challenge. "You've obviously thought about it." He stepped closer, frowning at the way she leaned away from him. Her chair was already up against the wall, so there was nowhere for her to go. "But I think it's time we found a bed, don't you?"

"I'm not having sex with you again." She said, even as her nipples pinched at his words.

Ace reached out and grabbed the back of her neck with one hand, as his other hand went under her chin to tilt her head for his kiss.

Sabrina knew what this was. It was about staking his claim. But she was not having any of it. He'd let her down. He hadn't looked hard enough. She pushed at his shoulders. But he wasn't letting her go, his lips stalking hers as she moved her head this way and that to avoid his mouth as he picked her up, sat her on the table, spread her legs and bent over her as she thumped at his back. But oh God, his hands were magical as one swept up her naked leg to skim the edge of her knickers.

Just then the room was filled with a loud, high pitched squealing noise and Ace, not prepared for the assault, was shoved off Sabrina and kicked in his shins by Heather, as she clamped on his arm with her teeth, not letting go.

"Heather no!" Sabrina tried to pull Heather off Ace, but she was kicking and hitting, her small fists flying at any place she could reach on him.

"Get her off me Sabrina before she hurts herself!" He yelled at Sabrina, as Heather went at him for all she was worth.

Sabrina grabbed Heather under her arms, moved away from the table, spun her around and on her knees got into her face.

Heather wasn't crying, no, her face was flushed with defiance as eyes just like Ace's, spat fire at him. Her little girl had been defending her. Sabrina wanted to cry, knowing how it must have looked to her daughter.

"It's okay baby," she soothed, stroking Heather's bare arms up and down. She signed it again, all the while stroking her arms until Heather finally looked at her. It was rare for Heather to initiate affection, but she flung herself at her mother for the second time that night and held on tight.

Sabrina picked her up, and Heather wrapped her legs around her waist to bury her head in her neck as she started to cry.

Sabrina rubbed circles on her back with the palm of her hand and rocked her back and forth and, even though Heather couldn't hear her, as she'd taken out her hearing aids, she used soothing words to calm her daughter.

"You'd better leave." She whispered, without emotion over her shoulder to Ace, as she walked out of the room and up the stairs.

She didn't come down again until she heard the front door close and her car driving off.

CHAPTER FOURTEEN

Sabrina had rung Sylvie Watson, the owner of the B and B, to tell her to expect Heather and herself after breakfast.

It was the next day, she was tired, completely jet-lagged, but having an almost seven-year-old, bounce on you ready to start the day at six in the morning, you got up no matter how tired you were.

They were both dressed in jeans, matching black wellies with green and red dots, and black tops. Sabrina had on her favourite bottled green body warmer and Heather her blue anorak. Summer had yet to catch up with the calendar, and the air was a bit nippy.

It wasn't a long walk, maybe fifteen minutes, if that, but by the time they stopped and chatted to other villagers out walking their dogs along the way or just getting some exercise, the walk had stretched to forty-five minutes.

"Ah, there you are pet," Sylvie Watson said, opening the front door to a house that was similar to Sabrina's in style and age. Sixteenth-century. She took Heather's coat and held her hand out for Sabrina's. "They're all in the living room," she whispered, leaning in close. "Do you want me to keep our Heather for a bit like?"

"No, that's okay Sylvie I'll just get it over with," Sabrina advised, appreciating how everyone looked out for them. They may be the only black people they knew, but they were treated like family and fiercely protected as if they'd been born in the village with a lineage that went back hundreds of years, like some of the residents in Frecknor Green.

Sabrina hadn't slept much last night, spending hours killing Ace off in different imaginary scenarios that even Stephen King wouldn't have thought of. This was Ace's fault. Yesterday had been a disaster, but all she knew today was that Heather needed to meet her family.

"Are you ready?" Sabrina signed to Heather. They'd had a long conversation about her conduct this morning. Heather had promised she was going to be on her best behaviour.

Sabrina had explained that her uncle Matthew was also deaf, just like her, and she was to help him with his British sign language as he signed in the American way and that can't be right. Heather had laughed, promising to teach him.

Heather nodded, and Sabrina watched as her little girl pulled herself up to her full height and pushed her shoulders back. Bless her!

Sabrina could hear the men talking in the living room and, with a nod, they went into the room.

"Morning, all." She told them, as they stopped talking, and all stood as they entered the room. Such lovely manners, Sabrina thought, as she went to hug Charles and Matthew and because she knew Heather was watching, allowed Ace to wrap his arms around her shoulders for a short hug too.

"Everyone, this is Heather, my favourite little munchkin." Sabrina introduced her daughter, who stood in front of her and signed her own hello to Matthew and Charles. Then turned to face Ace.

"I am not your friend," she signed, much to Sabrina's horror. So much for behaving. "You made my mummy cry."

Everyone looked at Ace, seeing something they had never seen before, embarrassment, but it was over in a flash. He went down to his knees in front of his daughter to smile at her softly.

"I'm sorry, Heather, I didn't mean to make your mummy cry. She's very special to me."

"How special?"

There was a chuckle from Matthew, and Ace threw him a dark look.

"Very special."

"So much special you won't make her cry anymore?"

"So much special sweetheart." He repeated.

"Yesterday you said you were going to call me Storm Cloud."

"I did, but sweetheart is nice too."

"No, I don't like it." She put her hands on his shoulders and went close to his face, almost nose to nose, before pulling back to sign with her eyes narrowed on his in warning. "You make sure to look after my mummy. She can dance on her toes, and I love her more than Eaton Mess. Come on, you can help me put my coat on. I don't like buttons. Do you like Eaton Mess?" She walked off, leaving all but Sabrina aghast. Yes, Heather was a right little miss, and they hadn't seen anything yet, she mused, as they filed out behind them.

"Where are we going?" Charles asked, as they walked through Frecknor Green, which took all of three minutes to walk on the single pavement through the heart of the village. Heather skipped ahead and led them down a leafy path with long scraggly nettles on each side, climbed over a low layered gritstone wall that was built hundreds of years ago and out into a field of grass dotted with cowpats.

"Over to my neighbours," Sabrina answered as she climbed over the wall.

They followed Heather who, looking behind and realising the adults weren't as close as she thought, ran back and captured Ace's hand to hurry him along.

Sabrina wanted to cry with the tender look Ace had shown his daughter. It was going to be okay.

They arrived at Stewart Harding's place. A working dairy farm with several labourers from Eastern Europe helping him.

Heather dashed off, going straight into the main house without knocking and coming back out with Stewart who was allowing himself to be pulled to the barn.

He waved his good morning and said. "I see our little Heather isn't any the worse for yesterday's plight like, is she?"

Sabrina laughed as she climbed the wooden fence that separated the field of horses from the yard. Stewart was teaching her how to ride. She sat on top and watched as Matthew and Charles shook hands with Stewart. Heather even said Stewart's name out loud, much to Sabrina's surprise. They'd practised for days saying his name for his birthday a few months ago, and this was the first time Heather had said it.

Stewart, bless him, didn't react but threw a wink over his shoulder at Sabrina when Heather wasn't looking.

"Thank you for that." Ace said as he walked to where she was sitting to lean his back against the fence.

He was one seriously good-looking bloke, Sabrina thought, liking the wind tousled look he was currently sporting and his die-hard profile. The country air suited him.

"We had a long chat this morning," she explained. "But just so you know, you're actually on probation."

He turned to look at her sharply.

"Not by me," she went on quickly, putting her hands up. "Your daughter informed me that if you ever make me upset, she will never speak to you again, so you've been warned, Alister Charles Edwards," Sabrina said lightly. She was in a good mood, she shouldn't be, her whole life was about to change, but for some reason, and for the first time since Heather had been born, she could relax and enjoy sharing the responsibility of parenting.

"She's a precocious little thing, isn't she?" Ace said, watching Heather show Matthew how to jump into a puddle to get the biggest splash.

"If that's what you would like to call it." Sabrina laughed. "I have a feeling she takes after you in more than just looks."

"She does," Ace smirked and nodded proudly and then turned to her, intentionally invading her space and leaning his forearms on her knees. "I'm sorry about last night." He said, looking up at her.

In a perfect world Sabrina would have, maybe, smoothed his wind tousled hair, cupped his face and pulled him up for a forgiveness kiss. But not in Sabrina's world.

"You need to respect my boundaries Ace. We are not a couple, and I don't want Heather to start getting any ideas."

They stared at each other, Ace noticing that Sabrina hadn't even tried to move his arms from her legs.

"Come on, let's see these kittens." He placed his hands on her hips to help her down and made her slide down his body before he let her go again.

"Is that the earring I gave you?" Ace asked suddenly, seeing the extra hole in one ear only. It was typical of Sabrina's past quirkiness, he thought. This Sabrina was sweet, but he missed the quirky Sabrina who'd called herself Nina Mae. He wasn't sure where he was with this Sabrina.

Sabrina touched the small gold stud self-consciously and nodded. She'd never taken it out.

They had a pleasant morning, staying with Stewart who packed Charles and Matthew up with plum jam from his collection and a bottle each of his apple cider he brewed in one of his out-houses.

They walked back, Heather bouncing between them all. She had yet to slow down, and Sabrina was waiting for the crash, hoping they would be home by then.

"We'll see you later?" Charles asked as they approached the B and B. "Is there anywhere we can go for dinner?"

"How about you come over to my house around six? I need to talk to you all anyway." She invited.

They agreed and, with hugs all around, went inside. It was Ace who stayed behind.

"I'll walk you back."

"We're fine."

"I'll still walk you back."

"Has anyone ever told you how stubborn you are?"

"Not really. You're the only one who can get away with it."

"Stop it Ace," Sabrina said.

Heather was holding each of their hands and swinging them as she walked between them.

"Bread and butter." He listed.

"I'm too tired to think Alister."

"I like it when you call me Alister."

"I guess I really am tired if I'm making you like me, huh," she said, without malice.

"I'm going to have to fly you all over the world, just to keep you this sweet." He drawled, lifting his daughter into his arms as she began to drag her feet.

Sabrina was surprised Heather hadn't objected to being picked up. She didn't do well with people touching her.

"Nah, I love my fields of sheep and horses; far away shores don't appeal to me these days. Morocco is as far as we go, and then I swap my fields for my argan trees."

"Are you going over in the summer?"

"That was the plan."

"When?"

"Not sure yet. I've got things to decide."

"We've got things to decide," he challenged.

Her house was in sight, and she nodded.

"How long will you stay in England?"

"For as long as it takes."

"What takes?"

"That's for me to know and you to find out." He winked over at her as she pushed open her wooden gate and opened the front door.

"Why isn't it locked?"

"This is Frecknor Green, Ace we have zero crime here."

"That's beside the point." He stepped inside and looked around for somewhere to put Heather down. She'd fallen asleep on his shoulder.

"Over here," Sabrina indicated the couch and watched as he put their daughter down with a gentleness that softened her even more towards him. He'd been doing that to her all morning. "Thank you." She said, as she pulled off her daughter's wellies and undid her coat. She wouldn't sleep for very long. Maybe half an hour if that.

Sabrina and Heather's safety brought to mind the rose she'd received in New York yesterday. Was it just yesterday, Ace thought?

"What's going on with the rose you got yesterday?" He followed her into the kitchen and watched as she put down her jars of jam.

"Rose?"

"Yeah, that rose you got as we were leaving your hotel."

"It's nothing."

"It was a whole lot of something at the time. You were scared shitless."

She sighed, knowing he wasn't about to let it go.

"I started to get a single rose whenever I did a book event. Whether it be in England, New York or wherever."

"Do you know who from?"

She shook her head.

"When did it start?"

"With my first book."

"How many books have you written?"

"Three. The first one didn't have a rose on the cover, but I received a rose, anyway. The messages are usually the same. 'I'm sorry. With love, or I miss you'" She shivered, remembering the first time she got the 'I miss you,' message. It made it feel all too sinister and creepy.

"Have you reported it to the police?"

She looked at him from below her lashes. They were talking nicely but knew he was going to get mad at her answer.

He narrowed his eyes at her, seeing her guilty flush. "You didn't did you?"

She shook her head.

"Fucking hell, Sabrina."

She poked her head out of the kitchen to ensure Heather was still sleeping.

"I have enough things to worry about. Why is your language so foul, anyway? Matthew and your dad are the epitome of gentlemen. But you? You have such a disgusting mouth."

Ace chuckled and kissed her lightly on the cheek before answering. "Matthew's language is worse than mine." He clarified. "I'll see you tonight." He said, walking over to Heather and kissing her forehead. "Tell her I'll see her later for me." He stopped suddenly and turned to Sabrina, who was standing in the doorway. "Thank you for my daughter." He turned and left, telling her to lock the door behind him.

CHAPTER FIFTEEN

Ace watched as Sabrina and Heather made their way down the street. He was sat at the window of the French-inspired coffee shop-cum-library-cum-meeting place, for the village.

The village was one of those quintessential villages with a single post office under the threat of closure, a butcher, a grocery store, this coffee shop and the church with an adjacent hall. That was it. For anything else, you had to go into Chesterfield or Derby or Manchester. Even the doctor's surgery was in another larger village six miles away.

Ace watched as Sabrina stopped yet again and was chatting to a lady he'd seen several times walking her three collies. Heather was busy patting the dogs' heads as they pushed against her hand, vying for her attention.

The pair set off again and almost managed to cross the street, would have to, if the butcher hadn't chosen that moment to go to the door. Ace looked on in frustration as another conversation took place.

Sabrina was dressed in a pair of worn jeans tucked into brown leather boots, a white T-shirt with long sleeves and a body warmer in deep red. Her hair was in plaits again. She looked like every other person in the village. Only *she* was sexy as hell.

He now knew Sabrina had moved here when Heather was three. Sylvie Watson, the lady that ran the B and B, had told him. Sylvie Watson wasn't really a gossip, she gave information in frustrating little drips, and he could tell she was suspicious of him. Hell, everyone in the village was, but there was some kind of tentative respect for being Heather's father, he knew. He had the feeling that if Sabrina hadn't welcomed him, neither would the village.

Heather started jumping up and down and pulling on her mother's arm when she spotted him.

Ace waved at her, and she smiled and waved back. She was a great kid. Today in her uniform of jeans, two T-shirts, the long-sleeved stripe under the short sleeve dots and yellow wellies with blue dogs on them. He smiled to himself, remembering Heather showing him her wellington boot collection when he'd asked what wellies were. She'd laughed so hard at him she'd had tears in her eyes, but they'd really connected when he'd sat on her bedroom floor, and she'd pulled several pairs of 'wellies' out to show him.

Sabrina looked down, then across the street. When she saw him, she didn't wave excitedly like their daughter. Instead, she walked Heather to the edge of the sidewalk, made her look up and down the street and watched keenly when Heather walked as fast as she could into the shop.

They'd been in England over a week now, his father Charles had gone off visiting friends down south today, and Matthew had flown back this morning.

Last week Sabrina had them all over for dinner and talked to them about Heather and her deafness and also where she was on the developmental spectrum. She explained her borderline PDDNOS.

It hadn't been easy hearing that his daughter was having such a problem socialising and being hindered by her deafness too, but Sabrina had told them about the programme she was on. Heather wasn't considered a stable enough candidate for the cochlear implant as her behaviour was too unpredictable, they said. When Ace had asked what the hell that meant, Sabrina went on to tell them how Heather taking off to do her own thing was a regular occurrence and how she always signs instead of talks, even though her deafness hadn't begun until she was almost four and her speech had been developing normally up to that point.

They even met Heather's speech therapist and care worker, an older woman called Hazel who lived in Eyam, a village known for its bravery as the villages had sacrificed themselves so that the bubonic plague wouldn't spread beyond the village boundaries in 1665.

With the summer holiday only a few days away it was agreed that Heather would not be going back to school, and that Ace would spend the summer in England getting to know his daughter. Sabrina had made it scathingly clear he didn't work, so it was not like he had anything to rush back to America for. He'd had to bite his tongue after that remark.

He still couldn't believe she had known where he was all that time, even having a Facebook page for him to find her, but knowing where he was? That didn't make sense. He'd lost years of getting to know his daughter, and he would never forgive her for that. She made it look like he was a womanising, selfish, adrenaline junkie, not good enough for her daughter.

That hurt. That hurt like nothing else.

His father had tried to make him see it from her side. She was a single mum, with no one. She hadn't had a chance to grieve for her parents before becoming a mother. She'd lost everything. Their daughter had a disability. He was just a guy she'd met briefly and got pregnant by.

But what his dad hadn't known was how magical that time had been. It may have been brief, but for Ace, it had been life-changing. Were those few days a game to Sabrina? Calling herself Nina Mae to take on a fun, carefree alter-ego? He hadn't thought so at the time. Now? Now he wasn't so sure. She was so different. Charles could see why Sabrina had been reluctant to contact him. Ace couldn't.

At least Sabrina wasn't visiting her ill feelings of him on his family. She'd had Charles and Matthew round for dinner. They'd gone on long walks across the fields together so Heather could get to know them better. She'd had Greta on the phone and Heather had met her grandmother via Skype.

Yep, there was no problem there. She just didn't want him, and he was okay with that.

He watched her laugh at something the butcher said, flinging back her head and giving Ace a view of her long neck. He gritted his teeth; did she have to touch her throat like that in front of the butcher? Ace turned away and focused on his daughter, who was looking at the cakes and silently counting them.

A black Lexus screeched to a halt across the street and Ace turned as Sabrina bent down to talk to the driver. From this angle, he couldn't make out who the driver was, but Sabrina seemed none too pleased. She stepped away from the vehicle and walked to the rear end. The driver, asswipe, got out, rushed to the back, trying to capture her hand.

Ace stood up, looked to make sure Heather was okay, before going outside. With his arms folded across his chest, he watched and was about to cross the street when Sabrina flashed asswipes hand off her arm.

She glared at Ace as though he were equal to the bastard and swept past him into the café.

Staring across the street, Ace caught asswipe giving him a smug knowing look, and was about to go stamp on his throat when the other man jumped into his car and sped off. Cowardly little shit, Ace thought, as he entered the café and sat down.

"Sorry about that." Sabrina took off her body warmer and placed it on the back of the dainty metal chair.

"Would you like a drink? A hot chocolate maybe?" He offered tightly.

"Please. Oh, and a tea cake please." She added, as he walked to the counter and placed their order as well as a small hot chocolate with marshmallows for Heather, before coming back.

"Did you find Derby okay?" She asked, knowing he'd gone there yesterday to do some business.

"The wonders of the Sat Nav Sabrina." He snarled.

"Okay, Ace," she sighed, rubbing her temples. "If you're going to be like that, I'll just go, and you can drop Heather off later." She stood to go.

"Sit down,"

She looked at him sharply, at his abrasive tone.

"A week ago, you told me you weren't fu—," he looked over at their daughter who was at a low plastic table reading a book. "Sleeping with him. That little tête-à-tête I just witnessed looks like you have a whole lot of something to me." He crossed his arms over his chest and pinned her with a chilling look.

"I don't owe you an explanation," she said tightly, fighting the feeling of letting him down, which was ludicrous. "I just need you to focus on Heather. Only Heather."

Ace glared at her, fighting all that he was feeling. She drove him so fucking mad! But he'd choose his battles.

"I've opened a new account for you." He said instead, holding up his hand when she was about to interrupt. "If you don't want to use it for yourself, fine. But Heather will want for nothing. Understand?" And, because he just couldn't help himself, added.

"And I don't want my daughter anywhere near that imbecile."

Her nod was to confirm his first request.

"No matter what," he continued. "And I know you're not going to like this, but you will need to move. The village is nice if you're retired, and I understand the security it gave you when Heather was a baby, but you've outgrown it. You're not on your own any more Sabrina. I can give you all that you need." He charged at her, bracing himself for an argument.

Sabrina had already resigned herself to the fact she would need to move once she'd calmed down from his high handedness last week. The school had lost her baby twice. Jonathan was becoming a nuisance, ringing her every day apologizing on the one hand and then blaming Heathers 'vagueness' on the other before asking her out to dinner or the cinema.

She bent to her bag on the floor and pulled out her iPad, smiling at him gently. "I've been looking at schools," she told him, pulling up web pages and showing them to him.

Before long he was on the phone, and they'd made arrangements to visit a few of them over the holidays.

They were amicable, they'd even laughed together, but there was an undercurrent of tension when their hands touched by mistake, or when there was a pause in the conversation, and neither one of them rushed to fill it. It was awkward, but at least they were talking.

CHAPTER SIXTEEN

Ace was bored. He was fine during the day when he had Heather all to himself, and they explored the area, but it was when he dropped her off, and he made his way to the B and B that the boredom set in. Rapidly.

He'd already taken a drive into Manchester last night and found a nice little pub, but because he was driving, he couldn't drink. He'd even been hit on by a cute little thing that invited him back to her flat, to give him a night he would never forget, her words, but he'd declined. There was only one person he wanted to hear those words from, but *she* was being stubborn.

The door opened to the living room that had the image of Queen Elizabeth on every plate, mug and tablecloth ever printed. Sylvie Watson was a proud royalist.

"I thought I heard you in here Alister." She said. She was a widow and had lived in the village all her life. She was in her sixties and hosted bingo down in the church hall on a Thursday night. He'd been invited along and was looking forward to it.

"Please call me Ace, Mrs Watson." He advised, not for the first time.

"Oh no, Alister makes you sound like a right ole gentleman. Proper English name Alister is. Strong and honourable." She went on as she sat across from him. "So how is our Heather?"

It had taken some getting used to everyone referring to each other as 'our' our Heather. Our Sabrina. It spoke of community and acceptance and security. These people looked out for each other. Ace liked it.

"We drove to Matlock today and walked by the River Derwent. Do you have many climbers up there?" He asked he'd noticed the topography was a climbers' dream, all steep, craggy rock faces of limestone and gritstone.

"Oh, Matlock is known for its crags, Alister. They get plenty of climbers and walkers through there. Did you see any motorbikes? As soon as the sun comes out, people from all bouts ride out there like, get an ice-cream and ride back out again. Pretty part of the county it is."

"Yeah," he looked at the time. It was barely seven o'clock. It was going to be a long night. He noticed Mrs Watson looking at the clock on the mantle too.

"Why don't you go for a little walk Alister, up by the church?"

"I've been up there already."

"Hmm, but tonight there will be something that might be of interest." She tapped the side of her nose and winked at him.

Ace had no idea what she was on about. But he stood up to go for this walk anyway as he had nothing else to do.

"I guess I'm going for that walk."

Sabrina locked the door to her house and walked towards the church. Heather was skipping ahead of her, well used to their routine. She'd been the one to remind her mother what day it was.

Sabrina pulled her jacket a little closer. There was a crispness in the air as the sun dipped behind the splendour of the Derbyshire hills.

It had been a good few weeks visiting schools with Ace, they'd narrowed it down to two, and were just waiting for Hazel, Heather's care worker, to take a look at them both. One was closer to Nottingham just off the A52 and the other on the outskirts of Manchester.

Sabrina was also house hunting with Ace driving them around the different areas. It had been nice. But if it weren't for his smartphone ringing every minute and the restless feeling she was getting from him, she would think he was enjoying himself being with them.

Heather was standing at the old building beside the church that they used as the church hall. It was the only space of any relevance that they had in the village.

Sabrina unlocked the door, as she was one of the four keepers of the keys, and turned on the lights.

She smiled, as she watched Heather fling her arms out and spin around and around with her head thrown back and her eyes closed.

Sabrina sneaked up behind her daughter and picked her up, much to Heather's squeals of laughter. They played around for a moment and then Sabrina went to the old music system in the corner.

She showed Heather the CD's she'd brought with her. Vivaldi's The Four Seasons, Madonna's Immaculate collection and one of Heather's.

She put the classical one on first, selecting *Spring*, then pulled off her coat, revealing her light pink leotard and tights. Heather followed, showing her identical costume, but she had on a white tutu and red satin dancing shoes.

Sabrina pulled on her old ballet slippers and laced them up her ankles.

"Ready baby?" Sabrina asked Heather and watched with pride as Heather put her little hands on the speakers to pick up the beat.

After a moment, Sabrina turned up the music so the vibrations could be felt all around and began to stretch. Heather followed, and then the two of them danced, going seamlessly into the choreography Sabrina had taught her daughter.

They danced and danced, Sabrina on her toes and Heather twirling around her.

***

Ace had seen them walk into the church hall and battled with himself whether he should go in or not. He was glad he hadn't, instead, watching through the window.

Sabrina took his breath away with her elegance and grace as she danced like a professional ballerina. She'd told him she used to dance and had danced and done gymnastics from a young age, but somehow Ace hadn't equated dancing and ballet.

She was beautiful, and little Heather was copying her mother's moves like the gem that she was.

Ace felt a lump in his throat. That was his little girl, and that was her mother. The feelings he was feeling crushed his heart in a very good way.

Heather touched the floor when the music stopped, then looked at her mother, who nodded and gave her a thumbs-up sign. Ace watched as Heather skipped over to the music centre and changed the CD.

That crazy song *Gangnam Style* blasted, and Sabrina laughed but went into position with her wrists crossed in the centre of the room and waited for Heather to stand beside her. Ace noticed Heather wasn't wearing her hearing aids.

Together they danced, doing all the moves and laughing. When it repeated, Ace slipped into the room. Heather saw him, but he put his finger to his lips in the universal don't say a word gesture, and she nodded before going into the horsey type moves again.

Ace sat on the floor by the door and watched.

When the song was about to repeat for the third time, Sabrina dashed to the music centre before Heather and put on Madonna's *Like a Prayer*.

Heather walked over to him and sat down between his legs, her back against his chest.

When Sabrina saw him, she stopped dancing, then with a look he hadn't seen in seven years, she started to dance.

Ace was riveted. He pulled Heather closer, tucking her head under his chin as they watched Sabrina twirl and leap around the perimeter of the room. She was beautiful; grace personified.

They clapped when she finished, and she dipped into a graceful curtsey, called Heather over and together the two of them curtsied for Ace.

He stood up and walked over to them, completely speechless. Completely overwhelmed. This was his family. His girls. Swallowing past the knuckle in his throat, he helped them with their coats and walked them home.

CHAPTER SEVENTEEN

Sabrina couldn't believe she'd been outmanoeuvred by Ace like this, she thought, as she got ready to go out. Dress to impress, he'd said. The bloody cheek of the man, she mused, as she swept bronzer all over her throat and shoulders as she remembered the conversation yesterday.

They'd been driving back from yet another outing around the countryside in his huge white Audi Q7. Not quite the people carrier she'd teased him with back in New York but was very 'him'. They'd been doing a lot of day trips, at first Sabrina had been reluctant to go along, not wanting to encourage any sort of 'togetherness' but Ace wanted her with him to help ease his roll into Heather's life.

They'd found a place for Heather at a specialist school on the edge of the A52 between Derby and Nottingham, where she would board during the week, and they had the rest of the summer to explore before Sabrina's planned trip to Morocco and Ace's return to America.

So, coming back from a day out at Skegness on the coastline, which was known for, well she couldn't think what it was known for, they'd been talking. Heather was asleep, and Ace had started to play pairs. He'd won, and Sabrina had suspected he'd been practising, as some of the pairs he'd come up with she hadn't thought of, and she was a pro at the game, I mean who were Laverne and Shirley? His prize was a dance from her on a proper dance floor as they had never shared a dance before.

When she agreed to that, thinking along the lines of the church hall, he'd then upped the ante and declared a night out in Manchester, before Charles went back to America and he could babysit.

So here she was, getting all dressed up in a posh frock she'd driven into Derby to buy, as her wardrobe was no longer a party girls paradise.

She wore a strapless bandage dress in soft gold; it shimmered against her brown skin and, stopping mid-thigh, made Sabrina feel all girly and sexy. She flat ironed her hair with a deep side parting and brushed it to one side, then added gold drop earrings that were left over from her party days. A bright red lip stain, liquid liner, loads of mascara, and she was ready.

She was nervous. She hadn't been out since that night seven years ago in New York. That gave her pause. Seven years. How the time had flown, she thought, as she spied Heather sulking at her bedroom door, she told her to come in. Heather was not happy if the fierce frown that was so like her fathers was anything to go by.

"What's up poppet?" Sabrina said. "Look at my lips," she advised and asked what was the matter again so that Heather could read her lips. It had been recommended by Hazel to lessen their use of sign language to encourage Heather to use other forms of communication and maybe her hearing aids. If they could get her settled with her aids, and confident about speaking, then they might be able to get the cochlear implants.

"I don't want you to go."

Sabrina sat beside her daughter, who was lying flat on her stomach on the bed. "Remember when you went to George's house and how much fun you had?"

Heather nodded.

"Well, I need to go out and have a little fun too. I'm going out with your daddy."

"Will you come back?"

"Of course, we'll be coming back."

"Will you dance and eat cake?"

"I'll dance, but I'm not sure about eating cake." She replied, then going for a distraction, knelt on the floor to look under the bed. She pulled out two pairs of high heeled platform shoes that hadn't seen the light of day in years.

"Which ones?" She asked Heather, slipping on a shoe from each pair.

Heather tipped her head this way, and that and told her mum to walk around. Her speech was slurred, and her pronunciation of the 'the' sound wasn't quite there, but she could be understood. Being around her speaking uncle Matthew had boosted her confidence, and they'd made a bet that he'd take her to 'hear' the Sequoia trees in America if he was happy with her progress.

Just then, the doorbell rang, and Sabrina went to answer it.

It was Ace.

"Where's Charles?" She asked as she led him into the living room.

"Talking to Stewart down the road. You look amazing." He finished, taking in her hair and dress. "But I don't get the shoes."

Sabrina laughed as she glanced down, seeing the patent nude and the suede black. "I was asking Heather which ones to wear."

"Where is she?"

"Sulking upstairs," Sabrina told him. "But she'll get over it once her granddad is here and we've left." She stuck out a leg to him. "Which one?"

"I like them both."

They were in a pretty good place. She felt comfortable talking and asking him anything. He was like her new best friend.

"Well you're a big help, aren't you?" She sassed as she went upstairs to her room to decide.

When Charles came in, she grabbed a black bolero and went downstairs, holding Heather's hand.

When Heather saw her granddad, she bolted over to him for her lift up and hug.

"See," Sabrina said to Ace. "We're already forgotten."

He smiled, looking over at the pair and going in for his own cuddle from his baby girl.

"You've got my number Charles if you need anything, okay?"

"I've done this a time or two Sabrina," Charles drawled with a twinkle in his hazel eyes, as he put his granddaughter down.

"Yes, I know but—" she started, then changed her mind at Ace's glance. "We'll go." She conceded on a laugh.

He nodded and after a quick goodnight to Heather, they left.

***

The drive into Manchester wasn't that long, Sabrina preferred the quieter cities of Derby or even Nottingham when she had to venture out of the village, so Manchester, especially at night, was a novelty for her.

"Do you know what I realised tonight, Ace?"

"What's that?"

"This is the first time I'm going out since New York."

"Three weeks ago?"

"No, seven years ago." She clarified. "The last time I dressed up like this was the night I met you."

Ace went quiet. He didn't like thinking of her alone during that time, struggling, while he'd been living it up, never forgetting her, but still living it up.

"I'm sorry."

"Oh no Ace," she consoled. "I don't mean to sound all pathetic or anything I'm just saying, I'm really looking forward to going out, and you look smashing by the way." She added, looking at his dark trousers and crisp white shirt with a subtle shiny stripe running through it.

"Smashing? As in I look hot?" He asked, not familiar with the term.

"You've really lost all of your Englishness, haven't you?" She teased.

"And you wouldn't have me any other way." He said, just as his phone started to buzz between them.

Sabrina looked at it, aware that he'd been ignoring all of his calls whenever she was around.

"Aren't you going to answer that?"

"I'm driving."

"Would you like me to answer it? Turn on the Bluetooth?"

"No. It's nothing. Whoever it is can wait."

They lapsed into silence. His phone rang several more times

as they drove along and with each vibration Sabrina wanted to scream at him.

"If it's another woman Ace, I won't mind." She said eventually, when it rang again for the fourth time, the unknown number flashing across the screen of his smartphone like an unwanted guest at a dinner party.

"It's not another woman Sabrina."

"Then why don't you answer it?"

He sighed. "It's an independent film company, and they want me to do a helicopter stunt for them."

"A helicopter stunt? I thought you said no one in the film industry would touch you since the accident?"

"True, but this is a tricky stunt for an indie film, and they want me."

"Why can't they get somebody else? Why can't they use one of those giant green screen things with special effects? I don't see why they need to use you."

"Because I'm the best."

"Best, or the one stupid enough to do it!" She accused.

He didn't reply, but his knuckles were showing white on the steering wheel, she noticed.

She swallowed, feeling the fear that had been with her every time she'd read about his adventures over the years. The same fear that kept her from contacting him. The same fear she didn't want Heather to ever feel.

"Maybe we should go back." She suggested quietly.

"No."

"It's not like you're in a good mood."

"We're not going back, Sabrina. You owe me a dance, and I want it."

"Fine, you get your dance."

Ace picked up his phone and turned it off, and they drove the rest of the way in silence.

***

The club that they went to was age appropriate. Sabrina had had thoughts of mingling with teenagers, but Ace had obviously done his homework. It was oldies night; their kind of oldies and Sabrina was having a grand ole time.

The décor was in red and black with black fringe curtains sectioning off individual booths, and a massive pink chandelier illuminated the circular dance floor.

She danced with Ace as he held her loosely, his hand on her back or holding her hand as she moved to the music. She was relieved that he danced with the loose confidence of a man who appreciated music and was not afraid to move his body.

Sabrina didn't have any shots, although he did offer with a twinkle in his golden gaze looking pointedly at the bar and she laughed, but she did have a few glasses of wine.

The oldies ranged from the early noughties up past the time they met, so a whole range of RnB and pop music kept everyone on the floor. *Holla Back Girl* came on, and Sabrina screamed and laughed, as she remembered the Blue Cadillac as she danced and sang it word for word.

A little later, the chandelier dimmed, and red lights glowed against the walls as slow jams started. Couples moved in close, their bodies touching, and Ace pulled her in close too with one hand holding hers, folded close to his heart, his other going around her waist.

They were barely moving, more like a gentle sway as Mariah Carey's *We Belong Together* spoke to each of them. Ace nudged her neck with his nose, and he skimmed his tongue behind her ear. Sabrina could feel his arousal, heavy with promise, against her hip. He was not embarrassed about it; in fact, she moved into it, encouraging the intimacy.

"Ace," she whispered.

"Sabrina." He answered.

The music was their conversation and when Mario's *Let Me Love you* came on Sabrina sighed, giving in to the emotion as tears welled up and she nipped along the strong column of Ace's neck until he turned his head and their lips met.

She let him inside, sweeping her tongue against his as he pulled her even closer, his arms even tighter.

"This was playing the first time I saw you when you stripped off in the middle of the parking lot." Ace said huskily, as he nibbled along her jaw. "And again, later that night in the pub."

She gasped, "I didn't think you noticed," she sniffed.

"I remember everything about our time together, Sabrina," he whispered into her hair behind her ear. "What you were wearing, who you danced with, what we talked about. Everything. I loved you."

A single tear dripped onto her cheek.

Ace cupped her face. "Hey, why are you crying?"

"I loved you too." She whispered. "I thought that time was only special to me. This was our song, but I didn't tell you it was."

"You didn't need to tell."

They kissed and held each other until the song ended and the genre changed to British pop, a time when Jamilia and Misteeq ruled the charts.

They moved apart, but not before Ace told her that he'd booked a hotel room for them and asked if she'd come with him.

She couldn't be mad at him. She really couldn't, and she nodded. He kissed her again and then excused himself to go to the bathroom.

Sabrina stayed on the dance floor, dancing by herself, that is until she felt a pair of hands on her bottom and thinking it was Ace, leaned into the hard body behind her, only when she looked down and saw the large hands of a black man on her stomach did she move away.

"Oh, I thought you were my friend."

"I can be your friend." He said, smiling down at her.

He was good looking, with dark skin, a shaved head and a nice wide smile. He wore two diamond looking earrings and a wide gold chain and was dressed all in black.

"No thanks, I have enough friends."

He leaned in closer. "What was that?"

Sabrina laughed at the tactic. She may not have been clubbing in years, but some things hadn't changed. He could hear her perfectly well but wanted to get closer. She pushed at his chest, stepping away to dance by herself as she waited for Ace.

The man came in close, gyrating his pelvis as he followed her.

Sabrina spied Ace over his shoulder. He was watching from the edge of the dance floor knitting his brow, his mouth tight and flat as he watched them. Oh, he was not happy, she knew.

"I'm going to my friend now." She told him and tried to step around him, but he held onto her arm, not hard, but he wasn't letting her go.

"My friend is waiting for me." She said again, as nicely as she could. Ace was walking towards them now, his face a blank mask.

"That's your friend?" The man said, glancing at Ace. He turned around, giving Ace his back in blatant disregard. "A gorgeous woman like you can do better than a guy like that."

Sabrina knew all that he wasn't saying. Black British men did not like to see black women with white men. But it was okay for black men to go out with who they pleased.

Ace was beside them now holding out his hand to her. She reached for it.

"What the hell man," the guy said. "Can't you see she's dancing with me?"

"I'm not." Sabrina retorted.

"What are you doing with a prick like this, anyway?" The man sneered.

"He's my—he's my—he's just a friend." Sabrina didn't know what to call Ace, and she had never used that hateful term, baby daddy. One, it was very American and two, very degrading for all concerned, she thought. She could have his baby but couldn't be his wife? No, she would never use the term.

"See, you don't even know what he is." The man caught on with a snarky smile.

Ace pulled her behind him, and, still without a word, punched the guy right in his face. The man, not expecting to be hit, went flying across the room to screams and glasses shattering as he crashed into a table. The music stopped.

Then, regaining his balance, he dived at Ace, who expertly side-stepped away from the right hook he'd tried to give him, and Ace slammed his fists into his stomach for his audacity. Ace was relentless, smashing his fists into the man's lower back and punching him in the face over and over.

Three bouncers came racing onto the dance floor, grabbing Ace and pulling him off the man, who hadn't really been defending himself and who now had blood pouring from his nose and a split lip.

As the bouncers took Ace away, he turned back to Sabrina and shouted over his shoulder the name of the hotel and that the room was booked in her name.

"Get the fuck off me!" Ace snarled, trying to wrench himself out of the vice grips the huge bouncers had on him, as they marched him out of the now silent room to the front exit.

Two paramedics came rushing in to revive the man on the floor. Luckily, he was moaning and trying to sit up by himself.

Everyone was looking at Sabrina and shaking their heads as if to say, what an idiot to be with a thug like that.

"Is he okay?" She asked the paramedics, tentatively.

"Not sure yet, we'll get him to the ambulance and look him over." The medic looked around. "Anyone with him?"

A girl came forward with tears in her eyes, and she had a pink Happy Eighteenth Birthday sash across her white dress. "I'm his sister."

CHAPTER EIGHTEEN

With a choked, *I'm sorry,* to the birthday girl, Sabrina pushed her way out of the club and onto the street, only stopping when she'd put enough distance between herself and the shame and embarrassment of Ace's thuggery.

People were milling around, shouting and laughing. England had a drunk culture that wasn't pretty. Every major city had problems at the weekend with people overindulging and becoming a nuisance for the authorities. They clogged the hospitals with their alcohol poisoning, bloodied faces and broken bones from all the fighting or falling.

She spotted Ace with a group of police officers across the street. There was some sort of mobile police station set up on the corner, with a large van, several cars and an ambulance parked in a semi-circle. Ace was sat in the back of the van with his head down low, beside a young lad who had a large red mark on the side of his face.

Then the van door closed with a slam, and she crossed the street to talk to one of the officers.

"Excuse me, my friend is in the van. What's going to happen to him?" She asked, deeply embarrassed she even had to ask such a thing. She was a mother for goodness' sake, why had he put her in this position?

"The young lad or the older guy?"

"The older one."

"Ah, the one with the temper, we've put him in there to cool down for a bit like. We might have to take him in if him in the club decides to press charges like."

That's what Sabrina had been afraid of.

"Can I see him? See if he's okay?"

The officer looked down at her and nodded. "Come on then," he said, turning away. "Just a peek like."

"Thank you."

He opened the van door again, and Sabrina rushed over. Ace turned to slice a look at her with eyes dark and vacant before looking down again, ignoring her.

Sabrina stumbled back with a gasp.

"See, he's okay like." The officer said, closing the door.

Sabrina thanked him again and rushed off. She wanted to go home, but Ace had the car keys, she had no money, and she'd been drinking. She made her way despondently to the hotel. Luckily, it wasn't far, and she knew where it was, as her toes were pinching, and a slight drizzle had started.

The hotel was a small boutique hotel in dark woods and traditional reds and greens. It wasn't to her taste, but once in the room, she appreciated the luxury of the heavy furniture and four-poster bed dressed in white linen and sheer curtains.

Ace had planned to seduce her tonight and had almost succeeded, she thought, as she stepped out of her shoes, leaving them by the door to walk to the bathroom to wash her hands and use the facilities, before going over to the bed. There was nothing she could do now but wait.

She must have dozed off, as a soft knock woke her, and she opened the door.

Ace stood there, looking fierce and possessive and not the least bit sorry for his brutal behaviour, she noticed, as she opened the door wider and then closed it behind him.

He turned to her and something–she didn't know what– flashed in his eyes, making her stumble backwards as he stalked towards her.

"You need to know who I am!"

Of all the things she'd expected him to say, that was not it.

She hadn't been expecting this rush of emotion from him either. It was as though he needed to ensure she was his. His kiss wasn't brutal, but it was the equivalent of a long lecture.

She was his, his mouth was saying, as he touched her all over. He'd never touched her like this ever before, with his hands up and down her body, hard and intent as he lifted the hem of her dress, his hand searching and finding the scrap of soft lace between her legs as he pushed it aside to bathe his fingers in her silky wetness.

She gasped at the urgency of it all. He wasn't giving her time to formulate any kind of thought, as he pushed her dress down to reveal her naked breasts, sucking first one nipple and then the other deep into his mouth. He scooped her up, but not to take them to the bed, he spread her on the floor and climbed over her.

She heard his zipper and then felt the blunt tip of him as he pushed inside her. Then he stopped, rearing up on his hands to look down at her with eyes bright and golden.

"I am not *just* your fucking friend!" He growled as he surged inside her.

She gasped at the fullness of him. His mouth covered hers and he moved rapidly, his hands going to her bottom to pull her even closer to his thrusts, as his hips pistoned between her legs.

Sabrina screamed at the intensity of her orgasm and, with a few more deep thrusts, Ace threw back his head as he climaxed with the biggest orgasm he'd ever had in his life.

For a moment he couldn't think. His whole body weak from the magnitude of it all, and he shifted onto his side to fling one arm over his eyes.

Sabrina shifted, about to get up, but gasped as Ace moved, picking her up lovingly, to place her on the bed with gentle tenderness.

He undressed her slowly, kissing every part of her body. Turning her over to rain kisses down her spine and over her bottom, sucking at the sensitive skin behind her knees, before moving her to swirl his tongue in her belly button and trailing kisses downwards as he pushed her legs further apart. He stroked his tongue over her sex, holding her hips still as she tried to pull away from his caress.

He watched her as she melted into another climax, her eyes rolling as her hands grabbed at the cotton sheet, while she tried to control the scream that was surging up her throat.

"Let it go damn it," Ace ordered as he sucked her hidden nub into his mouth and skimmed his finger inside her walls, seeking and stroking the small bundle of nerves at the same time.

She screamed and sighed as he moved over her naked body, now flushed and covered with a light layer of sweat.

He sucked one nipple while pinching and rolling the other, before kissing her deeply, stripping off his clothes and entering her body.

***

He must have fallen asleep for a moment, Ace thought, opening his eyes to see Sabrina facing him, her eyes closed, her mouth slightly open as she slept.

He looked at her, she was so beautiful, her skin so smooth and perfect and he couldn't resist pulling the sheet off her body to sweep his fingers into the dip of her waist and over the gentle curve of her hip and back again. Finally, he'd been able to make love to her completely.

He felt himself go hard again. They'd already made love for hours, he'd kissed and loved every part of her body, took a shower with her, made love to her under the spray of water and continued to love her some more, once he'd brought her back to the bed. He couldn't get enough of her. He never would.

He hadn't planned the night to be like this, well he had, he just hadn't expected to be locked up in a fucking police van for two hours and Sabrina having to go to the hotel alone. He'd been scared shitless she may have gone home instead.

He'd needed this night with her. They'd needed this night, he amended, to get back on track. His track. Ace had realised, pretty much from his first week in England, that she had relegated him to the friend category. By the third week, she'd even called him her new best friend to his fucking face. And last night? That was fucked up. Some guy was hitting on her, and she again calls him her friend after the kisses they'd shared moments earlier? It was no wonder he'd lost it. There was no way he was going to be her best fucking friend.

She moaned in her sleep and rolled onto her stomach. Ace continued to stroke her and massage her until she mewed again and consciously, or unconsciously, moved her legs apart and he moved over and into her, making love to her again.

***

When Sabrina woke, she was alone in the huge bed. It was late if the bright rays grappling through the velvet curtains were any indication.

She stretched her arms over her head, then stretched her whole body from fingers to toes. She ached all over. She was not an overly active person nowadays, but Ace had been insatiable, moving and bending her this way and that as he broadened her sexual experience in just a few short hours. She'd always known he was going to be a good lover and wow, she smiled to herself, he didn't disappoint.

She sat up, spying her gold dress spread over a chair. There was no way she was going to put that on, she thought, wrinkling her nose, then, wrapping the top sheet around herself went into the bathroom to have a shower.

She would have loved a bath, but the thought of sitting in a tub where naked strangers had been was a massive turn off, so a steaming hot shower would have to do.

Once finished, and with still no sign of Ace, she found her clutch bag and fished out her mobile, it was dead, so she sat in the centre of the bed, in the hotel robe, and waited for him.

She was reading the room service menu when Ace walked in, dressed in a pair of jeans and a clean T-shirt. She was about to demand new clothes when she noticed how pale he was as he walked to the edge of the bed.

"What's wrong?" She said with alarm, going onto her knees. "What is it, Ace?"

"It's Heather." He breathed. "She's missing."

CHAPTER NINETEEN

"What?"

"Come on," he said, his mouth pulling downwards. "I need you to get dressed."

Sabrina grabbed the plastic bag he held out to her and pulled out a pair of lacy knickers, a black pair of leggings, a large black T-shirt and white flip flops with decorative multicoloured gemstones on them. Supermarket couture.

"What happened?" She asked, as she scrambled into the clothes and shoved last nights dress, shoes and clutch into the bag.

"I'll tell you on the way." He said, going to the door. "Come on. I've already checked out."

They rushed out of the hotel and to the car. Ace had moved it to the hotel entrance.

Before long, they were whizzing home.

"Tell me."

"I forgot my cell phone in the car and went to get it. There were a lot of missed calls from my dad, I called him back, and he said he'd been trying to reach you."

"My phone is dead."

"He was making breakfast for Heather and called her to the table, but she was gone. That was about twenty-five minutes ago."

"Let me ring your dad."

Ace handed her the phone and listened as Sabrina told Charles where to find the list of telephone numbers for everyone in the village. He was to ring each one in order. She then asked him what they had been talking about before Heather had gone missing.

Sabrina screwed up her face as she thought, then gave Charles more orders, before she hung up.

"Where do you think she is?"

"I'm not sure, but my first bet would be Stewart's to see the kittens. They'd been talking about the value of family and good friends."

"Does she do this often?"

"More, now that she's getting older, she doesn't go far."

"Why does she do it?"

"Independence. She has a thought and just goes with it. Hazel and I have been trying to teach her to be more responsible, but she's so impulsive."

"Aren't you worried? You're very calm, considering."

"Of course I'm worried, but the village, everyone, look out for her and she won't have gotten far. We'll find her."

"Keep telling yourself that Sabrina, I'm sure you feel better for saying it!"

"Don't shout at me!"

"I mean, what the fuck?"

"And don't swear at me either."

"Okay, fine. I'm sorry. My little girl has gone walkabout, and I can't be as calm as you."

His phone rang, and Sabrina answered it. It was Charles.

"Good. Where?"

She turned to Ace. "They've found her."

Ace nodded.

"Thanks, Charles. We'll be home in about half an hour."

"Where was she?" Ace asked.

"On her way to see George."

"Her friend from school?"

"Yeah. Last night I reminded her how much fun it is to sometimes go out, this was after she told me she didn't want me to go." She told him. "And I explained everyone needs some time to be with their friends."

Ace growled, enough of the fucking friend business already, he seethed silently, wishing he could take the damn car up to full speed.

"It's just her trying to make me feel guilty Ace."

"So, she decided to visit George." He shifted gears and purposely slowed the car down. "Where does he live?"

"In long Eaton, closer to Derby. But she was heading in the direction of their school. This is my fault really. She never got to say goodbye to him."

Ace was quiet, Heather hadn't gotten far, but this kind of thing had to stop.

"What are we going to do?" He asked, feeling calmer.

"Have a play date with George."

"No, I mean after." He amended. "She can't keep running off like this. I know you keep saying the village is safe, but nowhere is one hundred per cent safe, Sabrina, you know this, and you've been living like a recluse in the security of Frecknor Green. The world is not a safe place for little children out on their own."

"I'm not totally clueless Ace, I have managed to bring her up all on my own for the past seven years."

"You don't want to go there with me right now, Sabrina." Ace drawled quietly, his temper simmering again.

"Look, she's going to board during the week at her new school. You said it was very secure. I'll talk to her."

"We'll talk to her," he interjected. "And she loses her iPad for a week."

Sabrina gasped. "You're going to punish her for something that was my fault?"

"How was it your fault? You weren't even there."

"But—"

"But nothing, she needs to know there is a consequence to her actions."

"But a week? She uses the speech therapy app on it."

"Okay two days and we'll tell her together. You won't be making me out to be the bad guy."

"There isn't a problem of that now is there Alister," Sabrina drawled sarcastically, crossing her arms over her chest.

"Careful Sabrina." Ace warned.

"You've been a dad for all of five minutes and for the second time in that five minutes you're telling me I'm a bad parent!"

"I never said you're a bad parent. You're doing amazingly,

considering. But saying no won't hurt once in a while."

"She's a good kid."

"I know she is, but she's also impulsive and doesn't understand the consequences to her actions."

"She has PDDNOS." She reminded him.

"Yes, but it's so mild Hazel thinks she'll be re-evaluated as normal when she gets older." He said, then added. "Heather plays you."

Sabrina turned to him with a puzzled frown. "What do you mean Hazel said she'll be re-evaluated? When did Hazel say this?"

"When I took her to lunch."

"You took Hazel to lunch?" She felt so betrayed by both of them. "Without me?"

"I wanted to know more about the PDDNOS spectrum thing without all the emotion and drama from you."

"Thank you very much, Ace, you are such an arsehole." She swore at him. "So, I'm an overly emotional, bad parent, whose seven-year-old runs rings around me?" She felt the sting of tears.

"Why are you spoiling for a fight?"

"I want you to explain."

Ace sighed dramatically.

"You baby her."

"She is a baby."

"She's almost seven and very bright."

"But she's also deaf."

"But can hear to a degree with her aids. She functions like a normal seven-year-old, but you baby her."

"I—" she didn't know what else to say and wiped at the tears that slipped down her face.

Alarmed, Ace glanced at her. "I'm sorry, Sabrina," he said, trying to capture her hand, but she moved it away. "I'm sorry I didn't mean to hur—"

"Yes, you did." She sniffed. "When does that film company want you again?"

"That isn't even funny."

"The end of summer can't come soon enough for me Ace."

"Why? What's happening end of summer?"

"You're going back to America."

"That's where you're wrong, sweetheart."

***

They drove the rest of the way home in silence. Not even the radio was on.

When they got to her house, Heather and Charles were out playing Swing-Ball in the back garden as though there hadn't been a crisis not even an hour ago. Heather was in a pair of denim shorts, a yellow vest and had on her blue fairy wings from her dressing-up box and her yellow wellies.

Sabrina made ham and cucumber sandwiches and a jug of Pimm's for lunch for the men and lemonade for Heather. Charles excused himself to go over to Stewart's, and Ace and Sabrina talked to Heather about always going off without telling anyone.

Heather narrowed her eyes to stare accusingly at her mother and, to Sabrina's dismay, said she had gone looking for her, as she didn't come home last night and had gone to find her herself.

Sabrina and been stricken with guilt and was about to apologise when Ace interjected, explaining that Sabrina is the mummy and mummies can change their minds. When he took her beloved iPad from her, there were tears and screams, with Heather flinging herself on the floor and basically behaving like the two-year-old Ace had accused Sabrina of allowing.

It had not been Heather's finest hour, and she'd pulled out her hearing aids and ignored them for the rest of the day. Ace had sent her to her room to think about her behaviour.

Sabrina walked Ace to his car when he was leaving.

"This wasn't how I planned our weekend to be." He admitted sardonically, leaning against his vehicle as she closed the low wooden gate behind him.

"Oh yeah, how was it supposed to be?"

He smirked. "I'd planned to keep you naked and in bed until I'd wrung every sigh out of you."

"That's rather presumptuous, don't you think?"

"Not really, I've waited a long time to get you into a bed." He shrugged. "It was only a matter of time."

"This conversation is rather distasteful, Ace; I don't like it."

"What's distasteful about two people who care about each other making love? We already have a kid together."

"We didn't make her in a conventional way, though did we?"

"It was memorable," he slashed her a grin. "Next time, you can take control." His gaze smouldered and Sabrina crossed her arms across her chest to hide her nipples peaking at his suggestive words. "I remember how well you do that." He finished in a voice one octave lower.

"Last night should not have happened Ace and I don't want Heather to get the wrong idea."

He tipped his head to the side. "And what idea is that?"

She rubbed her temples. "Last night was nice, but I'm happy being single. I don't want any man in my life."

"Glad to hear you have principles as I'm not 'any man' and I'll be the only man in your life." He moved closer and pulled at her arms, stroking her bare skin to lace their hands together. "But it will happen again."

He kissed her quickly before letting her go to pull his phone out of his back pocket. It must have been on vibrate as Sabrina hadn't heard it ring.

"Got to go. Get some rest sweetheart," he threw her a wink. "You didn't get much sleep last night."

CHAPTER TWENTY

Sabrina waited with Heather inside the cottage for Ace to arrive. They were going on yet another outing, and she'd seen more of England and Wales these last few weeks than she'd ever seen in her life.

To say Ace was a ball of energy would be an understatement. He was always on the go, always planning something. It was nice, and she did enjoy the outings, especially seeing Heather interact with her dad.

Heather was talking more confidently too, although she still took out her hearing aids just to go into her own little world. Otherwise, she was blooming.

Sabrina knew those periods when Heather shut them out was frustrating for Ace, as he didn't understand why, in the middle of a pleasant walk along the beach, or out to dinner, she would simply decide she didn't want to communicate with them. Then, an hour or two later come back to them as though nothing had happened.

Today was to be a surprise. Ace had said they weren't going too far and would be home by early evening. He'd had to get his head around not being so impulsive with having a young child, Sabrina knew, knowing if it were left up to him, they'd sleep in the car, or set up camp in a field without a change of clothes.

Sabrina preferred planned outings, not because she was boring, but because Heather liked some sort of routine and an explanation of the day's plans before they left the house. Although her daughter wasn't overly anxious like some PDDNOS kids, she did manage better with a routine.

Ace pulled up, and Sabrina opened the front door for Heather to meet her dad, while she locked up. Ace had given her a lecture on security and just to indulge him, she checked the windows and doors and locked the front door, even if she was just nipping into the village.

Heather was already buckled in on the back seat of Ace's car, and Sabrina walked down the path, with fragrant lavender on each side, going through the gate, conscious of him watching her as he made no bones about liking what he saw, as he whistled.

"Hi Sabrina," he said, as she made herself comfortable, he took the seatbelt buckle from her and secured her in place before kissing her on the cheek. "You look great and smell even better." He leaned into her neck to breathe in her unique scent of vanilla and lotus flower, he now knew. "What's in the bag?"

"A spare set of clothes for Heather, water and some snacks." She explained.

"Cool. I like the hat." He tapped the brim of the flat grey cap she had turned slightly off centre in what Ace was beginning to name her 'Nina Mae quirk', as there were some things she did that were so spontaneous it suited her Nina Mae persona more than straight-as-an-arrow Sabrina.

"Thank you." She re-adjusted it and wiped her palms down the front of her black leggings. "You said to dress casually. I hope this is okay?" She asked, biting the nail on her little finger. She was wearing a grey and white Aztec print long vest and a white lightweight jacket. "Do I need my boots?" She asked, looking at her black lacy flats and rotating her ankles.

He shook his head, admiring the hint of cleavage and wishing he could fondle her breasts. They'd fit his hands so perfectly, he remembered. "You look great, and you don't need your boots." He turned and started the vehicle. "How's our daughter been?" He liked referring to Heather like that. It made them seem more of a family.

"Fine, if a little quiet."

"She coming down with something?"

"I hope not." She said, turning in her seat to look at Heather, who was playing with the iPad. Sabrina touched Heather's knee to get her attention and signed if she was feeling okay.

Heather nodded then looked at her iPad again.

"She's fine. Where are we going?"

"It's a surprise."

"I don't like surprises."

"Then you'll just have to pretend that you do so as not to hurt my feelings." He went on with a smirk, taking his sunglasses that were tucked behind the sun visor, putting them on and turning on the radio, Beyoncé's *Love on Top* was playing.

Sabrina noted he was driving south, maybe to Nottinghamshire, she thought, as he had wanted to see the Major Oak in Sherwood Forest. When she'd informed him that Robin Hood was actually a fictitious character he'd been scandalised. She smiled to herself, as she remembered him telling her that she'd ruined his childhood. She had laughed so hard that day. He'd grumbled all the way home. But he still wanted to see the famous tree he'd said.

They drove for several miles down the M1 in silence, it was nice, the sun was shining, and traffic was light on the motorway. Ace drove the Q7 so expertly, Sabrina could fall asleep if she wanted to, she never did, but could if she needed to, which was a comfort.

Ace pulled off the motorway at junction twenty-four and Sabrina noticed they were in the Leicestershire, Derbyshire border area. She had no idea where they were going but tried to swallow away her misgiving when she spied the Donington Park road signs. Was he racing?

"Are we going to see some races?" She asked, as lightly as the single knot in her throat would allow.

"A friend of mine is over from Germany and invited me down to see his collection of super bikes."

"Oh, okay," she replied, feeling better now that he wasn't racing and so allowed the first stirring of excitement to relax her.

She had never been to Donington Park before and heard it was a great family day out. Not only did they hold bike, cars and mega truck races and championships, but there was also an extensive collection of Grand Prix cars on show and other exhibitions. The Sunday market used to be the best in the region.

Sabrina wondered if they still held it.

Ace parked the Q7 and helped Heather down from the large vehicle. He signed and said where they were to her, and she clapped her hands in excitement.

A tall, lanky, mixed-race man with the unusual combination of grey eyes and ebony skin walked towards them and Ace introduced them. His name was Erik and was so good-looking Sabrina had to drag her eyes away.

"Sabrina, beautiful name for a beautiful lady," Erik said smoothly, taking her hand to kiss her knuckles.

"Cut the shit Erik, she's my woman, and that's our daughter." Ace growled, completely unfazed by the look Sabrina sent him.

"Ah, apologies, my friend." Erik bowed, but sent a wink to Sabrina, making her giggle.

Ace scowled over at her.

"Come on, you need to see my new baby, Ace, she's beautiful," Erik said as he threw his arm around Ace's shoulders and they all walked towards a large fenced off area that Ace explained was the pit lane.

A huge grey and white building of multiple levels and a long row of double aspect garages ran parallel to the pit lane. They walked into one of the garages, where three aggressive-looking motorbikes stood centre stage.

Ace and Erik walked to a yellow and black motorbike with smooth wheels and began talking about suspensions, swing arms and cc's. The racetrack was empty, and Sabrina realised it must be a great day out for the family on race days. But she would never come here on a race day.

Heather was running around between the bikes and Sabrina watched her with one eye, but the other was on Ace.

He was so animated and enthusiastic, she thought, seeing yet another aspect of him, talking at length with a knowledge of engines that spoke of an expert. An excessive expert, she amended. She was bored out of her mind.

When Heather wanted to go to the toilet, she excused them

with a rush and went down a long white corridor. It was eerily quiet, and their feet tapped along the concrete flooring.

The bathroom was all-purpose white and black tile, and Sabrina took a moment to brush Heather's hair back into the pigtails she had started the day in, as they were now at odd angles and loose.

When they went back, the men now stood beside a blue and red bike, and Sabrina, holding Heather's hand walked to the pit lane side of the garage and walked the short distance to the stands to sit out in the sun.

Erik rolled out a red and neon green bike and was shouting something to Ace. Sabrina turned to concentrate on the game of baby scrabble she was playing with Heather on the iPad.

It was the loud revving of a bike engine sometime later, interrupting their game, that made Sabrina look over her shoulder to notice in dismay, that Erik had changed into one of those leather jumpsuit type uniforms in red and black with patches of logos on it that she couldn't make out from this distance. He waved when he saw her, then got onto the bike.

Ace walked out, and Sabrina was relieved to see he was still in his jeans and burgundy T-shirt that did amazing things to his shoulders. He was saying something to Erik, who revved the bike several times.

Sabrina tuned out again, really not interested in what was going on. Erik took the bike around the track, not at high speed, but fast enough to make Sabrina aware of it.

Erik went around the track two more times before pulling in. Ace came out with a headset on his head. They'd obviously been communicating while Erik rode.

Ace waved to her before disappearing inside the pit again.

Heather had had enough of scrabble and had put on a Disney film Ace had downloaded for her. Sabrina pulled out her notebook to read the notes she'd made for her next novel.

She barely looked up when she heard the bike start again and do several laps, but it was going faster now, and she watched it whiz past at high speed.

Distracted, Sabrina watched in fearful awe as Erik expertly went low around corners, almost skimming the asphalt with his knees and when he came closer, he slowed down before acceleratingly off again at high speed and doing a long wheelie. Show off, she thought, completely unimpressed.

She was digging in her bag, looking for a pen, when Erik walked casually out of the building.

She dropped her bag. Oh my God, she screamed silently, standing up as goose-bumps pinged along her arms. Ace was riding?!

Sabrina's stomach clenched tight, and she held it, trying to keep the nausea at bay as the fear of him getting hurt made her tremble.

Sweat broke out on her forehead and above her lip, but she was shivering. Pressing her hands into her stomach, Sabrina stumbled to the fence to hold onto the metal rail as she watched him.

No, no, no! *Please slow down, please slow down*, she chanted as he whizzed past yet again.

She was shaking and in tears now, unable to control the nausea that exploded out of her mouth. She gagged and retched, hearing the bike go past again and again. The acute smell of rubber and the loud revs took over her senses. *Please slow down. Please slow down!*

Sabrina felt Heather's hand on her arm, and she looked at her baby who was looking back at her with her own tears threatening.

Sabrina tried to calm the panic that was overtaking her. Her heart was racing so fast, and she could barely breathe. For her daughter's sake, she tried to smile and reassure her that she was okay, but knew she was failing.

Heather, bless her, pushed her into a chair and ran off. Sabrina watched, helpless, rocking back and forth, seeing the bike pass her again, Ace waving and doing wheelies, completely unaware of her distress as she hugged herself tighter. She was in a completely different place now, cold, as she held her arms around herself.

Some part of her knew she was being irrational, that he was safe, that he was only testing it, but like many times before, she couldn't watch him do any of the dangerous stuff he did that had millions of views on YouTube. The one time she did, she'd fainted. Luckily, Heather had been at school, and Sabrina had been sitting in a chair.

Heather came back with the water bottle Sabrina had left in the bag back in the building.

"Mummy?" Heather said, stroking her hair. "Drink." She put the bottle to Sabrina's lips.

"Thank you, baby." Sabrina managed, but another wave of nausea attacked her, and she quickly turned to the side, to retch again and again. Then knowing she couldn't stop it, she passed out.

***

Ace looked into the stands when he came around the track and waved to Sabrina as she watched him.

He'd never felt this good being on the track and knew it had everything to do with having Sabrina and Heather with him. He knew she was bored shitless, but she did hang around in the pit longer than he thought she would, trying to appear interested.

He smiled as he geared down, listening for the little cough Erik said the bike was making. He didn't hear it and went around again. He loved driving at high speed and missed test racing, but this summer was about his daughter and getting to know her. His needs would have to wait.

When he went around again, Sabrina was sat in a different place, Heather at her side. He looked on, but hearing the engine cough, went through the gears and went around again.

Halfway through the lap, Erik told him to come back. His daughter was crying and screaming, and he couldn't understand what she was saying.

Ace raced back to the pit lane.

"Daddy!" Heather yelled, flinging herself at him as soon as he came to a stop.

He'd never heard her call him that before, but didn't have time to appreciate it before she started talking, the words tumbling out and making no sense.

"Slow down," he urged, going down on one knee. "What is it, baby?" He signed.

"Mummy is dead!"

What?! Ace rocked back on his heels, feeling the life drain from him. Sabrina?

"Erik! Watch her!" He took off to the stands where he'd last seen Sabrina.

It was empty. In a panic, he raced up the steps and saw her slumped between the front row of chairs and the railings.

"Sabrina!" He yelled, scrambling over the chairs. He felt for a pulse and with relief, urged her up. She'd been sick. Vomit clung to the corner of her mouth and, using his shirt Ace wiped it off. "Baby?" He tapped her cheek and watched as she came back to him.

"Ace?"

Ace pulled her close then lifted her into his arms to carry her inside to the small makeshift office.

"Erik, some water." He ordered as he placed her down on the small couch.

"Sabrina?" He said as Erik came in with Heather hot on his heels. "She's okay baby," Ace signed to his daughter who was now clinging to his arm. "Mommy was just feeling a little poorly." He explained as Sabrina moaned.

Heather nodded then picked up Sabrina's hand.

"What happened?" Sabrina said, as she opened her eyes properly and focused on the three faces anxiously looking at her. "Ace, are you all right?" She asked worriedly, running her eyes over his body, cataloguing his limbs.

"Yeah babes," he said, his face creasing into a puzzled frown. "Why wouldn't I be?" He put his hand on her legs when she tried to get up. "You fainted. Don't move."

Sabrina lay back down, closing her eyes.

"Do you want more water?" Ace asked.

"Please," she sat up now, and Ace held the plastic cup to her mouth.

"Are you okay Mummy?" Heather asked her, her eyes so like her daddy's but red from crying. She was wringing Sabrina's cap in her little fingers.

"I am, munchkin. Sorry to scare you like that." She held out her arms. "Can I get a cuddle?" She asked, smiling when Heather flung herself into her arms and holding on to her for dear life. Sabrina looked over at Ace.

"How do you feel now?" Ace asked, watching her closely.

"Better. I was just feeling a little dizzy." Sabrina lied.

"Come on. Let's get you home." Ace said after he made her drink another cup of water and fed her a chocolate bar from the vending machine, to 'up her sugars' he said.

They said their goodbyes to Erik and made their way home.

***

Ace sorted out Heather's bed routine and had her tucked in and sleeping in under half an hour. Sabrina was impressed and told him so when he came downstairs again.

He'd made Heather a snack while Sabrina had a quick shower and changed into her pyjamas. It was barely nine o'clock, but her pyjamas were her comfort clothes.

She knew he was going to ask her what happened as she'd been fielding his questions on the drive home, before eventually feigning sleep.

He made her a cup of mint tea and some toast and sat opposite her in the living room.

"Are you pregnant?"

Sabrina spluttered her tea all over herself and Ace went to get a paper towel, clinically mopping up at the wet patches all over her chest.

"Well?" He prompted, going over to his chair again once he'd dispensed with the damp tissue.

"No Ace, I'm not pregnant."

"Are you sure?"

"I'm sure."

"I wouldn't mind if you were."

She looked at him. "I'm not pregnant." She reiterated.

"So, what happened?"

To tell him the truth or not? She'd been battling with herself on the drive back.

"I was scared for you." She admitted.

"What?" He hadn't been expecting that answer. "Me?"

"Yes. I can't watch you doing anything like that. It frightened me."

He chuckled, upset she wasn't pregnant, but happy she cared about him.

"I'm careful."

"That's beside the point."

"I'm not going to do anything stupid, Sabrina. I know what I'm doing."

She remained quiet, watching him under her lashes.

"You had a panic attack?" He began. "Was throwing up and fainted?"

She nodded.

"Because I was riding?"

She confirmed again by nodding.

"Baby," he began, going onto his knees in front of her to cup her face. "I'm okay," he soothed, rubbing her face with his thumbs. "I was in control. I wasn't even going fast."

She took a deep breath and moved her head away, leaning back against the chair to put some distance between them.

"You do stupid, unnecessary things Ace and I can't sit back and watch you do them. You could die!"

"I'm not going to die."

"You'd almost died when I met you." She began. "You almost died when you swam across that river in Australia, and that log hit you in the head, knocking you out!" She remembered feeling the fear when she'd watched that video, his body lifeless for a moment before he recovered enough to swim to shore. "I can't watch you flirt with death without a care in the world!"

"Sabrina, I'm always careful."

"You just don't get it, do you?" She sniffed.

"What?"

"I care about you."

He smiled and reached for her hand, lacing their fingers together. "I care about you too."

"But I can't live with the thought of anything happening to you." She admitted, pulling her hand away, but he held on.

"That's—"

"Let me finish," she took a deep, shaky breath cutting him off. "I didn't contact you because I wouldn't make you choose."

"Choose?" He asked. "Choose what?"

"Me. Me and Heather or your lifestyle." She replied, feeling the tears threatening. "I can't keep watching you flirt with death, Ace." The tears came. "I just can't be with you. Be around you! Did you see what happened to me? Did you see the state I was in? I couldn't even look after Heather! What would have happened if she went out onto the track to try and stop you, you could have run her over! You're dangerous to me. You're dangerous *for* me!"

"That's ridiculous." He scoffed.

"It's not. Once I was alone and watched the video of you scaling that stupid building, I passed out." She revealed. "No, I can't be around you," she shook her head and wiped at her tears with her fingers. "I won't watch you die."

"Sabrina—"

"I'm not going to be the one to tell you to change Ace. You have to do that on your own."

"You're cutting off your nose to spite your face Sabrina, and that's fucked up! What are you doing to us?"

"No Ace," she went on, feeling somehow cathartic now that she could tell him about her fears. "I'm saving myself." She admitted, through her tears.

"I've lost everyone I've ever loved," she went on. "And I won't risk my heart. It would kill me Ace." She sniffed loudly. "I barely survived seven years ago," she shook her head. "If it wasn't for Heather..." she breathed in deeply, trying to get her emotions under control before continuing.

"I love you and always will, but feeling this fear, even when I wasn't part of your life all these years was hard enough. I can't watch you jump out of helicopters and make you think that I'm okay with it because I can't. I won't. I'm terrified of anything happening to you." She admitted, on a hiccup.

"Nothing is going to happen to me."

She held up her hand and went on passionately. "Stop Ace, if we have a little fight, or you're worried about Heather and me and get distracted," she was shaking her head as she rubbed at her eyes. "I can't live like that. I'm scared for you." She pulled him closer and kissed him on the lips. "But I'm brave enough to let you go." She finished on a hoarse whisper. "When Heather starts school, I want you to go back to America."

"No." He said panicking. "You can't tell me what to do!"

"I've already lost my parents, and I'm not going to watch you walk out of the front door, with no telling if you're going to walk back through it again. I just won't. And I won't ask you to change."

"You couldn't in the fucking first place." He swore, his anger rising to the surface. What the fuck was she saying? "I was like this when we met, Sabrina."

She shook her head. "No, you weren't Ace, you were mending, and I was your distraction. I fell in love with the man in the wheelchair, but I can't love him again if he goes back in one."

"Too late, you already care about me." He shot back childishly. "You just said."

"But I don't have to live with you." She replied, rubbing her temples. A headache was threatening. "I think you should leave."

"Are you okay?"

"No, I'm not. But I will be."

"We'll talk about this tomorrow Sabrina. This conversation is not over." He charged, in frustration. He wanted to talk, argue, cajole his case, but she looked tired and upset and to be honest he needed to calm down as he was rolling with his emotions, something he always did around her. She tied him up in knots and verbally ran rings around him when he was this angry.

"It's over Ace."

He knew she wasn't referring to their conversation.

He looked into her eyes, trying to read what she was thinking she knew, but Sabrina shifted so that her head fell back against the armrest and she could curl her legs under herself.

"Don't get up. I'll lock the door on my way out." He kissed her forehead and smoothed her hair in much the same way he did with Heather.

"Bye, Ace."

CHAPTER TWENTY-ONE

Ace didn't get a chance to continue the conversation as, much to everyone's surprise, Matthew came back, and he'd brought their mother with him.

Within three days Greta was practically given the keys to the village, by the fifth day she was organising a village party in the church hall as a goodbye party for Heather and Sabrina.

He loved his mother, but she had completely blown his plans out of the window. He could not get Sabrina alone long enough to initiate a conversation, much less get her on a horizontal surface.

He watched her now, chatting away with his brother, hanging on to every damn word he was saying. Ace knew he was being unreasonable, it was his brother for shit's sake, but still, when had she ever hung on to any of his words? He frowned into his glass, then looked over at her again.

She was the only black person in the room, but you noticed her because she shone, she laughed and talked and sparkled as she mingled, attentive to everyone.

She was wearing a black strapless dress with blue and silver flowers on it, the skirt was full and skimmed her knees. The heels she wore weren't overly high, but high enough to tease the curves of her legs and taunt him.

Ace scowled when a farmer from the next village joined them, and she raised her face to accept his kiss on her cheek.

"Whatever it is you're thinking, stop it right now." His mother ordered, coming up to him.

"What?"

"You look as though you want to strangle somebody, and I don't want to deal with anyone's death tonight Alister, so you'd better stop it."

Ace smiled down at his diminutive mother, dressed in a long-sequined shirt in vibrant green and black pants, way over the top of an English village, but she did look nice.

Heather was holding her hand, dressed in a cute little pink and white dress and sparkly red shoes, that Greta had brought for her from America. He'd never seen her in a dress before, and her curls were on top of her head in a loose bun thing, she looked so cute.

"Hey baby," he went down onto one knee. "You look very pretty."

"Thanks, Daddy," she said, putting her hand on his shoulder and turning her head to show him her hearing aid.

Only yesterday they'd pimped it up with sparkly stickers and a large clip-on rhinestone star. Sabrina, doing some research, had hit on the idea and had ordered a kit. Heather had been wearing them normally ever since.

"Uncle Matthew bought me this from 'Merica," she touched her necklace, "and this," she showed him the matching bracelet with a pink heart on it. "And he says I don't have to wear them together, but I must wear one, so he'll always know I'm thinking about him. Have you danced with my mummy yet? She likes to dance, and so do I."

"Uncle Matthew has very good taste." He graciously admired the jewellery. There were also two hair clips and a matching ring he knew. "I'm not allowed to dance with your mummy until I've danced with you." He told her and watched her smile brighten. His heart tripped over. God, he loved this little person.

"Miss Heather?" He held out his hand and bowed deeply. "May I have this dance?"

She put her blue varnished nails to her lips, giggled, dipped into a perfect curtsy and took his hand to lead him to the centre of the room where they danced to an upbeat song with a girl talking about calling her maybe.

Sabrina watched Heather and Ace with a lump in her throat. Heather would be starting school next week, and Sabrina had found a house to rent close by, making the weekly commute less of an issue. She was going to miss Frecknor Green but knew it was time to move on.

"When are you going to Morocco?" Matthew asked, capturing her attention, as the farmer he'd been talking to excused himself.

"I've put it off until half term, and she's settled." She explained. "I have a young manager who's very reliable and we Skype daily," she laughed fondly, before going on. "She takes the laptop outside so I can see my trees and tell them hello."

"That's good. One of us can always come over if you need us."

"I know Matthew. Thank you." She said, taking a sip of her sparkling grape juice. "You have a wonderful family."

"You're a part of our family now Sabrina."

She smiled at him.

"Mummy?"

Sabrina looked down to see Heather with Ace.

"Yes, munchkin?"

"Daddy would like to dance. He wasn't allowed to ask you before because daughters, I'm his daughter, have to dance before mummy's, 'cause daughters are extra special."

Sabrina laughed. "Daughters are very, very special." She gave Matthew her glass and went into Ace's arms. He was wearing a pair of dark jeans, a white shirt open at the neck and a cream blazer. "Hi."

"Hey."

They'd barely been alone since that day at Donington Park.

One Direction's *What Makes You Beautiful* was on, and Matthew was dancing with Heather.

"Greta knows how to organise a party, doesn't she?" Sabrina said into the silence, as he was looking at her intently.

He didn't answer but said instead. "Sabrina?"

"Hmm,"

"For years I've resisted asking anyone," he began, "or even googling what dandelion and that other thing you wrote on that note was."

"Dandelion and Burdock?" She answered, her dark eyes sparkling with amusement. "It's a drink."

"Never heard of it."

"It's a British thing."

"I'll have to try it."

They swayed to the music, even though everyone around them was dancing enthusiastically, including his parents.

"Ace?"

"Sabrina?"

"There's something I have to tell. Well, two things," she added. "But I'll tell you later after the party."

He groaned, pulling her even closer.

"You can't do that to me. I have zero patience," he took her hand and pulled her outside, walking the short distance to the church entrance that had an old bench by the door. He pulled her down onto it but kept a hold of her hand. "What?"

"Remember when you met me properly that night in New York?" She started.

"Yeah," he smiled, remembering her dancing on the bar and those tiny red shorts.

"Andy and I weren't supposed to be there."

"What do you mean?"

"We had fake ID's."

He frowned over at her. "Fake ID's?" He repeated faintly.

"Yeah, too young to be drinking in America."

"How young?"

"Not yet, twenty." She admitted, giving him a wide-eyed innocent look, that he didn't seem impressed by.

"What the hell Sabrina?!"

"It's not something I really thought about until recently Ace."

He was pissed off. She was just a baby. She'd had his kid when she was a fucking teenager. Jesus Christ, if he'd known back then he'd never have gone back to her hotel, he thought guiltily. Stop lying Ace, he told himself, she'd been his fucking beacon of light. His distraction. He would have followed her anywhere.

"What's the second thing you need to tell me?" He asked reluctantly as he still pondered her age. She was so young.

She was chewing her nail, he noticed and looking at the

ground before she pulled her phone out of her pocket and with one hand, negotiated an app and then gave him her phone.

"Several months ago," She began, now chewing her bottom lip. "I re-applied for Oxford as a mature student. I just got the email."

He laughed, going back seven years to the computer room in the hotel. "We've come full circle." He said chuckling. "I'm so proud of you."

"I know."

He looked at her phone. "Do you want me to read it?"

She nodded and watched as he tapped the screen, but then she snatched it from him before he could read anything. "No. No, I don't. It doesn't matter. I can't go, anyway."

"Why not?"

"Heather."

"It's not just you any more Nina Mae," he called her that on purpose. It just seemed fitting. Nina Mae was her adventurous persona, and she needed to be reminded of that. "You have a whole family who loves her and you, and we'll make it work for you."

Sabrina started crying. She had no idea why and let Ace gather her in his arms and pull her onto his knee.

"This is really stupid, Ace." She began on a sniff, he smelled so good, all-male, and she breathed him in before moving away. "I don't even know why I applied. I don't have the time to study linguistics. I've got my business."

"And your writing."

"Nah, my writing was a fluke, something I did when Heather was a baby. between you and me," she dropped her voice. "I don't really have a passion for it."

"But you write so well."

"Have you read any of my books?"

"No," he admitted ruefully. "But my mom and sisters have." He added quickly.

She pinched him playfully on the arm. "I feel like a fraud writing, Ace. At first, it gave me a small income and then *The Beholden* took off and made our lives easier." She leaned forward in the chair putting her elbows on her knees as she focussed on the pink and white hydrangeas the village had planted four years ago. "I don't even know who Sabrina is, Ace." She admitted quietly.

"What do you mean?"

"I was a party Essex girl one day and a grieving mum to be the next. I don't know who I am. I don't know what I want. I don't even know if I want Oxford. It was my dream back then. Is it my dream now? I'm really not sure. I need some time."

"Time alone? I can take Heather—"

"No." She shook her head and reached for his hand. "Time to get to know me. I know it's a horrible thing to say, but Heather going to boarding school will free up some time for me to get to know me. Who I really am."

"It's not a horrible thing to say, Sabrina. I'm your friend, and I understand." He felt comfort in those words. She was his friend. His best friend. "You know you can tell me anything."

She took a deep breath and turned to look at him again. She couldn't see the colour of his eyes as it was already dark. The summer solstice had gone by weeks ago, and the days were getting shorter again.

"I know you want us to be together." She put her hands on his shoulders. "And I'd wanted that too, Ace. Once." She sniffed. "Being around you like this has reminded me of that time years ago, I feel the attraction now as much as I did then, and I also have this horrible fear of the things you do. I can't cope."

She put her fingers to his lips when he was about to speak.

"But also," she took a deep breath.

He knew what she was going to say.

"But it's time for me. I need to be selfish. Even your mother said that. Mothers need to be selfish sometimes in order to cope. In order to grow."

Thanks, mom, Ace thought bitterly. But nodded at her words.

"Maybe one day we'll get to a place where maybe…" Her smile was small. "I'll always love you, Ace. But it's time for me to be selfish and get to know me." The tears dripped onto her cheeks.

He pulled her close, tucking her head into his neck as he couldn't speak. What she was saying was true, she'd single-handedly raised their daughter. She was so young. He had to step back.

"I love you too." He whispered in her hair before pulling back so he could see her face.

"I won't ask you to wait for me Ace."

His smile didn't reach his eyes. She was breaking his fucking heart.

"Shall we open that email?" He suggested instead.

She sniffed, laughed self-consciously and nodded, holding her phone out to him to read.

"I'm sorry, Sabrina. You didn't get in."

Her shoulders slumped, and she leaned back against the bench.

"I'm sorry." Ace said again, taking her hand.

"It's okay. It's not like I can zip off to Oxford all willy nilly. I don't know why I even applied in the first place."

"What are you going to do now?"

"Find out who Sabrina Mavis Forrester really is." The smile she bestowed on him was the brightest one he'd seen since that night he'd said he'd go to the hotel with her.

He laced their fingers together and kissed her knuckles. "The one I know is fucking awesome."

She laughed.

"Thanks." She leaned over and kissed him on the cheek. "Come on Alister Charles Edwards they're probably wondering where we got to." She hauled him up, suddenly feeling light-hearted and carefree. "Ace?"

"Sabrina."

"Thank you for understanding I know this isn't what you wanted."

He shrugged. "Dandelion and Burdock. You and Me." He tugged playfully at her hair. "Always, Sabrina."

She hugged him, wrapping her arms around his neck, not knowing that her heart was close to the small box he'd had in his jacket pocket to give to her all evening.

CHAPTER TWENTY-TWO

"Hi, Daddy!"

"Hey, baby. What have you been up to?"

Ace eased back into the cracked plastic chair he was sitting on, trying to get comfortable in the stifling café. It was the first time in three weeks that he could see her in more than just the screen on his smartphone, plus he had the added bonus of being in an internet café in La Paz with coffee on tap.

"I'm getting married."

His coffee went down the wrong way, and he coughed and coughed trying to clear the fire in his throat.

"Wha-what did you just say?"

"I'm getting married to Aiden, Daddy." She said seriously, then moving closer to the screen added dreamily. "Daddy he is so cute."

"Aren't you a bit young to be thinking of marriage?" He choked. "I thought I had to escort you to your prom, then engagement party then wedding."

She giggled and Ace smiled. She was so beautiful. At ten, she was tall and lanky; her hair had settled into a deep auburn colour, and all the clothes she wore had to have some sort of sparkle on them.

"Not a real wedding Daddy. We're going up to secondary school, and Aiden thinks I might like another boy. He's going to a school for the deaf in Nottingham, and I'm going to a regular school."

What Ace was hearing was that she had been re-evaluated just like Hazel had said, and she was going to a mainstream school.

"Are you looking forward to it?"

"Not really. They might not understand me." She chewed on the side of her lip, much like her mother did from time to time.

"Of course, they'll understand you." He promised her. "Your speech wasn't bad, to begin with, and since you got the cochlear implant, you sound even better."

She'd gotten the implant just before her eighth birthday. "Sing me a song." He asked, knowing that had been her favourite way of learning pronunciation.

"Dad!"

"Go on, baby," he coaxed. "I've not heard your pretty voice since before I went into the jungle."

She screwed her nose at him, looked over her shoulder then leaned closer to the screen.

"Did you hurt yourself?" She asked, instead.

He rolled his eyes at her. She was becoming as bad as her mother.

"No."

"Promise me, Daddy, 'because I don't want to tell mummy any fibs."

"I didn't hurt myself. I went to a coffee farm to check on things, that's all."

"No swimming in piranha-infested waters? No leeches between your toes?"

He chuckled, shaking his head. "What have you been watching?"

"There's this programme on the telly, and the men do all that kind of stuff like catching fish with their bare hands. Stuff like that. Mummy can't watch it."

"I didn't go fishing. Besides, I have to keep myself safe so that I can walk you down the aislc."

She laughed at him. "Daddy, you're so funny. I miss you."

"I miss you too, baby."

"When are you coming to get me?"

"When do you finish school again?"

"Not sure," she got up, and Ace could see she was wearing a pink leopard print onesie. She went out of view, but he heard a loud shout. "Mum!"

He heard a muffled answer from Sabrina.

"When do I finish school? Daddy is on Skype!"

Another muffled answer then she came skipping back to him.

"Week and a half away." She advised, bouncing on her bed.

"Okay."

"Daddy?"

"Yes, baby."

"Don't tell her I told you, but mummy keeps getting these really awful headaches and once her nose started bleeding."

Ace felt a cold shiver race through him.

"When?"

"Just the other day," she whispered. "I think the business is stressing her out. I told her she doesn't have to work so hard and that you've got tonnes of money and she said she knows you have, but she needs to feel secure, or something like that and said she had to be able to look after herself in old age and won't depend on anyone." She came closer to the screen again. "Daddy I'm scared."

"When did she have the last headache?" He asked with concern. "Has she been to the doctors?"

"I don't think so. The last one was when I came back from the cinema, do you know they have a showing for deaf children now on a Saturday afternoon? Mummy got the local cinema to do it."

"Your mom is awesome." Ace praised. "When was her last headache?" He asked again.

"Saturday. Aiden's mum dropped me off. We went for dinner after the film and had to wait for mummy to open the door. Aiden's mum was with me because it took mummy ages to come to the door. Aiden's mum had to ring her mobile for ages."

Ace frowned. That was so unlike Sabrina.

"How did she look?"

"Her eyes were all puffy and red, and she could hardly see. I made her some tea, and I mean Daddy," she went on in a concerted rush. "She *let* me use the kettle and make her tea, then I put her to bed, and that's when I saw it."

"What?"

"Bloody tissues," she slapped her hands over her mouth before continuing. "Not bloody the swear word Daddy," she clarified swiftly. "Blood on the tissues."

"What did she say happened?" He hated asking these questions, but Sabrina barely talked to him about anything other than Heather.

"She had a little nosebleed. But Daddy, it was a lot of blood. I felt faint." She put her hand to her head dramatically.

This month Heather wanted to be an actor.

"It'll be okay."

"But she has nobody Daddy, and I'm worried."

"I know you are, sweetheart."

"Will you come to Morocco with us?"

"Depends on your mother."

"She won't mind. We built a beautiful little house there. Did you see the pictures I emailed?"

"I did. I like the pool."

"Daddy?"

He knew by the look in her face that she was coming with a whopper of a question.

"Yep?" The screen froze for a second, and her face was distorted into thousands of tiny squares.

"Can you hear me?" She started moving, and Ace tried to figure out what she was saying and where she was going.

"Mum! Daddy's on Skype." The screen cleared. "Say hello." Heather turned the laptop around to face the room.

Ace chuckled. Sabrina hated being ambushed like this; she had just come out of the shower and was covered in a bright pink towel and pink and white shower cap with lace around the edges.

"Heather!" She admonished, pulling the old-fashioned cap off her head and allowing her hair to fall around her shoulders.

God, she was so beautiful, if a little thin, Ace thought, as he watched her wag her finger at their daughter who was laughing.

He got a sweeping view of Sabrina's bedroom of soft creams before Heather settled at the head of the bed to lean against the padded velvet headboard and propped the laptop on her knees.

"Can you see me now, Daddy?"

"Yes, baby."

Ace was surprised when Sabrina came into view. She'd replaced the towel with a white satin robe. It reached her knees. Ace felt himself harden. It had been so long since he'd had sex and seeing her like this sent a rush of blood to his groin.

"Hi, Ace,"

"Hey, beautiful."

He watched as Sabrina put her arm around their daughter, kissed her hair and hugged her close.

"Hey! Daddy!" Heather shouted, sticking out her bottom lip. "You call me beautiful!"

He laughed. "You get your good looks from your mother, baby."

"Oh, okay." She smiled, happy with his explanation. "Mummy, tell daddy about the house we built in Morocco."

"I thought you sent him pictures?"

"Yeah, but it's better coming from you. You have such a way with words. And tell him about the new book you wrote that came into your head one night and you wrote practically nonstop for six weeks. Daddy, it's fab."

"And how would you know it's fab young lady?" Her mother asked.

"I've not read it," Heather defended quickly. "But Aiden's mum said she can't wait for your next title as she loves your style of writing and you're fab. That's what she said."

Ace watched the two women he loved most in the world banter back and forth, glad to witness their relationship. It was so rare that the three of them were ever together like this and his heart tripped. He missed them. He missed seeing Heather regularly, and he only ever saw Sabrina for maybe a day or two, when she flew Heather to his parents for the holidays.

"Say goodnight to your dad," Sabrina ordered. "It's late, and you have school in the morning."

"Goodnight Daddy." Heather blew him a kiss then kissed the screen. "I'm glad you didn't go swimming with the piranhas." She slapped her hands over her mouth, hearing her mother's loud gasp.

"You went swimming with piranhas?" Sabrina asked faintly.

She avoided every article about him, and they'd come to an agreement that he wouldn't tell her what he was doing.

She still wasn't over her fear for him. He found it ridiculous, but also endearing and knew he'd be in trouble if she ever got over that fear as that could only mean one thing. She was over him.

"I didn't go swimming with piranhas. Heather saw a program on TV." Ace explained quickly.

Sabrina pinned a glare at him. "You're not lying to me?"

"Ooh, Mummy you said lying," Heather chimed in. "You told me to use fibbing instead. It's more ladylike, you said."

"Sorry, Heather, and yes, it is." She kissed her daughter's head again. "Say goodnight and don't forget to brush your teeth."

"Okay. Love you, Daddy." She blew him a kiss again, and Ace was glad to see her wearing the bracelet he had Matthew make for her. "Love you, Mummy." She kissed her mother on the cheek.

"Love you too, baby." Both Sabrina and Ace said together. They laughed as Heather bounced off the bed and slammed the bedroom door.

Ace noticed Sabrina's wince, which gave him the perfect opening.

"You okay?"

"Just a bit of a headache." She rubbed her temples in circular motions and then slid further down into the bed, making herself comfortable against the pillows.

She moved the laptop a little further away, but Ace was able to see more of her.

"You've lost weight."

She looked down at herself and adjusted her robe over her breasts. "And how would you know?"

"I got a good glimpse of you in the towel." He revealed, wriggling his eyebrows suggestively.

She laughed, and Ace watched as a delicate touch of red entered her cheeks, he noticed because he was looking for it. Her skin was dark, but he knew where to look.

"Are you still perving on me, Ace?" Sabrina said with a laugh and then gasped. "Forget I even said that!" She playfully slapped her head then winced again, shifting even deeper into the pillows.

"Your hot body helps me go to sleep at night." He whispered and watched as she closed her eyes briefly and touched her bottom lip with her tongue. Damn it to hell. He wished he wasn't in a public place. They'd never had a conversation like this, and he wanted to push her further.

"Yeah, well, err." She stuttered. "Where are you anyway?"

Ace sighed, knowing the moment was lost. But it had been interesting. "Bolivia. I'm flying home in a couple of days."

"New York?"

"I guess."

"Aren't you tired of not having a base?"

He shrugged, they'd had this conversation before, only this time he was more honest with her. "When I have someone to go home to, then maybe I will."

"Are you seeing anyone?"

"No."

She had never asked him that before either. Was she fishing? Or did she have something to tell him? "Are you?" He growled.

"I went out to dinner with this guy about three weeks ago, but he kept talking about this expedition he was going on." She revealed, with a shudder. "One adventurer in my life is enough thank you very much."

Ace didn't like the fact that she was even dating but didn't say anything. Silence was golden in this case.

They looked at each other, both silent, Sabrina was the first to break the silence.

"I was talking to your mum today. She's planning a family reunion for the end of summer."

"Oh yeah."

"She was worried you won't be there."

"What date?"

"Not sure yet."

"Are you going?"

She'd been to a few of his family gatherings, and he loved seeing her there.

"Depends."

"On?"

"On a few things."

"I don't see why you can't just confirm with me now that you'll be there!"

"Are you seriously shouting at me, Alister?"

"No."

She smiled tightly. "I thought not."

Silence.

"Your beard is really bright." She watched him stroke the long wiry hair. She'd never seen it this long. His hair was tied back too. "I'd forgotten that you are a true redhead." She joked.

"You laughing at my red beard?"

"I wouldn't dream of it.

"I like your hair like that." He said instead. He wanted the intimacy of their conversation back.

Sabrina touched her hair, sat up and gathered a fistful where she started to plait it.

"I've got the hairdresser coming around tomorrow."

"What's the occasion?" Ace asked, trying for a light, easy note. If she were going on another date, he'd fly out tonight and be on her doorstep first thing.

"No reason," she bit the corner of her nail. "Well, there is a reason."

He waited, one brow lifting in arched enquiry.

"Have you ever heard of Regalia Cosmetics?"

"Nope."

"It's a European cosmetic company, and they want to buy me out."

"That's great!"

"I'm not sure Ace," she said. "I love my trees, and I love my oil. I've worked so hard to get argan oil noticed and accepted as a primary ingredient for a whole range of things."

"How much are they offering?"

She named a figure and grinned when he whistled.

"You're going to be rich."

"I would not be so vulgar to say I'm rich, Alister." She winked at him, as they both remembered a similar conversation when they were younger.

"Richer than me, maybe?"

"Hopefully."

"Has that always been your end game Sabrina?" He asked curiously. "Because you never let me look after you."

"You know I had to do this by myself Ace."

"I know sweetheart."

Sabrina was touched by his endearment.

"Will you bring Heather out or shall I come over?"

"You come over. I've also got this publishing thing to sort out. They like the book."

"Congratulations. You always said writing was a fluke, but boy are you great at it!"

She laughed, tipping her head back as she plaited another section of her hair.

"You always were good for me, Ace."

"Yeah, well."

"Ace?"

"Sabrina."

"This was nice."

He smiled at her, then frowned, his brow knitting tightly, as he watched a tiny drop of blood drip slowly from her nose.

"Erm Sabrina?"

"Hmm?"

"You've got a nosebleed."

Sabrina scrambled from the bed and Ace waited in frustration, seeing just the pillows but hearing her in the bathroom and water running.

She came back minutes later.

"I'm so sorry." She apologised with a bundle of tissue at her nose. The nosebleed had stopped.

"Why did you get a nosebleed like that?" He asked. "You feeling okay?"

She nodded, pinching her nose and leaning forward. "I'm just tired, that's all."

"Sure?"

"Yeah, I'd better go now. It's late."

Ace wanted to keep her talking. They hadn't had a conversation like this in years.

"Will you go to the doctor to get checked out?"

She laughed. "Don't be silly. It was just a little nosebleed."

To say any more would be to reveal what Heather had told him, so he remained quiet.

"I'll tell you what. You get ready for bed, and I'll keep you company until you fall asleep."

"Isn't that a bit creepy Alister?"

"It would be creepy if I didn't care about you. Go on," Ace urged. "Get your nightshirt or whatever it is you wear to bed on, and I'll keep you company."

He didn't think she was going to do it, but that Nina Mae persona arrived just when he wanted it to, and she giggled.

"Wait there."

"Can I watch you get dressed?" He pressed.

"Yes." She turned the laptop to face the room, and he looked over his shoulder to make sure no one was watching and moved closer.

She turned her back to him, slid her robe off her shoulders and, just as he caught a glimpse of her slender brown back, she threw her robe over the screen, and all he could see was white.

"Hey!"

He could hear her laugh then she came back moments later in a long cream and blue V-necked T-shirt.

"Ace?"

"That wasn't very nice Sabrina." He admonished, but his golden eyes were sparkling.

"I enjoyed it." She smiled playfully at him, as she arranged herself on the pillows. "You really didn't think I'd let the people of Bolivia see my naked self, did you?"

"I'm sure the people of Bolivia would be eternally grateful to see you pleasing me."

She laughed and turned away to turn off her bedside light.

She was bathed in the blue-white glow of the laptop. It wasn't a clear picture, but he could see her well enough.

"Okay Ace, put me to bed."

The image of putting her to bed burned in his brain, oh the possibilities. But he didn't push it.

"Pairs. I'll start."

"What's the prize?"

"A kiss when I see you next." He waited, okay, maybe a little push.

"Okay."

She was full of surprises tonight, but he hid his by saying. "I'll start. Bonnie and Clyde."

"Batman and Robin."

"Horse and Cart."

"Coat and Hat."

"What I suffered from in the jungle. Vomiting and Diarrhoea."

"Ew," she grimaced. "I've got one, Mary Kate and Ashley."

"Who are they?"

"Those twins, they used to be in an American family series years ago, now they have their own brand of cosmetics and clothing."

"I'll take your word for it." He drawled, his face creasing as he thought. "Rest and Relaxation."

"Tia and Tamera."

"Now you're just making up names."

"I'm not. They also started in an American sitcom years ago, but one of them is now in this other thing, and the other one is on a talk show. It's on BET."

"Okay, Sabrina." He sent her a sceptical glance.

"All right, next time we're together I'll show you."

"Sure. Mario and Luigi."

"Who are they?"

"They're in a game."

"You can't use gaming personalities," she challenged. "I don't play video games."

"I don't watch American sitcoms." Ace shot back with a grin.

She sighed dramatically. "I thought you were going to relax me, not shout at me?"

"If I were alone and in my hotel room, I'd definitely have you purring right about now."

"Oh, Ace."

"Let's play Sabrina. No names and I've upped the prize."

"Oh yeah to what?"

"You'll have to trust me on this."

"So, I must play without knowing what the prize is? Dream on, action man."

He laughed.

"Remember when you called me hot wheels?"

She laughed. "You should have seen your face!" She laughed again, "Oh Ace, those were the days."

"I don't know Sabrina," he said. "We're at a pretty good place right now."

"Surf and Turf."

"Burger and fries."

They played on and on, and Ace could see her lids getting heavy until she finally closed her eyes.

He watched her sleep. Her face relaxed with a tiny smile pulling at the corner of her mouth.

He was satisfied that he had put that smile there.

She worked so damn hard, raising their daughter, doing her course, she was still at Oxford. She hadn't got in for that autumn term, and if he'd read a little more of her email, they would have been celebrating, as Oxford had invited her to start the winter term instead. She'd switched to an online course, only having to physically go there on occasion.

He was so damn proud of her. He only wished she wasn't so stubborn and would let him help her financially. The only way she let him help was via Heather. He bought 'Heather', a nice little house. He purchased 'Heather', a new car every year.

He knew Sabrina was only indulging him, but at least it was something.

A woman tapped him on the shoulder and shouted at him in Spanish. She'd obviously seen him looking at Sabrina's sleeping form, as she threatened to call the police.

He quickly ended the Skype call, before the ruckus woke Sabrina and explained to the woman, and the rest of the café now, that he hadn't seen his woman in three weeks and needed to put her to sleep. The whole place practically sighed dreamily, and the women told him that he was so romantic and would he please come home with her to talk to her husband.

Ace left with a spring in his step, stopped, looked around and suddenly wondered what the hell was he doing in South America.

CHAPTER TWENTY-THREE

He'd never done it before, but he couldn't wait. A murderous thirty-six hours travelling and, still in his travel gear, he knocked on her door. She wasn't expecting him.

Her silver Q7–she preferred silver–was parked on the drive, so he knocked and rang the bell simultaneously.

He hadn't given a thought to her not being in. He just needed to get here.

Then he heard footsteps, and the door swung open. He took in the pencils stuck at odd angles in her hair, a light blue shirt, grey jeans and white slipper boots.

"Ace?"

He stepped over the threshold before she could ask anything else.

"Where's Heather?"

"School."

"Anyone here?"

"No."

With her hand still on the door handle, Ace pulled her into his arms with one hand and nudged the front door shut with the other, before gathering her up and kissing her like there was no tomorrow.

She didn't have a chance to formulate any words as he plundered, yes there was no other word for it, he plundered her mouth and lifted her leg to grind his arousal into her.

She moaned against his mouth, bumping her lips against his before he swooped down to her throat, raining kisses along her neck to the vee of her shirt and back up again.

She felt the wall at her back as he lifted her totally and she wrapped her legs around his waist as he kissed her, anchoring her against the wall as he used his hands to pull her shirt apart to rub his hands over her throat then shoulders, pulling the straps of her bra down along the way as he dipped his head to trail kisses along the soft cushions of her breasts, cupped in delicate pink lace as he pushed them together to bury his face in her cleavage.

She rubbed her hands over his red beard, then moved her hands to the back of his head to release the leather tie that had imprisoned his hair, allowing her to tunnel her fingers into the long soft strands.

"Ace."

"Sabrina."

Ace couldn't get enough of her, he didn't know where to touch first, all he knew in some small part of his brain, was that he should find her bed, but he couldn't navigate the stairs in this state. And he couldn't wait.

Sabrina pushed his battered brown leather jacket off his shoulders, then tore at his shirt. Finally, to feel the solid wall of his chest, her hands grazing over the defined wall of his pecs, his stomach and his back, tracing his scars, smoothing his hot skin, feeling his light chest hair tickle her palms as she stroked him. She bit his neck only to bathe the slight pucker with her tongue. He growled against her mouth.

She moved to another spot and nipped at his heated skin again, and he moved up to punish her mouth with his for her tenacity.

Sabrina felt his hands smooth along her sex, pressing into her before planing her taut stomach and reaching downwards, pulling her soft jeans and knickers with him as he rubbed his hand against her sex again, feeling her silky moisture against his fingertips.

He moved back slightly, giving her room to unbuckle his belt, and he growled deep in his throat when her small hands clasped around him, hard. He rocked into her hands in invitation and then, re-adjusting them both, his hands on her bottom he plunged into her, moving rapidly as she held onto his shoulders and bounced against him.

There was nothing Sabrina could do but hold on tightly. He

was merciless. It was as though he couldn't get enough of her and was racing away, at high speed, to the end of time.

He latched onto her neck, kissing and sucking the delicate skin below her ear. He moved back so that only her shoulders were supported and widened his stance. She was looking at him, and Ace felt the first stirring of his orgasm as she watched him with eyes half-open, teeth biting the corner of her bottom lip as she gripped him inside her.

She was coming, her eyes closed as he pounded into her, giving her everything that he had.

She was his, was his last thought as she screamed his name and came apart in his arms, a moment before he gave in to the hot rush and joined her.

***

"Hi, Sabrina." Ace said, several moments later.

Sabrina leaned back to smile at him. "Hello, Ace."

They grinned at each other. Their clothes were in disarray, her legs were still wrapped around his hips, and he was still pulsating inside her, yet they were grinning like idiots at each other.

Sabrina smoothed his long hair out of his face, then kissed him softly.

"Are you going to let me down?" She asked, on a whisper.

"Only if you promise to come back here later."

"I promise." Sabrina watched, fascinated, as Ace's eyes went from golden brown to a deeper burnished bronze at her promise.

He let her go, bending to pull up her panties and jeans before attending to his own clothes.

She looked at him properly. His clothes were all dusty and wrinkled, and he was wearing the scuffed leather boots he only ever wore on his many expeditions.

"Are you coming straight from the airport?" She asked, moving away from the wall.

"Yeah." He refused to break his habit and told her the truth.

"After talking to you I stood on the sidewalk in La Paz, one of my favourite cities, Sabrina," he shook his head and reached out to tenderly stroke her face with the side of his thumb. "And knew I didn't want to do it anymore." He admitted. "I felt a crippling loneliness." He went on. "I didn't want to be there. I wanted to be with you and Heather." He watched, waiting for her reaction, seeing her slight accepting nod and finally letting out the breath he hadn't realised he'd been holding.

Sabrina picked up his large rucksack bag, slung it over her shoulder, almost lost her balance and laughed when he took it from her.

"Come on, action man." She walked ahead of him. "Shower? Food? Bed?"

"How long until Heather gets here?" He asked, appreciating her ass as he followed her up the stairs. He was aware Heather came home via the school bus but wasn't sure of the time.

"Not for another three hours."

He stopped on the stairs. "Shower first, then bed." He listed, before adding. "With you in it."

And he was rewarded by her quietly saying.

"Okay."

***

"Why is daddy in your bed?" Ace heard Heather ask her mother. "You never let me sleep in your bed."

"Daddy flew all the way from South America. He's tired."

Ace heard Sabrina explain.

"Why couldn't he sleep in the spare bedroom?"

"Because mine is bigger and the en-suite is just there in case he wakes up and has forgotten where he is."

"That makes no sense Mummy. My daddy can read maps upside down."

"Will you be quiet and let him sleep? I've let you see him, and he's really here, so come on."

"Okay." Came the grumpy reply. "When will he wake up? Can I

touch him?"

Ace heard Sabrina sigh and could picture her rolling her eyes. He opened one eye slightly to peek at Heather, and when he felt her tiny fingers stroke his face, he growled loudly and pulled her down onto the bed as she screamed.

"Daddy!"

"Hey, baby."

He was strangled, smothered in kisses and strangled some more before she finally let him go with tears in her eyes.

"I thought you weren't coming until the week after next. I love that you're here. Don't ever leave!" She flung herself at him again, and Ace held her tight but looked over her shoulder to see Sabrina smiling through her own tears.

It was time to put his family back together.

CHAPTER TWENTY-FOUR

Ace closed the front door with a quiet click, unsure whether Sabrina was still sleeping or not.

He'd woken early, due to the time difference, sneaked into her bed, made love to her for a couple of hours, before sneaking out again, to go back into the spare room, just as Heather's alarm went off.

He'd had a fun morning, making his daughter breakfast and seeing her off to school. Then, as Sabrina had slept through the whole morning routine, drove her car into Derby, went to the bank, picked up some stuff from the supermarket and here he was.

The house was still quiet. Sabrina must have been even more tired than he initially thought, as it was now mid-morning, and she was still sleeping.

He had another long shower, appreciating the sting of hot water against his skin after weeks of simple river washing and he washed his hair and had a much-needed shave.

Feeling better, dressed in clean clothes, he went and looked in on Sabrina, thought about joining her in bed, but, with a guilty smirk dismissed it as he'd kept her up most of the night. He went downstairs to grill some mushrooms and bacon for her breakfast but would leave the eggs until she woke up.

When she'd showed him a photo of the house a few years ago, it had been a beige new build. A modest, detached, three bedroomed in a cul-de-sac position. A family home, only without him.

She'd decorated it nicely, Ace thought, walking around. Gone were all the original beige walls, replaced by mostly white walls, but then your senses were hit by a bright wall of yellow, or purple or orange. He loved it. It encapsulated both Sabrina and Nina Mae perfectly.

One entire wall in the living room was devoted to family photographs, and he was pleased to see many of himself with Heather, or some of just him alone. It was heart-warming to be included like this and only confirmed what he'd known all along.

Ace was glad when he heard her walking around upstairs. Finally, he thought.

She was brushing her teeth when he went upstairs and wearing nothing more than a pair of white lacy panties that could double as a pair of shorts, a very sexy pair of shorts, he amended, looking at her long legs before travelling upwards to appreciate the simple white top which moulded and clung and showed off her perfect breasts and shoulders.

When she spied his reflection in the mirror, she smiled around the red toothbrush in her mouth, at his sexy wink. Aside from the deep tan, he looked just as he did when they'd first met with his auburn hair loose and touching his shoulders. Sabrina felt a thrill of something delicious dance down to her core.

"Remember when we'd just met, and you lived by the moment?" Ace asked casually, as he leant against the door frame.

Sabrina nodded.

"But you had dared to think past that, to a future of me and you together?"

She nodded again but stopped brushing her teeth as she watched him produce a small velvet box from behind his back. He opened it to reveal a large marquise diamond mounted on an infinity shaped band, also with diamonds. It was breath-taking.

"I had this made three years ago as I wanted that moment then," he admitted. "But you weren't ready. Now you are. I love you; you love me, and I want us both to start planning more than just a fucking day ahead. Marry me and let's make this right."

Sabrina turned to the basin and spat out the minty foam from her mouth. Waving her toothbrush in the air, she addressed his reflection.

"You're asking me to marry you in the bathroom, with me half-naked and brushing my teeth?!"

He smirked. "Sounds about right."

Sabrina rinsed her mouth and dried her face with a towel before looking at him again, with her hands on her narrow hips.

He moved up behind her, put the box on the counter and wrapped his arms around her waist, pulling her flush against him.

"Here's the version you won't tell our grandkids," he whispered in her ear. "Grandpa was so romantic he couldn't wait for dinner and proposed in the bathroom with you half-naked, your lovely breasts," he cupped her breasts and pulled at her nipples. "Hard and pressing into my hands. Your knees giving way, as I do this." He swept a hand into her panties and played within her folds that were already damp and inviting. "And you turning your head to whisper yes against my lips as I kiss you."

With her knees trembling she leaned against his hard body for support, then turned her head to kiss him deeply, dragging her tongue against his as he continued to rub his fingers in small circular motions against her sex.

He spun her around and lifted her onto the counter, stepping into the space between her thighs before leaning back, his golden gaze staring into her dark eyes. "Well?" He demanded, none too gently.

She smiled, grabbed his head with both hands to pull him forward to nip at his bottom lip with her teeth.

"In a language that you rarely use Alister, absolutely." She said in Italian, then laughed, as he scooped her off the counter, wrapped her legs around his waist, walked back to her bed to make love to her again.

***

"What date have you got in mind for the wedding?" Ace asked casually, as they lay in bed, sedated and mellow after a marathon session making love. Sabrina had yet to go downstairs for her promised breakfast of eggs, mushrooms and bacon.

"I was thinking March would be nice."

"No flipping way." Ace said as he stroked her fat plaits

methodically. "I've waited ten years to get you where I want you and I'm not waiting until next year. No," he repeated adamantly. "Forget it."

"Did you just say flipping?" Sabrina asked, chuckling.

Ace wriggled his eyebrows comically.

Sabrina knew he was trying hard to stop swearing as Heather had caught him out and told him off about it last summer.

Sabrina pulled on his nipple before saying. "Okay, later this year."

"You've got what? Another year of studies?"

"Well, err," she began feeling her cheeks warm. "I finished early."

"What do you mean?"

"I kind of have an aptitude for linguistics, as you know, and I'll graduate this summer."

"So, I'm lying in bed with a genius, is that what you're saying?"

"Sort of."

"Jesus Christ Sabrina," he laughed. "I think you just got sexier."

She laughed, and they settled into the silence for a while, both content to just lie there, stroking each other, each lost in their own thoughts.

"Sabrina?"

"Hmm,"

"Tell me about that date you went on a few weeks ago," Ace asked.

The finger that had been going around and around his nipple stopped.

"Do you really want to know?"

"No," he admitted. "But I need to know."

"Okay," she began. "He's a Boy Scout leader for the school, and he caught me at a weak moment."

"How d'ya mean?" Ace asked. "What moment?"

"I'd gone to pick Heather up after school," she remembered. "It was badge night and the Brownies mixed with the Cubs for a bonfire and games. You know they socialise, Ace? Well anyway, all the parents were milling around as couples, and then there was me, all alone." She shrugged, remembering the feeling. She'd known these past years had been self-inflicted, that she was alone out of choice, but still.

"Did you sleep with him?" Ace asked quietly.

"No." She admitted. "From the moment I said I'd go out to dinner with him, I regretted it." She revealed. "How about you? Have you been out with anyone?"

"No."

"What about sex?" She turned to rest her chin on his broad chest as she looked up at him. "You're highly sexed if the marathon sessions you do with me are anything to go by." Her smile was that of a satisfied woman. "I won't be mad Ace." She promised sincerely. "I don't have a right to be mad."

"Thanks, but you don't have a reason to be." He told her. "I didn't have sex with anyone."

She gasped. "No sex?" She raised onto her elbows. "In three years?"

"Why do you think I fell on you like a fucking animal?" He explained, staring into her dark eyes. "I got one taste of you three years ago and will only ever sleep with you."

"Oh Ace," she breathed, his words were even better than any 'I love you's' he'd ever said.

"Have you slept with anyone?" He watched her closely and waited. He didn't know if he could be so forgiving. He would be mad.

"I do have Percy," Sabrina admitted, mapping the circular tattoos on his broad chest with tender kisses.

Ace moved to get up. He'd tried to keep tabs on her, surreptitiously asking Heather if her mother was going out with anyone and now to hear she'd had a boyfriend. Percy. What the hell kind of fucked up name was that? He shouldn't be mad, but the thought of her sharing her body with another man, made acidic bile rise in his throat.

Sabrina moved over him, her naked chest against his as she reached into her bedside cabinet, rummaged around and pulled out a large velvet pouch in deep purple.

She sat on his lap and smiled as she pulled out a bright purple vibrator and waved it around.

"Meet Percy." She said, laughing at his ferocious yet amused look. "I had you then didn't I Ace."

"Don't do that to me again, Sabrina. My heart can't take it."

"I love you, Alister always have."

"And you'd better not forget it." He said sternly, as he rocked her hips backwards and forwards until she got the hint, picked up her own pace, lifted onto her knees then sank slowly onto him.

**

The next time they woke, they made it out of bed, had a shower, got dressed and ate the now dry bacon and shrivelled mushrooms. Sabrina had offered to toss them into an omelette, but Ace took over and made scrambled eggs. They were the fluffiest scrambled eggs she'd ever eaten.

"Heather is going to be over the moon," Sabrina said, waving her left hand in the air and watching as the light bounced off her new diamond ring. It was beautiful, so her. "This is a beautiful ring Ace."

He turned to her, smiling, his eyes clear and golden. "You really like it?"

"Hmm, mm."

"Good, 'because you'll never be taking it off. You are mine. Have always been mine."

"It's a good job I don't have a problem with that isn't it Alister?"

"What time will that daughter of ours be here." He asked, before adding darkly. "Do you know she's got a boyfriend?"

"Please," Sabrina flicked her newly bejewelled hand in the air. "Christopher is a boy who's a friend."

"Not him, Aiden." Ace advised. "Apparently, he asked her to marry him as she's going to a new school."

Sabrina laughed, looking at the clock above the kitchen door. "She'll be here in two minutes."

"Two minutes," he pulled her out of her chair and wrapped his arms around her. "Hmm, I wonder how we can fill two minutes." He asked, dipping his head to capture her mouth.

**

The rest of the day flew by, and Ace tried to keep himself awake by going for a run with Heather riding her bike beside him.

By the time they got back, Sabrina had made a midweek roast beef dinner in celebration of Ace being home, even making her Yorkshire puddings from scratch.

As they knew she was going to be, Heather was over the moon about the wedding and jumped straight online to look for bridesmaid dresses. That's when the questions started.

Where would they get married? When Sabrina said his parents' house in America, he laughed and said no way. He was not getting married in his parents' back yard, which was practically a pet cemetery he said, telling them about the numerous pet cats and rabbits buried there over the years.

Then came the question of where they were going to live. Ace said he was happy wherever she wanted to be. It was Heather who said she wouldn't mind living close to her grandparents.

"You don't mind?" Ace asked quietly when Heather went off to do her homework.

"Mind what?"

"I remember a time when you said you would never live with me over there."

"I love you and your family Ace," she said. "I just want to be wherever you are. Besides," she shrugged. "I have my own money. I'm rich," she gave him a wink. "Well, I will be in a couple of weeks."

"You've decided to sell?" He asked, chuckling at her 'rich' comment.

"It makes sense really," she said. "There is so much more I want to do. Want to give." She started passionately. "I've had this dream of supplying hearing aids to children in third-world countries then..."

Ace listened, watching how lively she became as she listed all the good they were going to do in the world. God, he loved her.

CHAPTER TWENTY-FIVE

Sabrina and Heather were having a mother-daughter day out in Derby. Shopping, then lunch, was the order of the day.

Ace had gone off to Donington Park, and Sabrina smiled, remembering how nervous he'd been this morning when he'd told her his plans. She'd patted him on the back and sent him on his way with only the promise of him coming back to her with all limbs duly accounted for. He'd grinned and sealed his promise with a kiss.

Heather was in dire need of some clothes for the summer, as well as a few outfits for her eleventh birthday, Sabrina's graduation and another outfit for the book event in London. Sabrina's latest novel *The Beginnings* had been launched last week and was doing very well.

The shopping mall had a decent array of shops with all the major High Street names available to them. But for Sabrina, who had shopped in some of the best cities in the world, Derby was seriously lacking, but it would have to do for now.

It had been a crazy few weeks, they had finally agreed on a wedding date and were currently liaising with a celebrity wedding planner in New York, via Skype. Heather had left primary school and was looking forward to seeing her grandparents and cousins in America over the summer holidays. The book launch, and the meetings with Regalia Cosmetics regarding the sale of her business, had all guaranteed Sabrina was feeling stressed out.

With both of them laden with bags, Sabrina announced it was lunch-time. They had a simple bacon butty from a café and then went to the luxurious dessert shop, where Sabrina had a double chocolate cheesecake and Heather a waffle, fresh strawberries and cream concoction, with a shot of white chocolate on the side.

It was a beautiful day. They walked around at a relaxed pace, walking outside to peruse the few shops in the oldest part of the city centre.

Derby was a young city compared to others in the region, as it had been known as a town up until the mid-70s. Unfortunately, the older part of the town centre was dying out, rows upon rows of shops closed, due in part to the bright and shiny enclosed mall. Pity, Sabrina mused, feeling a slight headache coming on as they walked along St. Peters Street, down past the church, towards Albert Street.

She'd had a nosebleed last night while taking a bath. Luckily, Ace had been showing Heather places he'd been to on Google Earth, and Sabrina had simply flushed away the bloodied tissue, but she did make a mental note to go in for a check-up once things had settled down.

This would be her third headache this week, and she was reluctant to take any more painkillers, but knew, if she didn't get in front of the pain right now, it would become a blinding headache in no time at all.

Stopping off in an over packed Newsagent, she bought a packet of fast relief migraine capsules, downed three with some bottled water, and bought Heather a chocolate bar to distract her from watching her.

They walked back and Sabrina, trying hard not to dwell on it, was resigned to the fact that she was feeling seriously ill.

She needed to get to the car and home before it became worse.

"Heather baby," she said to her daughter, who hadn't been distracted at all, and who was looking at her with eyes full of concern. "I'm not feeling so great, so we'll finish shopping in London okay?"

"Okay, Mummy." Heather agreed, taking her hand. "Shall I ring daddy?"

"No, that's okay," Sabrina said, as cheerily as she could. "Let's get to the car."

The walk should only have been five minutes, but it dragged. It was too hot, the crowds too close. Her head was pulsating in deep long throbs, the pain radiating down the back of her neck and on one side of her face. Used to how her migraines now worked, Sabrina knew she was going to be in for a rough time.

They walked through the mall and waited for the elevator that a lady with silver hair, cut in a pixie style, with as many bags as themselves, had already called.

As they all entered the elevator, a shady looking man in a shabby navy-blue tracksuit with two wide stripes on the legs and sleeves, walked in behind them. He'd pulled the hood low, so only his chin could really be seen.

Sabrina grabbed Heather's hand and held her daughter close. Car parks were notorious places for robberies, she knew, even with all the CCTV cameras about.

They left the elevator, leaving the man inside and Sabrina squinted against the harsh brightness of the blue and yellow car park. She stood in the queue and waited as the stupid pay point machine spat out the paper note from the pixie cut lady and Sabrina went into her purse and looked for some coins but didn't have enough. When it was her turn, she smoothed the ten-pound note she had as flat as she could, but the machine still spat it out several times, before Heather, taking it from her, fed the money into the machine, slowly. Very slowly.

Grabbing the exit ticket, Sabrina turned and glimpsed the same man from the elevator. He'd returned via the stairs.

She looked at him, making it obvious that she was, but he turned and left the small area with his shoulders hunched and his head down low. She hadn't got a good look at his face but knew he was up to no good.

They were parked at the far side of the level. The one time Sabrina had thought to get a little exercise in by parking at the far end of the car park she had become ill. Typical, she thought.

"Come on baby," Sabrina said, urging Heather forward.

They walked quickly. White spots were distracting Sabrina's vision as though she were peering through a curtain of fairy lights, and she was feeling nauseous. She wasn't going to make it.

Spying her Q7 with relief, she got her keys out and, glancing over her shoulder to ensure no one was nearby, pressed the key to open the vehicle, got in after Heather and quickly locked all the doors.

She started the car, took several swigs of water and knew she was going to be sick so, opening the door again, leaned out and vomited.

"What can I do Mummy?" Heather said, with concern, from the back seat.

"Stay in the car Heather," Sabrina ordered, aware of movement around them. She could barely see now as the pain was blinding, literally.

From the corner of her eye, she watched pixie cut lady put her bags in her red sports car.

Sabrina heaved and fanned herself, before turning off the engine and getting totally out of the vehicle but leaving the door open.

Bending at the waist and with her hands on her knees, she inhaled deeply, trying to alleviate the feeling of light-headedness, thinking how was it that her head felt as though cement was being poured on it, yet she was feeling light-headed?

Sabrina watched the flashy red car drive off, looked over at Heather who was watching her and then took some more deep breaths as she heard another car approach. She turned and saw the same man from the elevator watching her from a small black car with an old-style registration plate. He drove off very slowly, and Sabrina could have sworn she'd seen him take a picture of her from his phone before disappearing down the ramp with a smirk on his pale face.

The hairs on Sabrina's neck stood on end, and she shivered. That was really weird. "I'm going to ring your dad," Sabrina told her daughter, then watched gratefully when Heather took out her own basic mobile phone to ring him and tell them what was happening.

"He says he's coming. He was on his way back anyway and not far away." She told her worriedly. "Come sit down Mummy,"

Heather instructed, climbing into the passenger seat from the back.

Sabrina, with effort, got into the vehicle, locked all the doors and waited with her eyes closed and her head leaning against the black leather headrest.

It seemed liked hours before Ace came and Sabrina had gone from thinking that she should have just called a taxi to take them home, to wanting to curl up and cry.

She was aware of a blur of motion, a white vehicle identical to hers screeching to a stop and Ace, jumping out and tapping on her window.

It was Heather who unlocked the doors.

"Hey baby," Ace said to Heather, then felt Sabrina's forehead. She didn't have a temperature, but she looked like hell. "What's wrong?"

"Mummy has a headache Daddy," Heather told him. "We were walking along and bam, it struck just like that." She said. "She was sick too."

With his brows knitted tightly and a decision made, Ace lifted Sabrina from her car to his, settling her in the back seat and telling Heather to sit beside her mother. He transferred their bags to his vehicle and locked hers up before driving straight to the hospital.

Sabrina was seriously ill, Ace thought worriedly, as she didn't offer any objections to going, in fact, she was barely coherent when the male nurse in A&E asked her to confirm her name, age, address and the name of her doctor's surgery, before telling them to sit down and wait.

Ace, about to demand they see to her now, was thankful that Sabrina threw up beside the reception desk and the nurses went into action like a swarm of ants, whisking her away to be seen by the doctor on duty.

Dr Adekaunsi, a young black doctor from South Africa, Ace knew by the accent, came back within ten minutes to tell him they were admitting her as her blood pressure was dangerously high, and they needed to intervene quickly. He was advised to go home and come back tomorrow as they were going to sedate her.

***

When they'd got home, Heather had shown him the emergency list Sabrina always kept in the kitchen drawer and reassured him that they'd never had to use it and that auntie Sylvie came and stayed with them all the time. Then Heather had calmly gone upstairs, asked him to pull down a small suitcase from the closet and began to pack for her mother.

Ace had never been so proud. Without a word, they packed the bag and sat on the bottom step of the stairs waiting for Sylvie Watson to drive down from Frecknor Green.

When she arrived, Ace kissed Heather, promised to ring her no matter what time it was and left.

Dr Adekaunsi was still on duty and was able to tell him more. Sabrina had been walking around like a pressure cooker, the doctor explained, the nose bleeds and headaches were symptoms that something more was going on than a general migraine. He said she was very lucky as she could have had a stroke today.

Numbly, Ace thanked the doctor, went into the men's toilet and ran cold water over his hands.

He wasn't feeling anything, his landscape was as stark as the Siberian winter. Ace had never been able to picture a life without her in it. No matter how many miles were between them, Sabrina was his beacon.

He walked into the private room he'd arranged for her, pulled the blue padded chair as close as it would get to the bed, sat down and held her hand as she slept.

It was just two days ago at the climbing centre that he'd held her hand ready to ease her fears and reassure her it was safe to climb, only for her to grin at him, pull on the ropes and climb the resin, fifteen-metre rock face like a pro. She'd stopped halfway up and asked if he was coming—the minx.

When she'd climbed down, she'd put her hand on his shoulder, looked him dead in the eye and said the past three years had not only been about getting to know herself but also facing her fears as she wanted to be able to do things with him too.

Ace felt the stinging tears behind his eyes now, as he remembered the feeling of tenderness that flowed between the two of them at that moment. People milling all around them, yet they'd never been closer.

Then, as she walked to sort out Heather's helmet, told him how she was learning to ride a motorbike.

"God, please," he prayed as the tears fell onto their entwined hands. "God, please don't let anything happen to her. She's my life."

***

It was in the wee hours of the morning when Ace, with his head resting on the side of the bed, felt Sabrina stir. He watched as her long lashes fluttered open to reveal tired, confused eyes.

"Hi beautiful," he said, leaning forward and kissing her knuckles as she turned to him.

"What happened?"

"Shh, don't move." He ordered when she moved to pull herself up. "You're in the hospital. Don't you remember?"

"No," she scrunched her eyes up in confusion, trying to remember, then she looked at him. "I remember locking the car door. Wh-where's Heather?"

"At home," Ace confirmed. "We called Sylvie," he kissed her hand. Every emotion he was now feeling lodging in his throat like a ball of elastic bands. "You should have seen her, babes, Heather took control, didn't cry and calmly packed you a bag and told me about your plans in case of an emergency. She was awesome."

Sabrina smiled tiredly with pride. "I feel all floaty. What happened to me?"

"All those headaches you were getting, and the nose bleeds you didn't tell me about?" He pointed out with a dark frown. "Were symptoms of your blood pressure rising." He disclosed. "I should be mad at you, but I won't shout until I have you home and you're well again. The doctor sedated you."

"Blood pressure?"

"Yeah, you went into what Dr Adekaunsi called a Hypertensive crisis. Did any of your parents have it? Do you remember?" He asked. "It's hereditary and common in African Caribbean communities, but yours went undiagnosed for too long."

"I think my dad may have had it." She told him. "Can I have some water, please?"

"I'm not sure," he looked around, as though able to pluck the answer from the air. "I need to tell the nurses you're awake." He said, kissing her knuckles again before standing beside her bed to stare down at her with his hands shoved deep into his jeans pockets. "Sabrina?"

"Hmm?"

"I never understood," he told her truthfully, running his hands through his hair. "Now, I do."

She knew what he was referring to, the almost debilitating fearfulness for her well-being. She merely nodded and watched him leave to get the nurse when he could have simply pressed the button beside the bed.

***

When Sabrina next opened her eyes, it was to see Greta beside her.

"Hi," she said, focussing on the older lady who was reading from her e-reader beside her.

"She wakes," Greta smiled, putting her e-reader down to pour Sabrina a glass of water. "How are you feeling sweetheart?"

With Greta's help, Sabrina pulled herself up and arranged and fluffed the pillows behind her back.

"Feeling?" Sabrina closed her eyes as though calculating the presence of every ailment that had plagued her these past few weeks. "A lot better. When did you get here? What day is it?" She asked, turning to the window, it was dark outside, she noted in confusion. "Where's Heather and Ace?"

Greta laughed. "One thing at a time Sabrina." She held the cup out to Sabrina and waited until she had finished it before answering. "I got in yesterday morning. It's Tuesday, and Heather is at home with Sylvie. I sent Alister home to bed. He hadn't slept since you were admitted, and his temper was beginning to show. Those poor nurses didn't know what to do with him."

"Tuesday?"

"You slept for practically two days straight." She explained as she went back to her chair. "The nurses have been monitoring you, but more or less, they let you sleep. You obviously needed it."

"I do feel better. When can I leave? Do you know? I've got a wedding to plan and a book to promote and a business to sort out."

"And it was all of that, that got you into this mess in the first place, young lady," Greta told her sternly, frowning over at her. "You are not to worry; we are all here now."

"We who?"

"Me, Charles, Kelly and Charlene and all the kids. Maddie is in New Zealand and sends her love and Sophia has just started her internship so can't be here." She explained, before going on. "Matthew will be here next week with Kyle."

"Staying where? I've only got a three bedroo—"

"Mom, didn't I tell you to call me when she woke up?" Ace asked, striding into the room, sending his mother an annoyed look before going over to the bed to kiss Sabrina on the forehead and smile tenderly down at her.

"I'll forgive you your tone this time young man, but watch it," Greta said. "She's only just woken up."

Ace went to kiss his mother in apology, before walking over to the bed again. "Hey baby," he said, looking into Sabrina's dark eyes and kissing her, on the lips this time.

"Ew, Ace," she glanced over at Greta. "I mean Alister," with a sorry expression at Greta, belatedly remembering calling him Ace was not allowed around her. "My mouth feels as though fur is growing inside it."

He grinned and kissed her again on the mouth. Loudly.

"I'm just going to go and get myself a coffee," Greta said. "I'll tell the nurses that you're awake on my way-out Sabrina."

Sabrina smiled her thanks and turned to look at Ace.

"You look tired." She commented, reaching up to smooth his brow.

"Yeah well, you decided to frighten the heavenly fuck out of me, and I couldn't sleep without you in our bed."

For him to swear meant he was distraught, and her smile was soft as she laced her fingers through his, tugging him down to the bed. "Sit down. I'm okay."

He sat beside her legs but was scowling over at her. "Do not frighten me like that ever again. I can't handle it."

"Sorry."

"And don't think I'm going to let you out of this bed until your blood pressure is normal and your heartbeat isn't skipping at odd beats either."

"What are you talking about?"

"You've been walking around with a messed-up heart. Your blood pressure was so high, for so damn long that your heart was struggling to cope."

"Sorry."

"Yeah well, you've got the rest of your life to make it up to me."

"Where is everyone staying?" She asked, wanting to change the subject. When she'd been admitted, the doctor did say she could have had a stroke at any moment, and her heart needed to be monitored. That was frightening enough, especially for her age.

"At a hotel," Ace explained. "Now that you aren't about to explode—"

"Explode?!"

"Explode," he pursed his lips before continuing. "You're going to be transferred to London where a specialist is waiting for you. I've rented a house large enough for everyone nearby."

"I'm sorry, Ace."

"Will you stop fu-saying that." He instructed as he looked sheepishly towards the door as a thin young nurse with jet black hair and bright blue eyes came into the room.

"I will still get you banned from my ward if you continue to harass my staff *and* my patient Mr Edwards." She said sternly, her Irish accent evident.

She looked as though she had barely left nursing school, but the look she pinned on Ace had years of practice behind it, Sabrina mused.

"My apologies."

The nurse glanced tellingly at the door, and as soon as he left, she grinned down at Sabrina who was looking on in amazement.

"Handful isn't he that one?"

"You could say that," Sabrina replied with a small smile and watched as the nurse fiddled with the machine Sabrina was hooked up to.

"The poor lad has been out of his mind with worry."

"Was he a nuisance?"

Sabrina watched her take a reading and make a note on her electronic pad. "Only because he loves ya. How're you feeling? Headache? Woozy?"

"I feel fine, in need of the bathroom though, and I'd love to have a shower.

"Okay." The nurse pulled back the sheets and helped Sabrina move to the edge of the bed. "Take your time. You're a little weak." She advised as they walked steadily to the adjacent bathroom. "No shower just yet as Dr Adekaunsi will need to see you first. But you can have a little wash. Everything is in there, give me a shout if you need me."

"Thank you."

***

In the end, Sabrina spent an additional ten days in a hospital down in the capital, to ensure she hadn't suffered any organ damage, as her blood pressure had gone undiagnosed for so long.

She missed her graduation and with a new management team and lawyers, Ace had brought in to help her, she sold her company for three times the amount Regalia Cosmetics had initially offered.

The eight bedroomed house Ace had rented came with two cooks and a housekeeper and was overflowing with his family. Kelly had been coming to her graduation as a surprise anyway, and as Sabrina wasn't allowed to fly anywhere at the moment, everyone stayed to enjoy the summer holidays in England.

Alongside the family, Sabrina played tour guide as well as casually looking at houses for them to buy online in America, although Ace had told her to take her time with that, as he had somewhere in mind.

Together, they had started running. Ace couldn't believe how unfit she'd become and immediately started waking her up at an ungodly hour to go running with him. All in the interest of her health, he said. The only bonus Sabrina got was the joy in chasing after his hard backside to pinch, every time she caught up with him.

What she didn't know, and had only just learned, was that Ace was a patron to several large international charities.

She had laughingly referred to his globetrotting lifestyle in conversation one evening, only for Greta to speak up for her son and tell her about his work. Not only did he give his money, but he also gave his time.

Later in bed that night, Sabrina had made him tell her everything he'd been doing. He'd done an excellent job of distracting her these past few weeks, what with his sudden appearance and then her illness, and she had never felt so small or so proud of him. He'd actually been busy with his charities these last three years, telling her that he had needed a direction as much as she had.

He also shared his long-term vision for the first time, and together they made plans.

CHAPTER TWENTY-SIX

Sabrina was at the signing table and smiled at the next fan who requested a selfie with her. This one even had the requisite stick with her bejewelled phone already positioned at the end.

She didn't mind, but after two hours of this, she was beginning to flag.

She herself had insisted she was capable of doing the event and was reluctant to let Ace know how tired she was. Just seven more people in the queue she counted, smiling for the picture.

The Beginnings was currently topping the bestseller charts here and in North America, and this was the only book event she was going to do in England.

Natalia had flown over from New York, and once she realised Sabrina was reluctant to promote more than one event, her publicist had made this a big one. A reading, a Q&A, three live radio broadcasts and several newspaper interviews all in one day.

Sabrina was stressed out and beginning to feel the first throbs of a headache. Only six more people, she counted, smiling through her pain as she stood for another picture.

Greta, Charles, Charlene and Kelly had taken the children to get something to eat, leaving Ace behind. She noted that he was making no bones about watching her, as he was stood off to one side, leaning against a display of cookery books and looking all gorgeous. Whenever she caught his eye, he winked, and she blushed.

She felt loads better, and now that they'd found a combination of blood pressure meds that were keeping her readings stable, not to mention all the new physical activity, green juices and healthy eating plans Ace had insisted on, she felt fine, that is until today. It had been too much.

She signed another copy of the book, smiled, chit chatted

and stood for yet another photograph. Four people to go, she counted, tiredly.

When the event was finally over, and Natalia had locked the doors, Sabrina collapsed in the chair and toed off her heels.

Ace stood in front of the desk with his hands on his hips with an 'I told you so' expression on his face, but Sabrina would be damned if she would give him the satisfaction of telling him he was right.

"Did I tell you how scrumptious you look today?" She said, to throw him off. He did look good though, black trousers, a pale pink shirt and a black leather blazer. At her insistence, he'd left his hair loose to sweep his shoulders, and every time she looked over at him, she felt her heart skip a beat that had nothing to do with her health, but all to do with how turned on he made her feel.

"Hungry?" He asked instead, onto her tactics, but deciding the battle wasn't worth it now that the event was over.

"Starving," Sabrina replied. "But I'd rather eat something light at home." She sneakily put her heels back on and got up to roll the kinks from her shoulders and stretch her lower back.

"You were amazing," Ace told her, tucking her into his side as he kissed her forehead and led her to the back of the enormous book shop in Piccadilly.

"Thank you."

"Tired?" He asked.

"A little." She replied honestly. "Home?"

"Sure." He turned to Natalia who was hovering nearby. "We're heading out."

"Oh but—" Natalia started, taking a step forward with an armful of books, then backing off completely at Ace's fierce glance over Sabrina's head.

Sabrina's mouth fell open in amazement. Natalia always had something more for her to do.

"I'll see you tomorrow," Natalia said instead, smiling tightly over at Ace. "You did great Sabrina." She finished, then turned to the cluttered desk beside her. "Oh, this came for you."

Sabrina had already received a huge bouquet of tiger lilies from Ace and a summery bouquet of yellows and reds from the family today and, as she watched Natalia pick up the thin white box, her heart sank. It could only be a single rose from her so-called fan.

She took it from her publicist and opened the box, knowing what she would find and wasn't surprised, her fan was anything but consistent. A single peach coloured rose to match the cover of her latest novel. The card read 'Forgive me'.

She flung the whole ensemble onto the desk and walked away, not caring how it looked.

"What the hell," Ace said, as he reached over to read the card. "Is this from the same person Sabrina?"

"Yes." She replied numbly, wrapping her arms around herself. "Come on, Ace, let's go home."

But he wasn't listening.

"Natalia, do you know who brought this?" He asked.

"No, it was waiting for us after that BBC Radio interview this afternoon. Why? What's wrong?"

"Some fucking asswipe has been tormenting her over the years. Didn't you know?"

"No."

They both turned to Sabrina, both scowling at her.

"What?" Sabrina defended. "It's not like it happened all the time."

"I'm going to deal with this shit." Ace said, picking up the box with a paper napkin.

"Ace?"

"What?! This is fucked up Sabrina," he charged, completely losing it. "I don't like some jacked-up stalker following you and thinking that it's okay!"

"Fine. Whatever." She said, grabbing her coat and putting it on. "Let's go home."

The ride home was made in rigid silence. For Sabrina, all but the last few minutes of the day had been a triumph. She wasn't going to write any more books for now and had told Natalia and her publisher, even under pressure from both, but she'd stuck to her objective, despite their insistence.

She was going to help run Ace's charities and together they planned to collaborate and help even more children with hearing loss around the world by supplying hearing aids and offering sign language classes to teachers. 'Hear our words' was the name of Ace's main charity, which he had started three years ago and which they were going to build on.

The house was quiet when they got home. Ace made her a cheese and chorizo omelette as the staff had gone home, then ran her a bath.

She was soaking away all the day's stresses, surrounded by vanilla scented candles and listening to old school slow jams that Ace had added to her playlist. She could practically feel the tension floating away.

He was such a good man, Sabrina mused, as she thought about how cherished and loved he made her feel, and she loved him with all that she had. She couldn't wait to be Mrs Alister Charles Edwards in a few weeks.

The front door slamming and voices shouting made her sit up suddenly and listen keenly. Then she heard the distress in Greta's voice and Charles booming out orders. Something was wrong.

Getting out of the now tepid water, she quickly threw on Ace's T-shirt and grey flannel tracksuit bottoms, as they were already on the bed, and promptly made her way downstairs.

Greta was pale and crying, as were the children and everyone looked worried. Kelly, with tears in her own eyes, was trying to comfort the children.

"What's going on?" Sabrina asked, from the bottom step of the stairs.

Ace turned to her, his face pale and his golden eyes dead.

"Heather has gone missing."

***

Sabrina felt herself sway but held onto the mahogany newel on the stairs for support, looking, but not seeing, the spreading opulence of the massive foyer crowded with Ace's family.

"What do you mean gone missing?" She voiced, as her throat tightened. Heather didn't run off anymore, hadn't run off since she got her cochlear implants. The last time had been the weekend when Ace had taken Sabrina for that night out in Manchester. "She can't have gone missing."

Matthew stepped forward and signed instead of speaking. Signing was always faster for him when he was stressed, she knew.

Heather had gone to the bathroom in the restaurant and hadn't come back out, Matthew explained. Charlene had gone to find her, but she wasn't there. CCTV from the restaurant had shown Heather being pulled into a waiting vehicle at the back entrance by a man in dark clothing.

The blood roared through Sabrina's head. "What?" She whispered, sinking to the bottom step. "Where's the police? Why aren't they here?" She looked at them all, noting the way Ace looked at Matthew, who looked at Charles who looked back at her. "Charles? What the hell is going on, and where is my baby?!" She reached out her hand pleadingly to Ace. "Ace?"

Charles stepped forward, his face so, like Ace's ashen in distress, he went down onto his haunches in front of her, taking her cold, trembling hands into his. "We're tracking her," he explained calmly. "I've got people out there now."

"What people? Tracking her where?" She asked, to upset to cry. "Ace?!" She yelled, looking around Charles's form to speak to him. "Why aren't you out there looking for our baby?!"

"Sabrina," Charles said, with such an authoritative tone Sabrina's raising hysteria temporally quelled itself and her head snapped round to him. "I can do more than the police," he explained calmly. "I need you to trust me." He waited for her to acknowledge what he'd said. "Good girl," he said, at her nod of confirmation. "You know all the jewellery Matthew has given her over the years?"

"Yes," Sabrina said.

"They're tracking devices. Each and every one of them.

Tonight, she was wearing the hairpins and bracelet, wasn't she?"

Sabrina nodded, remembering Heather skipping into her bedroom to show off the new set her uncle had brought for her.

"I'll not let anything happen to my granddaughter Sabrina, do you hear me?" Charles tightened his hands around her fingers. "I've got this. We've got this."

He turned to Matthew, Charlene and Ace. Sabrina hadn't noticed Charlene hovering over an industrial-looking laptop on top of the small table by the front door. She was talking on a phone.

"Its stopped Dad." She turned to her father, who, with quick strides, made his way to the laptop and took the phone from her to talk to the person at the other end. When he repeated an address, Sabrina's head shot up.

Ace, Charles, Charlene and Matthew made their way quickly to the front door, and Sabrina moved determinedly towards them.

"I'm coming."

"No," Ace objected, putting his arm out to stop her. "You're staying here."

"I'm coming, Alister." Sabrina shoved her feet into her trainers and pushed past him.

Ace sighed dramatically, his golden eyes blazing. "Okay," he relented. "But you stay in the car," he ordered, as they made their way outside and into his brand new white Q7.

Charlene was speaking rapid Italian into the phone, giving orders and telling whoever was on the other end that they were minutes away and they were to wait.

If the situation weren't so serious, Sabrina would be wondering who these people were and asking questions. She knew Charles had had to deal with certain people from that time Heather had gone missing from school all those years ago. She knew Matthew worked for the American government, but she didn't know or had never thought to ask, in what capacity.

Charlene's husband was a detective in the police force, and Charlene was a stay at home mum. But what had she done before she had her three children? Sabrina wondered, watching, as Charlene swept her dark hair into a ponytail with quick efficiency, giving out instructions at the same time.

Now, Sabrina had all these questions that would have to wait as she tried to control the hysteria that had been churning inside her since she came downstairs.

Ace was quiet, but she could see his jaw ticking, and she reached for his hand, folding her fingers over his as they drove swiftly through the quiet streets of London to a wide street with mature trees and wrought-iron gates.

Charles turned off the vehicle lights as they approached a house on the right and parked close to the crumbling wall. The gates were open and a set of men, all in dark clothing and balaclavas, quietly approached their vehicle, and Charles gave orders as he got out.

Ace turned to her. "Stay here." He ordered quietly.

"But—"

"I need you to stay here, baby, okay." He said, softer now as he gently cupped her face with one hand and smoothed his thumb over her cheek.

"Okay."

He nodded, his golden eyes blazing into hers. "Lock the doors." Then he was gone.

Sabrina reached over to the front to lock herself in, knowing which button it was even in the dark, as his car was the same as hers.

She peered at the dark silhouette of the house and then, just when she thought nothing was happening, the front door was busted open, and everyone rushed inside.

There was shouting and screaming, and within seconds Ace was hurriedly carrying Heather out.

Sabrina sprang out of the vehicle and ran to her family.

"Are you okay? Did they hurt you? Let me see you?" She ordered through her tears.

"Mummy I'm fine. I just got here." Heather said matter-of-factly, and Sabrina catalogued her limbs and checked for any cuts or bruises all within one sweeping, grateful, motherly glance.

"She's okay, Sabrina," Ace added.

Charlene came out, and Sabrina could have sworn she saw her tuck a gun behind her back.

"I'll take her home Ace," Charlene said, pulling Heather from him and carrying her to the car as though she were a toddler instead of a gangly ten-year-old.

"What just happened?" Sabrina said, staring after Charlene. "And why was Charlene carrying a gun? Guns are illegal in England. Did you know that?" Sabrina stammered, trying to make sense of it all.

The men in balaclavas came pouring out of the house, not saying anything, but they all nodded or gave her the thumbs up as they passed her.

"Who are they?" She asked, watching as they piled into two blacked-out SUV's and sped off. "Ace? What's going on?"

Ace sighed. "They're dad's friends." He said, by way of explanation. "But I'll tell you more another time." He grasped her arm lightly, turning towards his vehicle. "Come on."

"Not on your life." She pulled away from his grasp and stormed her way into the house and straight to the living room, where all the lights were on.

"How could you take my daughter?"

***

She was massive, at least twenty-four stone. Her once pretty face rolled into one lump on her thick, rounded shoulders. Her once vibrant dark hair was practically grey and pulled back into a tight ponytail that hung thread-like down her back.

She wore an old red jumper that stretched across her chest and leggings that were thin and cheap with a scattering of holes in the seam of one leg. The straw flip flops she wore were frayed at the edges and looked a size too small.

Sabrina had not seen her former best friend in years, and she would have never recognised her now either.

"Andy," Sabrina said, moving into the room. The same room that held memories of their childhood laughter and whispered secrets.

This house had been a second home for her growing up. Because Sabrina's parents lived mainly in Essex, whenever Andy and Sabrina came home for the holidays, they stayed at either of their houses and always slept over. They'd once made a camp-site right beside the electric fire when they were nine, Sabrina remembered, seeing the same fire now dull with tarnished brass trimmings.

The wallpaper was the same. The Laura Ashley motifs faded to dull blobs on the wall. The red 80s Axminster carpet, also the same, still held its thread, but it was grimy with dirt and was stained here and there. Part of the ceiling was sagging, and Sabrina knew the upstairs bathroom was directly overhead. And where there were once thick velvet red curtains, now hung netting over one window and a large piece of plywood board covered the other.

Andy was watching her, waiting, her eyes overflowing with tears.

Sabrina watched, detached, as Andy suddenly struggled out of Charles' and Matthew's grip to throw herself onto the floor by her feet. She held Sabrina's ankles, almost making her stumble over.

When Ace rushed forward, Sabrina shook her head at him.

"I didn't want to do it, Nina!" Andy cried. "I swear!"

Sabrina looked at her, unable to see the person she once knew.

"You kidnapped my daughter?" She said calmly. "Frightened her, for what?"

"Gareth did it. He wanted to get money from you. He'd been keeping tabs on you and said that you're rich again." Andy explained. "But I made sure she was okay. I made sure he didn't hurt her, Nina." Andy pleaded. "When he brought her here, he just said to lock her up, downstairs in the cellar. But I didn't do it. He left straight away, and I gave her some water and told her I wouldn't hurt her, that you and I are friends. I showed her the picture, see?" Andy reasoned, pointing to a faded photograph of the two of them in identical swimsuits at the beach.

That picture had been taken in Italy the year they'd turned fourteen, Sabrina remembered.

"I told her that she must, must, must do whatever Gareth says," she went on, suddenly looking around and whispering. "He's not a nice person if he gets mad Nina, and I try so hard not to make him mad." Andy rambled on.

Sabrina disengaged herself from Andy's grip and stepped away. "Andy get up!" She ordered and waited for the other woman to move, but Sabrina was horrified to see Andy cower at her tone and cover her head as though expecting to be hit.

"Please get up," Sabrina asked, softening her voice as she took Andy's hand and hauled her up to her feet, trying to ignore the sweaty stench coming from her, then led her to the only sofa in the room.

She kept hold of Andy's hand, stroking it as her agitation eased. They had once been inseparable, Sabrina thought guiltily. Andy's life had come to this?

"Andy? Would you like some water? Something to eat?"

"Oh I can't eat, Nina, it's Thursday. Gareth doesn't let me eat on a Thursday."

Sabrina turned to look at the three men in the room and watched as all but Ace filed out.

Ace, using sign language, told her that Charlene and Heather were home and Heather was having a bath. She was fine. Gareth had been apprehended moments before they'd stormed the house. Sabrina nodded at his explanation but was confused by the words he used. It sounded so military.

"How are you, Andy? What have you been doing all these years?" Sabrina asked and listened as Andy told her that her mother had died eight years ago and that her father had re-married, left her the house and moved to Australia. She learned that she and Gareth were now married, with Andy rapidly explaining that Gareth doesn't believe in wedding rings. She told her how she had been reading her books and was so happy for her but wanted to know why Sabrina had never come to see her, that they had always promised to be friends no matter what.

That promise had been made the first night they'd gone to boarding school in France. The two odd girls. One black, the other chubby. They'd gravitated towards each other, grateful to find a friendship that had lasted right through boarding school and beyond.

"How?" Sabrina asked. "You made it plain you didn't want anything to do with me, Andy."

"But I sent you the roses."

"You sent the roses!" Ace roared, from the corner of the room where he'd been leaning against the wall listening, ready to drag Sabrina out of there if Andy became hostile, as she'd been when they'd stormed the house.

Both women jumped, forgetting he was there.

"Yes, Ace," Andy smiled at him, but quickly covered her mouth. "Do you remember me? I remember you. I'm so happy you found each other again, and I'm glad you didn't end up in that wheelchair. That would have been just horrible."

Sabrina could see the annoyance and impatience in his eyes and quickly turned back to Andy.

"You sent me the roses?"

"Well," she smiled, covering her teeth with her hand again, hiding the blackened edges of her gum line. "When I'm good and have lost a bit of weight, Gareth takes me to the library to see what you're doing, and then I ask Gareth, really really nicely, if he would send you a rose. The message is always the same. I wish we could be friends again, and my phone number, I only have a landline. Gareth says he does it."

"I get the roses Andy, but the message is different," Sabrina explained, hating to see her old friend like this. "Would you like me to make you something to eat, or I can order some food for you?" Sabrina said, hearing the other girl's stomach rumble for the second time.

"No, I'm not allowed to eat on Thursdays."

Sabrina turned to look at Ace who frowned at her.

"How about I make you a nice cup of tea?"

Andy smiled behind her hand again and, getting up, reached out to pull Sabrina from the sofa with surprising swiftness. "Hot water," she said instead. "Come on. I'll show you my children."

"You have kids?" Sabrina asked, allowing herself to be pulled.

Ace was close behind.

"Yes." They walked into the second sitting room that Andy's mother had always called The Parlour. They had never been allowed to play in here as there used to be a huge collection of blue and white porcelain figurines of Victorian boys and girls. Now the shelves and display cabinets were bare.

Sabrina walked to the picture frames on the mantle and saw with alarm, the black and white images you get from ultrasounds. There were at least eleven of them.

"Oh, Andy." Sabrina breathed sadly, picking up a frame and noting the date, then picking up another. They were taken barely a year apart.

"That's why I'm not allowed to eat every day. Gareth says I'm too fat and kill my babies." She walked out of the room, into the kitchen.

Sabrina passed Ace, who was murmuring into his phone and followed Andy into the kitchen where she stopped.

All the cupboards and the fridge had padlocks on them.

"Oh, Andy," Sabrina repeated, unable to stop the tears.

"Don't cry Nina Mae," Andy soothed, hugging her close and rubbing her back. "This is how it's supposed to be. I'm not allowed to eat on Thursdays."

***

The ride back to the house was made in silence. It had been a harrowing four hours. No matter what Sabrina said, Andy refused to eat and only had half a cup of hot water.

After a conversation with Ace, Sabrina asked if Andy would like to go to the hospital and Andy had become so agitated, pulling her hair and walking up and down the room, that it took thirty minutes to calm her down.

That's when Andy told her that she didn't go out and when Sabrina had asked her when was the last time she'd been out, she told her four years ago. Gareth took her to the library where he checked out *The Beholden* for her, but he hadn't taken it back yet.

Charles and Ace had arranged for a private ambulance to take Andy to a private clinic. She required special care, as much a victim in all of this, as Heather had been. She cried and screamed and fought to stay inside the house, repeating that it was Thursday until the male nurses held her down and sedated her, only then could they take her away.

"She'll be okay now Sabrina." Ace said quietly as they drove away from the private clinic.

"I feel so guilty."

"Why?"

"She was my friend. I knew something was up with Gareth from the moment I met him."

"You stop right there!" Ace yelled, gripping the steering wheel. "Remember what you were going through? Your dad? Your mother, the pregnancy?" He reminded her. "You weren't in a position to help her, and she is her own person."

"I know, it's just..."

"No, don't go blaming yourself. You didn't know, Sabrina."

Sabrina sighed and closed her eyes. She didn't think that she would ever be able to sleep again without seeing Andy screaming and crying and begging to stay in the house.

"We can help her now," he added gently, squeezing her knee reassuringly.

Sabrina sighed. Yes, they could.

"What's going to happen to Gareth?" Sabrina asked, after a moment.

"He's in custody."

"Where?"

"Someplace where he can never get to my daughter or you or hurt anyone ever again."

"Is it legal?"

"Sometimes, babes," Ace advised lightly. "What you don't know won't hurt you, and this is one of those things. Trust me on this."

"Okay." She confirmed. "I think I saw him that day I was admitted into the hospital," she said, going on to tell him about the weird feelings she'd had, but had forgotten all about due to her illness and everything that came after.

"Why did you put a tracking device on Heather and how come you never told me?" She asked suddenly.

"When she went missing from school, I asked Matthew to get it done, not just for her safety because she was wondering off, but because you both could be targeted."

"Targeted?"

"I'm a rich man, Sabrina." Was all Ace said in his defence.

Sabrina nodded, then asked. "Has my engagement ring got a tracking device in it?" She held up her hand to look at her ring.

Ace smiled, rubbed her knee as they pulled into the wide driveway of their temporary home before turning to her. "Nah, you have my heart, that's the only beacon I need." He leaned over and kissed her.

CHAPTER TWENTY-SEVEN

Ace lay poolside with his arm flung tiredly across his face, as he listened carefully to the gentle breeze playing with the leaves of Sabrina's beloved argan trees on the other side of the walled garden.

He'd finally got to see the house she'd built. It was traditional, to look at from the outside, completely surrounded by a wall, with a massive wooden gate with brass bolts dotted around it.

They'd landed in Marrakesh a week ago and only today had they ventured outside of the house as Sabrina wanted to take him to Jemma El Fna Square, one of her favourite places in the whole world, she'd told him excitedly this morning. She'd dressed carefully in a pale blue cotton kaftan, heavily embroidered with gold thread and pulled her hair into a ponytail.

He'd only ever passed through Morocco once before, and even then, he'd been racing through the desert with an international rally circuit, but this, meeting the people, eating the food and soaking up the culture was something else.

He could see why she loved it so much. She was greeted by name and given large glasses of freshly squeezed orange juice as she introduced him to her friends in the square.

She'd taken him into the winding souks, where he wondered if they could ever find their way out again, as the narrow paths with an array of brightly coloured stalls twisted and turned in every direction.

Sabrina bought sweet pastries for 'later,' laughingly bargaining with the traders and talking carefully in Arabic, much to their appreciation. He'd said before that her brain was the sexiest thing about her and fucking wow, it was.

Now, back at home, the Moroccan dust showered off their bodies, Ace dozed with a smile on his face as he remembered what she'd done to him just last week.

Sabrina played the starring role in almost all of his favourite memories, but last week she'd blown his mind. He settled deeper into the pillows and closed his eyes to remember every detail.

"I hope you're not peeking Ace," Sabrina warned as he felt the car come to a complete stop.

"Woman, you've become so demanding since I locked you down."

Sabrina giggled, checked his blindfold, got out of the vehicle and walked round to his door to guide him from the car.

Minutes later, and with him continuously moaning just to piss her off, she sat him in a padded chair without handles and left him there. He could smell engine oil and rubber but had no idea where he was as she'd blindfolded him from the house. It was fucking unnerving hearing her reminding herself to drive on the right.

"Okay," she said, breathless with excitement. "Take it off."

Ace took off the black blindfold and squinted, expecting blinding sunlight, but quickly realising he was in an enclosed building, before zeroing in on his wife as she stood in front of him, looking the sexiest he had ever seen her, and that was something as only two days ago, she'd looked sensational in her wedding dress. But fucking wow, this?

She was dressed in black and gold leathers that hugged every curve and contoured her body. His mouth watered as he took in her breasts and hips. He didn't think he had a thing for leather, but fuck me!

"You like?" She asked, quirking a single brow as she stood with her legs apart, the leather stretching over her supple thighs.

He swallowed. "I like."

She pulled a remote from her breast pocket, and the soothing sound of Mario singing Let Me Love You, their song, filled the large room from an audio system somewhere behind him. They were in a large garage, he noted vaguely.

Sabrina glided forward, her body swaying to the music as she approached him, holding his gaze as she moved to the music.

Ace reached out to touch her, but she stepped back and shook her head, waving a finger in his face as a warning. No touching.

Ace, with his hands fisted at his side, felt himself grow even harder than he'd ever been in his life.

She undulated around him, going in close, nipping at his ear or his throat before twirling away.

She was a fucking tease. Ace groaned, loving every minute of it.

She began to strip. Very slowly, flirting with the puller of the zip as she slid it down and then up and then further down again. Ace growled.

He couldn't take it. He could feel a trickle of sweat drip from his temple down the side of his face. He was going to combust when he glimpsed the soft pink satin of her bra. The colour looked amazing against her dark skin.

The zipper had opened to her belly button, and she wiggled her hips, tucking her thumbs into the folds of the leather, and as the music changed to an old Mariah Carey tune, she stepped out of the suit.

Ace was a mess. A tiny triangle of pink barely covered her sex, and thin straps held it in place on her luscious hips. She was walking sex.

Ace bit his tongue, wanting to pant as she neared him. She flashed her hair over his face, and he breathed it in, smelling the argan oil hair lotion she put in it at night. He loved her hair wild like this. He'd plaited it for her last night, and she simply undid the plaits and finger-combed it this morning. It was dark and wild, and he buried his hands in it every chance he got.

She placed her long legs on either side of his chair and, leaning over him, licked his neck from the base, up behind his ear and back down again.

"You want me?" She whispered.

"Ye—" he coughed. "Yeah."

She skimmed her tongue over the seam of his lips then pushed her way inside. At his groan, she grabbed his hair and angled his face up to her. It was an aggressive move; one she had never done before, and Ace loved it.

Just as he was about to grab her, she twirled away, laughing at his fierce look. He could feel the rising heat in his body, taste her on his tongue and feel the pulsating throb where she'd sucked hard on his bottom lip.

She stepped forward and brought her leg all the way up to her ear, reminding him of the gymnast she once was as she held the pose.

Ace got a sweeping glance at the shadow of her sex, and placing her foot on his thigh, placed her hands on his broad shoulders and leaned forward, allowing him to breathe in her aroused scent as he dipped his head to her.

"Touch me now baby," Sabrina ordered and sighed with relief when his large hands went straight to her hips to pull her into his face. He smothered her sex with his kisses before, using his nose, nudged away the satin scrap covering, to tease her swollen nub out to play.

He kept her there. His hands hard on her smooth hips as he slipped one of her legs over his shoulders to continue his assault on her glistening folds.

Her legs began to tremble, and a slight sheen of sweat covered her body. Planting the heel of one hand up her taut stomach, Ace moved to knead her breasts, first one and then the other, tweaking her hard nipples in turn.

Her whimpers became louder, the grip she had in his hair tighter. He knew she was close, so he pushed a finger inside her and swirled it around and around until she fell apart against his hand.

When she moved again, it was to undo his trousers, climb over him and ride him like he'd wanted her to ride him that first night in the pub.

It was wild. It was loud. It was dirty. It was rough.

They didn't make love; they had sex, feeding off each other like never before.

***

Much later, with Ace in leathers that matched hers, he walked around the gold and black motorbike that was his wedding present. It came as a set of 'His and Hers' Sabrina told him, looking anxiously on.

"Do you really like it?" She asked again, biting the nail on her little finger. Ace plucked it from her mouth and kissed it.

"I like it," he traced the word 'His' scripted in flowing font on the gold tank and smiled, smoothing his hand over the machine. "How long have we got?" He asked, itching to get on the super bike and do some laps. It had been years since he was last on a professional track.

"It's ours until midnight." She told him, picking up her black with gold trim helmet and putting it on.

Ace watched; he hadn't seen her ride yet. Her bike was identical to his in colour, but that was about it, thank God. The cc's much lower.

She'd told him about her lessons, and she got her licence before they left England, but still...

"You go first," He said, observing her. He wasn't even sure if he wanted her on a motorbike at all but kept his thoughts to himself.

"Don't you trust me, Alister?" She asked, obviously catching his nervousness.

"It's not that. It's just this is a powerful machine. I need to make sure you can handle it."

"Oh, I can handle it," she replied confidently, zipping up her jumpsuit.

"Where did you say you got lessons again?"

"I didn't," she dipped her head, not knowing how he was going to react to her next statement. "With Erik."

He frowned over at her, not liking that she took lessons from his friend.

"Don't do that again." He said darkly, not caring if he sounded like a Neanderthal. "Anything you need to learn, I'll teach you."

Sabrina came forward, wrapped her arms around his neck to kiss him, but forgetting the helmet she was wearing and ended up bumping his chin instead. She reached up and smoothed the annoyed creases from his brow. "Okay."

Ace watched closely, as Sabrina got on the bike, started it, and ever so slowly rode out of the pit lane to the track. When she stopped and turned to him, he got on his own bike and joined her. They did a whole lap together very slowly. So slowly, Ace could have walked around and still beat her, he mused affectionately.

When they got back to the pit, Sabrina parked, took off her helmet and grinned at him.

"Okay Alister, that's enough riding for me. Go show me what you can do, baby." She ordered and laughed, as his face lit up and he *pulled down the sun visor and roared off.*

He went around twice more then stopped in front of her, telling her to get on the back.

It was a massive turn on, the speed, having her cling to his waist and the heavy vibrations of the powerful engine.

He heard her moan, and she tightened her arms around his waist, pressing her breasts against his back.

Ace pulled over mid-track, pulled her off, rushed her between two low triangular advertising boards on the grass, where he made quick love to her before taking her back to the pit and making love to her again against the wall.

They'd spent that same night in their new apartment in New York. Four Thirty-Two Park Avenue was her wedding present. The new super-skinny high-rise that had changed the New York skyline.

She'd once told him how she'd like to see inside the building but had never dreamed of owning one and had spent most of the night oohing and ahh-ing over the oak herringbone floors and massive windows. It was an exclusive address with one penthouse selling for the price of a Greek Island. They were on the thirty-eighth floor, an apartment not nearly as expensive, but they did overlook Central Park.

Ace felt a shadow cross him, blocking the African sun and opened his eyes. "How is she?" He asked, squinting up at her.

Sabrina, wearing a different kaftan in a semi-transparent fabric of swirling greens, put the plate of dates and pastries onto the low wooden table beside him and sat at his feet on the lounger.

"Her doctor says she's doing well. Lost more weight and is eating three meals a day now."

Ace watched as she put on her wide-brimmed straw hat before looking at him.

"But?" He asked.

"I'm not allowed to see or talk to her just yet. He says she's riddled with guilt and seeing me might set her back some."

Ace reached for her hand and squeezed, knowing how difficult it was for her. It had been two months since the incident with Andy back in London. They'd moved to America since then, finally got married and enrolled Heather into the same school as two of her cousins. They'd also bought a house half an hour away from his parents, with the requisite garden for Sabrina.

"Ace?"

"Sabrina?"

"Let's play." She went on, scooting up beside him and curling her body around his to trace the tattoos on his chest. "I'll start. Pencil and paper."

"Sweet and sour."

"Teeth and gums."

"Dandelion and Burdock." He kissed her forehead.

"Nappies and bums."

"Huh?" He frowned but went on, knowing she was likely to win as her brain was the sexiest ever. "Husband and wife."

"Boy and girl."

"Hot and cold."

"Teddy and blanket."

"Laurel and Hardy." He said but was still processing her last pair.

"Pitter and patter."

That stumped him completely. "What's pitter and patter?"

She turned, moving up and over to sit on his broad chest, licked her finger and traced it around one nipple and then the other.

"The pitter and patter of tiny feet?"

"Huh?"

"Come on, babes, keep up." She leaned in close to whisper. "I'm having your baby, Ace."

He sat up, pulling her with him and watching her closely. "We're pregnant?"

She nodded, smiling as he breathed in deep, his whiskey coloured eyes intense as he released the most peaceful, heartfelt breath before pulling her close.

"Sabrina."

"Ace."

The End

I usually leave it there, but please consider
leaving a review. I'm seriously lacking.
Thanks!

The second in the International Heroes books,
Convincing Kyle, (excerpt below) is now available.

CONVINCING KYLE
(unedited)

Kyle dropped his aunt and cousins off and drove through the not so quiet streets of Manhattan. Now that Ace had bought an apartment in the exclusive Four Thirty-Two Park Avenue building, Kyle stayed at his old apartment whenever he was in New York.

He parked and rushed inside. The magazine was burning a hole in his back pocket, and he only stopped to pour himself a whiskey and grab his tablet before sitting on the couch.

He did a Google search on the film, an Indian adaptation of Wuthering Heights, called *The Mumbai Plains.* It had gained five stars. Camikara, Camille, was playing the lead and was apparently Oscar Nominee amazing.

Kyle went to images, and there she was. It was her, the dark skin, even darker hair and startling grey eyes and the dimple in her chin. There was no mistaking her. She was still incredibly beautiful, if not more so.

She was in town. A premier of the movie was showing not far from where the apartment was. Kyle looked at the time. It would still be going on.

Now that the wait was over and the baby had finally arrived safely and a sweet six pounds eight ounces, Kyle was free. He was going to the Premiere. He wanted, no needed to see Camille. It had been nine years.

All the pomp had died down when he got there half an hour later, but hundreds of people were still waiting around, and the air was filled with a spicy, succulent fragrance, that made him remember the flower stands in Jaipur market.

As Kyle waited for the film to end, he got talking to a paparazzi reporter from England. His name was Kev Taylor and didn't look what Kyle thought a sleazy pap would look like. Kev Taylor wore a dark suit, white shirt, red bow tie and a tweed flap cap, turned slightly backwards. A dangly earring in his right ear and a full beard completed the look. He was character personified.

Kyle had lived in England for three months and hated everything about it. He was a New Yorker born and bred. The boarding school had been in Derbyshire. Surrounded by miles upon miles of fucking green fields of various shades, but still green. He hated green.

There was nothing for a city boy like him to do. That was until he'd discovered the sister school, St Ann of Hope for Girls, just a tiny green field away.

Every night, in the last of his three-month term, he took a bunch of guys and would sneak out to meet up with some girls. Kyle smiled at the memory. Boarding school girls were just as hot and kinky as the porno videos made out. The things they all did. Fucking A.

Then he'd met Camille. She'd been out riding a massive chestnut coloured horse. A special privilege one of the other girl's had said scornfully.

Camille had sat, with her back straight, looking down her elegant nose at them all. Kyle had actually hidden his cigarette behind his back, hoping she hadn't seen it. She had, and the look of distaste on her face made him feel all sorts of embarrassment.

With a flick of her riding crop, directed at them, she'd trotted off.

He didn't see her again until the official school fête, and the two schools met in the middle field to play traditional games like apple bobbing, conkers and a game of rounders.

Camille had been sat on a bale of hay, looking bored out of her mind. She'd been wearing tan coloured pants, a light blue shirt, tucked into the waistband, a brown jacket and brogues. Brogues in a field. Kyle smiled at the memory. Her hair had been in a long thick braid over one shoulder.

He'd bought her some pink cotton candy and went to talk to her. She'd ignored him at first, but he'd continued to talk and talk, exaggerating his accent until she'd laughed. She'd looked at him then and accepted the cotton candy that seemed to have lost some of its fluffiness. They'd argued over the proper name for it cotton candy versus candy floss. He'd let her win.

They'd been inseparable after that. Meeting in the village for ice-cream. He'd gone to a 'revision group' he knew she'd be in and fell in love for the first time in his life—two fucking weeks before he was to leave England.

"They'll be coming out in a minute, mate." Kev Taylor said, lifting his camera and jolting Kyle out of his memories. The pap scrabbled about in his hunt for a better view of the double doors. "Get ready."

Kyle tipped his head at him, then said. "Nice to meet you and thanks for the info." That pap knew more details about Camille than the Google search he'd done earlier.

She was Bollywood royalty. Super rich and it was rumoured she was retiring. This was to be her last film, hence all the interest. But there was also the rumour that she was going to play a role as a smouldering sex siren in a Hollywood film that would be frowned upon in conservative India.

There was movement from the inside of the building and straightening up behind the gold velvet rope, that matched the gold carpet, Kyle watched as the huge 20s style glass doors opened. The long tubular brass handles reflected and threw candlelight into the crowd from the millions of fake tea lights on the ground. Beautiful people-that matched the pages of the magazine he'd been reading earlier-came pouring out.

Kyle was pushed out of the way, and his feet trampled on, by a group of teenaged girls who had somehow managed to stand in front of him, their phones at the ready. Just then, their screams got louder, and they started jumping up and down excitedly, shouting the name Camikara and declaring their love for Parmer Christopher Abdul.

Camille came out on the arm of a tall, handsome dark-haired Asian man. They looked like a couple, laughing and leaning into one another. Kyle felt a fire ignite in his lower belly as he watched.

Camille wasn't in traditional Indian dress, but she was in a shiny white gown, elaborately embroidered with dark gold threading, sequins and stones, from the hem to the knee. The skirt was full, hanging from her shapely hips and fell to the ground. When she walked one long slender leg played hide and seek within the folds. She was wearing sky-high heels, with barely there gold straps.

There was a gold stone in her belly button, and her stomach was bare right up to the low-cut white bodice type thing, with tiny sleeves on her shoulders. He didn't know what to call it, as it had a bit more fabric than a bra, but not much more. He just knew it displayed a whole lot of skin and the guy beside her was busy looking at her boobs. Kyle wanted to punch him in the face.

They walked slowly down the steps to shouts and flashing lights, all smiles, stopping now and then to take pictures with fans or sign autographs. It took them fifteen minutes to walk twelve steps, Kyle knew because he'd been counting. This was fucking ridiculous.

Then she was there, taking pictures with the group of girls in front of him. Her beautiful long hair, still as long as he remembered was parted in the centre, reaching the curve of her bottom and covered by some sort of glittering gold headdress of small pearls and gold gemstones. A thick gold chain sat along her parting to cascade in an array of intricate chains to lie on top of her hair. A large tear-drop shaped gemstone lay perfectly centre on her forehead.

Nothing she wore could detract from her natural beauty.

"Camille," Kyle said clearly, over the din of gushing. She heard him.

Kyle watched as she looked through the crowd, still smiling, still taking pictures but looking for him. He knew she was. She would never forget his voice, and he would never forget hers. She'd whispered to him and screamed at him. She'd cried to him and said goodbye to him. He would never forget her voice.

She saw him then. Her body froze for the millisecond she looked into his eyes. Recognising him, and just like that, turned her back to be swept away by a tide of people wearing black with orange lanyards swinging around their necks, to a waiting limousine.

Kyle didn't move. She'd blanked him?! She'd fucking blanked him! After everything, they had shared?! He watched as the gold limo pulled into the street and he stood still as the crowd dispersed and he lost sight of the car.

Only then did Kyle turn to walk back to the apartment. Hurt beyond belief.

THE END
(for now)

Scan Me

Join Caroline's influencer list for more fun reads and freebies!

ABOUT THE AUTHOR

Caroline Bell Foster

Caroline Bell Foster was born in Derby, England, and went on a six-week holiday to Jamaica with her family. She stayed for years!

Ever the adventurer, Caroline bought her first pair of high heels in Toronto, Canada and traded her pink sunglasses for a bus ride in the Rift Valley, Kenya by the age of 18.

A self-proclaimed cat person, Caroline is looking forward to one day being called 'The Mad Cat Lady. She enjoys writing sweet or spicy romances.

The multi-award-winning writer is also the author of the Amazon Bestselling Call Centre Series, Call Me Royal and Call Me Lucky, where she pays tribute to all those who work the night shift in call centres as she has done.

With themes of substance, Caroline's latest novels defy convention and celebrate modern-day Britain, with several titles set primarily in the East Midlands. Caroline has been listed as one of the most influential creatives in her region.

Caroline has come full circle and lives in Nottingham, England, just twelve miles from where she was born. She married her college sweetheart David (Mr Sunshine) and they have two children.

If you would like to keep up to date with Caroline's new releases, please sign up to her twice-yearly newsletter via her website.

www.carolinebellfoster.com

BOOKS BY THIS AUTHOR

Sweey & Spicy Books For Every Mood

Love To Belong - How could one little lie cause so much chaos?

Distracting Ace – (International Heroes Book 1) It took thirty-six hours for Ace to fall in love. But longer to find it again and keep it.

Convincing Kyle – (International Heroes Book 2)
First, love and family interference spelt disaster for Kyle and Camille. Years later, they tried again, but even more, interference threatens their love.

Avoiding Matthew – (International Heroes Book 3)
Special Government Operatives Matthew and Lacy hooked up every chance they got. But wanting to make the world a better place, Lacy has to avoid Matthew at all costs. But it's so hard!

The Pussycat Trap - 3 stories in one - Who knew the pitter-patter of tiny paws could melt the hearts of these powerful men. (Sweet Romance)

The Cat Café - London banker Blake enters the cat café by mistake. Not only is he shocked to see so many cats in one place, but to also fall in love with the mad cat lady Trinity Peters.

Amazon bestselling Call Centre Series:

Call Me Lucky - Teddy could not believe the foul-mouthed girl he once knew had changed so little. He needed to show Felicity the world could be better and brighter with him.

Call Me Royal - Della now lived her life by one word, safe. Could long lost love Spencer remind her how it used to be?

Spicy Tropical Romances:

Saffron's Choice - . Engaged to a man she hadn't seen in 5 years. Saffron gives in and falls in love with the man that had always been in front of her.

Caribbean Whispers - Could Merrissa escape her past and take a chance on Alex, or does her past continue to haunt her?

Ladies Jamaican. - Three friends, three kinds of love. Could they make it?

www.ingramcontent.com/pod-product-compliance
Lightning Source LLC
Chambersburg PA
CBHW051422170626
46809CB00006B/2279